Natural Born Readers

VICTORIA CONNELLY

Cover design by J D Smith.

Published by Cuthland Press
in association with Notting Hill Press.

ISBN: 978-1-910522-13-4

To Jan Cramer – my wonderful narrator
and a natural born reader!

ACKNOWLEDGEMENTS

Thanks, once again, to the great team who help put my books together: Roy, Catri, Jane and Jan. Also special thanks to Ros Byam Shaw and her wonderful book *Perfect English Farmhouse* which inspired the braying donkeys in this novel.

CHAPTER 1

Bryony Nightingale leaned into the bow window at the front of her children's bookshop and replaced the titles which had enjoyed their time in the limelight. If only she could fit all the children's books in the world into her little shop, she thought, not for the first time. There were so many delectable ones from the classics to the very latest chart-topping titles. It was a constant source of frustration that her limited shelving couldn't accommodate everything.

The bookshop, which was on Church Street in the small market town of Castle Clare, was Bryony's pride and joy. Simply called 'Nightingale's', it sat opposite her brother Sam's shop with Josh's next to that but, unlike their classic dark green painted woodwork, Bryony had chosen mustard yellow for her window and door. It was such a happy, jolly colour and had proved a magnet to the children of the town and its neighbouring villages. It looked, Bryony thought, like the kind of place a Beatrix Potter character would own.

Indeed, Bryony looked as if she might have stepped right out of one of the colourful children's books she sold. With her long, dark hair clipped back or up with an assortment of colourful bands or pins, her patchwork skirts in an array of bold fabrics, and her enormous silver belts teamed with biker boots, Bryony was a vision to behold and children adored her because she looked so unlike their parents and teachers. Bryony's motto was 'why wear one colour when you can wear seven?'

Today, which was a cold April day, she was wearing one of her favourite skirts which was a swirl of blues, greens and silvers. Her hair was tied back with a lemon-yellow scarf, and enormous silver hoops dangled from her ears. Her sister Polly had popped in to the bookshop after dropping her son at school and had said that Bryony looked like a fortune teller who'd walked through a paint factory at the precise moment it had exploded. Bryony had laughed. Polly had always favoured a much quieter, more conservative palette.

Bryony had been running the children's bookshop full-time since graduating although she'd worked there part-time since she was fourteen, learning everything there was to learn from her mother, Eleanor.

'This is your place now, Bryony,' her mother had told her that summer and Bryony still remembered her sense of awe and excitement and the strange, potent silence that had filled the shop after her mother had left it and the little bell above the door had stopped ringing. She'd stood in the middle of the floor, her head spinning at the thought that this was her very own little world now and she was in charge of it. She'd immediately got to work, painting the shelves in primary colours, buying beanbags and colourful rugs so that her little customers could sit or sprawl in comfort as they perused the shelves and made their choices. The result was a little heaven and she loved it.

She couldn't imagine any other life and she was proud of what she'd achieved in the six years since she'd taken over the shop, including the children's reading club she'd set up which was going from strength to strength. Twice a week, after school, parents would come into the shop with their children. Some would stay and some would take advantage of the safe environment and nip across the road for a quick cup of tea at The Golden Biscuit, leaving their children in Bryony's care. She didn't mind. She encouraged it, in fact. She found that she could be much more free and open in her readings if the parents weren't around, often feeling self-conscious about her dramatic performances and sound effects if there was a po-faced parent staring at her.

She thought back to when she'd started the reading club and it didn't take her long to remember because it was in the summer six years ago when she'd taken over the bookshop. The same summer that Ben Stratton had left.

Ben. The man she'd loved since primary school. Not that she loved him anymore, she told herself as she chose a few new titles to showcase in the window. Those feelings had been crushed the moment he'd walked out on her all those years ago. He'd wanted to travel, he'd said, to leave Castle Clare far behind him. Well, fine. If he didn't want to stay with her, then it was better that he went. The fact that he'd begged her to go with him didn't weigh much with Bryony. His departure had been a betrayal. He'd loved something else more than her and she could never forgive that. Nor forget it.

The little bell tinkled above the door, breaking into Bryony's thoughts. It was her eldest brother, Sam.

'Hey!' she said from the top of the small step ladder. She was shelving a new display of children's mystery books and was admiring each and every cover as she placed them carefully.

'Hey,' he said and she watched as he shuffled around the shop for a moment.

'You okay?' she asked.

'Sure,' he said.

'Quiet at yours?'

'Yes,' he said. 'Grandpa's keeping an eye on things. He's got the morning off as Mum's taking Grandma to get her hair done. They're getting manicures and pedicures too.'

'Fancy!'

'Although Mum said she didn't know why she was bothering as her feet are always shoved into a pair of wellies and her hands will be ruined in no time in the potting shed. Dad's roped her into sowing seeds.'

Bryony laughed and continued with the job in hand, aware that Sam was still hovering.

'Did you want a cup of tea?' she asked him.

'Er, no thanks.'

She nodded, scrutinising him. He didn't look right. He looked decidedly uneasy like he had something on his mind.

'What is it, Sam?'

'Pardon?'

'Is there something you want to tell me?'

'No.'

'Okay.' She turned back to her shelves, not quite believing him and that was when he cleared his throat.

'Ben's back,' he said.

Bryony's right hand, which was holding a copy of a book about a group of Egyptian mummies on the run, stopped and stiffened, as if she'd been caught in the glare of the Medusa.

'Right,' she said at last, her voice devoid of colour and emotion.

'Got back last night,' Sam continued, kicking one of his boots against the other. 'Gave me a call to let me know. I guess he knew I'd tell you.'

Bryony only half-heard the words her brother was saying. Her mind was still stuck on the first two: *Ben's back.*

'Bry?'

'What? What do you want me to say?'

'I don't know,' he said. 'Something angry? Something rude?'

'Not going to happen.'

'Okay.'

'Was that it, then? Was that what you wanted to tell me?'

'Yes. I just thought you should know, that's all.' There was a pause full of awkwardness. 'Okay. I'll leave you to it, then.'

Bryony heard the sound of the shop bell and waited before slowly climbing off the steps.

So, Ben was back, was he? Well, that didn't make any difference to her. She doubted very much that he'd dare to walk into the bookshop so, as long as she stayed within its safe confines, all would be well.

She walked to the door and locked it, turning the sign round to 'Closed' even though lunchtime was a good couple of hours away, and then she went into the storeroom at the back of the shop and promptly burst into tears.

The April evening was chilly and Callie Logan had lit the wood burner at Owl Cottage to brighten things up a bit. After a day writing in one of the tiny upstairs bedrooms she'd turned into a study since moving to Suffolk in September, she loved spending time in the living room with the curtains drawn and a fire blazing. She also loved spending time with Sam and it was a rare evening that they didn't spend together these days either with him visiting Owl Cottage or her driving the short distance in to Castle Clare to his flat above the bookshop.

'I got a call today,' Sam called from the kitchen where he was cooking rice from a recipe in a book he'd pulled from one of the shop shelves just before leaving. He had a habit of doing that. Callie kept telling him not to bring any more books over but book lovers never heard commands like that, did they? Or Sam certainly didn't. Telling him to stop bringing her books would be like telling him to stop breathing.

'Who was your call from?' Callie asked as she threw another log into the wood burner.

'Ben.'

Callie frowned. 'Ben who?'

'Ben Stratton,' Sam said, coming into the living room and sitting in the chair by the fire.

'*Bryony's* Ben?'

'The very one.'

'What does Bryony think?'

'She didn't say anything when I told her. She went all quiet on me.'

'Oh, dear.'

'I'm a bit worried about her to be honest.'

'Isn't she seeing Colin the baker?'

'Kind of.'

'What do you mean, "kind of"?'

'I think it's a bit half-hearted on her side which is a shame as he's a pretty decent bloke. I hope she's not leading him on.'

'She wouldn't do that, would she?'

'You'd be amazed what people do to stave off loneliness,' he said.

'But you didn't do that when you were on your own, did you?'

'Of course not,' he said. 'I knew you were on your way to me.'

Callie smiled at him. 'You always say exactly the right thing at the right time, don't you?'

'Comes from a lifetime of reading.' He kneeled down on the floor and kissed her before returning to the rice in the kitchen. Ten minutes later and they were eating. The rice was very good indeed.

'So tell me about Ben,' Callie said.

'What do you want to know?'

'Everything! I've only heard bits and pieces from your family and it's kind of hard to put it all together in the right order,' she said.

'Well,' Sam began, 'Bryony and Ben were best friends growing up. They met at primary school and they did absolutely everything together, even making sure they went to the same college in Cambridge to study English. He was a good friend to me and Josh too, but he was always Bryony's friend first and everyone just expected them to become a couple. There was never any talk of getting engaged or married or anything – it was just a given that they'd be together forever.'

'So what happened?' Callie asked.

'Ben took off. Got this idea that he had to leave Castle Clare and go travelling. It was so sudden. Nobody had seen it coming.'

Callie frowned. 'And how did Bryony react?'

'That was the odd thing,' Sam said. 'She didn't really react at all – not in any way you'd expect. There was no screaming or tears. She just kind of went quiet and threw herself into the bookshop and none of us were allowed to mention Ben ever again.'

'And that was it? No news from Ben?'

'He sent Bryony postcards from all over the world but, being Ben, he did something a bit different with them. Each postcard came inside a book.' Sam smiled at the memory. 'Whichever country he was in, he'd find some classic book in its language and send it to her.'

'Really? Callie said, her eyes lighting up as she fell a little bit in love with the mysterious Ben herself.

'But the books stopped arriving after about two years and we never heard from him again. Bryony moved on, started dating a line of hopeless cases and forgot about Ben.'

'So you think,' Callie said.

'No, I'm sure she did.'

'Sam, Ben was Bryony's first love. You don't ever forget that!'

Sam sighed. 'Maybe you're right.'

'And now he's back.'

'Yes.'

'What do you think will happen?'

Sam shrugged. 'I don't know. I don't think Bryony will want to see him, but I'm sure my family will. He was like an honorary member.'

'I'd like to meet him too.'

'Then you shall,' Sam said with a grin.

Callie's writer's mind couldn't help but find it all fascinating. 'I wonder if she kept all the books and postcards he sent her,' she said. 'Do you know?'

He shook his head. 'She probably made a big bonfire of them all.'

'No!' Callie said aghast. 'Do you really think so?'

'I think Ben is very much a part of Bryony's past,' Sam said, but Callie couldn't help wondering if he was right.

After sharing a small house with her cousin Megan for years, Bryony had recently moved into a place of her own – a tiny house in Springfield Terrace on the Great Tallington Road. She missed having the constant companionship of Megan, but there was something rather wonderful about closing your door at the end of a day's work and having silence greet you. Plus, of course, her enormous book collection had demanded a larger premises. Megan ran Castle Clare's library and, like the rest of the Nightingale family, had books in abundance. Their tiny place simply hadn't been able to cope with two bibliophiles.

Bryony drew the living room curtains. It had been dark for a few hours but she'd been lost in the pages of the latest Lucy Lamont novel. She was one of the most popular middle-grade authors around and Bryony could see why with her lovable characters and hilarious storylines in which adults were most definitely second-class citizens.

She'd known what she'd been doing by picking up the novel: she'd been putting off the inevitable. Ever since Sam had come into her shop with the news, she couldn't stop thinking about it. She'd managed to put it out of her mind whilst she was reading – that was the magic of books; they could whisk you away from your troubles for a few blissful hours – but you always had to return, didn't you? And, for her, that meant going upstairs into the second bedroom. It was still full of boxes of books yet to be unpacked, but it wasn't a box she was looking for – it was a battered old suitcase from her student days. It had belonged to her mother years ago and had been passed down to Polly and then Bryony university. Lara had escaped the old suitcase by being so much younger than her sisters and it had kind of attached itself to Bryony.

She saw it as soon as she walked into the bedroom. Cracked and faded, it still held a kind of beauty and her hands reached for it now, pulling it out into a space on the carpet where she could kneel down before it and open it up.

A silver and sea-green scarf greeted her eyes. It was one which a young Hardy, her parents' pointer, had once got hold of and ripped right down the middle. Bryony hadn't been able to part with it and so it lived in the suitcase as a protective layer over the treasure trove of books within. Books which Ben had sent her.

She removed the scarf now and she saw the stacks of titles. There was *A Room with a View* in Italian, *Romeo and Juliet* in French, *Madame Bovary* in Spanish, *Pride and Prejudice* in... actually Bryony wasn't too sure what that language was. All the great love stories of the world found by Ben on his travels and posted to her bookshop in Castle Clare.

She held each one gently in her hands, knowing that Ben had touched every single one. And then she opened up the copy of *A*

Room with a View, her hand hovering over the postcard that had been sleeping inside it for so long since she'd last read it. The first few lines were about his travels. He'd had his wallet stolen in Rome. He'd eaten far too much pizza than was good for a human being in Naples and he'd climbed Vesuvius. Her eyes read the words once again, rushing towards the final line which she knew was coming.

I wish you'd come with me. I love you. Ben. x

Every single postcard ended with that same message. For two whole years. And then the packages and the postcards had stopped and Bryony's heart had broken.

CHAPTER 2

At seven years old, Bryony was already a bookworm. It was a foregone conclusion when your family owned a bookshop, and very few Christmases or birthdays passed without her receiving books. So, when she saw the school library, she felt an immediate affinity with it. She might not understand arithmetic, but she did understand books. This was a world she was familiar with and she remembered feeling rather proprietorial as she entered and saw the shelves of books for the first time, as if she was scared that the other pupils might manhandle them and that, perhaps, she should be put in charge of them, deciding which pupil could have which book and for how long.

She was anxious about the way some of her classmates treated the books – tearing them from the shelves as if they were common items and not the glorious things she knew they were. They dropped them, threw them at each other, left them open – spine up – and squashed them into their dirty bags. It was awful. Didn't they instinctively feel what she felt toward them: that they should be handled gently and with great reverence? That their value was more than the price they had cost? That the words and pictures inside them could be read only once, but live with you forever? She knew all this and it baffled her that her classmates didn't. Well, perhaps one did. Ben Stratton.

Ben sat somewhere behind her in class. She wasn't sure where because she didn't like boys very much. It was quite enough for a girl to have to put up with two older brothers at home without having to deal with even more boys at school. They were always so rough, she thought. Pushing and pulling each other in the playground and making rude noises in class. It was frustrating to Bryony that she had to have anything to do with boys.

It was during one of their library sessions when she met Ben properly for the first time. She was just about to reach for a book she'd been longing to read for ages. It had caught her eye the last time, but she'd been told that she couldn't take more than three books at once which was a very silly rule, she thought. One could read three books in one sitting and then what were you meant to do with the rest of the week?

So, she'd just been about to reach for the longed-for book when the bulk of Damian Anderson pushed in front of her and his big chubby fist claimed her book.

'Hey!' she cried.

'Hey what?' he cried back.

'I want to read that.'

'Yeah?' He gave her a taunting look which made his face look even uglier than before and then he threw the book into the air, catching it in his meaty paws a moment later.

'Don't throw it!' Bryony said in alarm. 'You shouldn't throw books.'

'Sez who?'

'Anybody with a brain.'

Somebody behind her laughed at that and Damian frowned.

'Give her the book,' a voice said.

Bryony turned around and saw Ben Stratton standing there. The expression in his dark eyes was that of somebody not to be messed with.

'I said, give her the book.'

Damian seemed to be weighing his options. He was easily twice the size of Ben, but he seemed to sense that he shouldn't mess with him.

'Here!' he snarled, throwing the book on the floor. 'I didn't want the stupid book anyway.' He turned and walked away as fast as his bulk would allow him to.

Ben stepped forward and picked up the book before handing it to Bryony.

'Thanks,' she said and he gave a little shrug.

Bryony stroked the book, checking to see if Damian had harmed it in any way.

'Why did you want the book so much?' Ben asked her. 'There are loads of others.'

'I know, but I set my heart on this one.'

'You're funny,' he said.

'No I'm not. I just love books.'

He continued to stare at her as if he was trying to work her out. 'I'm Ben,' he said at last.

'I know,' she said. 'I'm Bryony.'

'I know,' he said and they smiled at each other.

'You can read it after me if you like,' she said, holding the book up. He glanced at it and nodded.

'Okay,' he said.

It was shortly after the incident with the library book that Ben gave Kelly Smailes a packet of gobstoppers to get her to swap seats with him so he could sit next to Bryony. The teacher, Miss Percival, wasn't impressed and made him move right back. Of course, Kelly didn't give Ben his gobstoppers back, but she took his wine gums the next time he persuaded her to move when Miss Percival's back was turned, and half a packet of Polos the third time. Finally, Miss Percival admitted defeat.

'I've got no sweets left now,' Ben told Bryony.

'Don't blame me,' she said.

'I'm not,' he said. 'Anyway, it was worth it.'

The Well Bread bakery in Castle Clare was always busy and rightly so because of Colin Wriothesley. He was known simply as 'Colin the baker' because nobody really knew how to pronounce his surname. Rizley? Risely? Wrothsley? The jury was still out and so he became 'Colin the baker'. That he was the best baker for miles around was something that everybody was sure about. There was no doubting that and the morning and lunchtime queues were well worth putting up with to get hold of one of his farmhouse loaves, custard slices or chocolate eclairs.

Bryony often cursed that her shop was next door to the bakery because the scent of freshly baked goods was almost too much to bear and no amount of climbing up and down her little stepladder was going to make up for the calories she consumed on a daily basis especially since Colin had started paying her special attention.

'Morning,' he said, leaning forward to kiss her cheek as he came into the shop.

'Colin!' she said, pushing him away. 'Someone may come in.' But it wasn't just the fear of somebody seeing him kiss her that made her push him away. He was getting far too tactile for her liking. They'd had dinner out together a few times and the odd date, but that didn't mean that they were a couple, did it?

He gave her a mournful sort of look with those big grey eyes of his and she instantly felt bad. He had the knack of making her feel guilty and she didn't like him for that either.

Her mum had told Bryony to bring him to Sunday lunch, but that was getting far too familiar, Bryony had decided. Sunday lunch was for when you were practically engaged like her brother Sam and Callie. It wasn't for someone who you were just casually sort of, kind of, dating like she was with Colin. Sunday lunch would give both Colin and her family the totally wrong impression and that wouldn't be fair at all.

'I've made you a raspberry sponge,' he told her as she found something to busy herself with behind the till. 'Can I get you a slice now or shall we save it for later?'

'Oh, Colin! You mustn't keep making me cakes. My waistline's going to balloon!'

'Nonsense! You're absolutely perfect,' he said with a tender smile.

Oh, how she wished he wouldn't say things like that. 'I'm not perfect,' she said. 'There's at least half a stone of me that shouldn't exist at all.'

'That's rubbish,' he said with a laugh.

'And my nose is too big and I'm not tall enough.'

'What?'

'I always wanted to be taller and slimmer. Like Polly. But I'm the shorter, plumper one.'

Colin shook his head.

'And I'll get even plumper if you keep baking me sugary treats.'

'How about some savoury ones instead? I've got some cheese straws just out of the oven.'

Bryony's mouth watered at the thought of Colin's cheese straws. The temptation was almost too much as she pictured the perfect golden crumbliness of them and that hit of tangy cheese.

'No!' she said, the word shooting out of her mouth and startling him. 'I've brought a sandwich for lunch.'

'I can make you lunch,' he said. 'I've told you.'

She shook her head. 'I'm quite capable of making my own lunch.'

He held his hands up as if in defeat. 'Okay, okay! I just thought...' he stopped. 'I'd better get back to the shop.'

Instantly, Bryony felt bad for throwing his kind gestures back in his face.

'Call me later,' she said and winced inwardly. She didn't really want him to call her later.

He gave a little smile which looked half hope, half frustration and left the shop.

Bryony released a long sigh she'd obviously been holding in. Why was she so mean to Colin? She should just put him out of his misery. Polly was always telling her to because she could see that Bryony wasn't in love with him and yet she kept him dangling as if having somebody there in the wings was better than living as a hopeless case. And she did feel hopeless too, what with Sam finding Callie and Polly getting all cosy with Jago. Josh was still single, but he seemed quite happy married to his books, truth be told. It would take a very special person to catch his attention. Even her younger sister Lara was living it up at university. Bryony was quite sure that she got through as many boyfriends as she did term papers.

Whereas she was a big fat failure in the romance department, resorting to online dating agencies and half-hearted attempts at a relationship with Colin the baker. It shouldn't have happened, of course. She shouldn't be single. She wouldn't have been either if Ben hadn't –

No! She wasn't going to think about that, but boy was it hard not to think about Ben when she knew he was back in town. And, in her experience, there was one way to banish a nasty thought from your mind: you ordered books. That was the one sure-fire way of taking your mind off your troubles and so that's what Bryony focussed on, making a selection of golden oldies and debut titles, series books and standalones. Her mother had once told her not to make rash decisions when it came to buying.

'Remember, you must think about your customers and not just what you want.'

It was good advice, but Bryony usually made up her own mind because she knew that the passion she had for each and every book she stocked could easily be transmitted to her customers. She felt sorry for the ones who sometimes just came in to browse when it was raining because they'd invariably leave with a big bag of books by the time Bryony had finished with them. She was passionate about her stock and that meant that everything she ordered in would be sold.

But even ordering a big stack of beautiful books could only keep her thoughts at bay for a limited time and Ben Stratton soon wiggled his way back into them. There was a part of Bryony which had hoped that this day would never come and that Ben would find a job and make a home somewhere abroad. Maybe he had, she thought. Maybe he was just visiting or collecting some of his things before heading off again. But something told her that wasn't the case. She instinctively seemed to know that Ben Stratton was back for good and that was highly unsettling.

Ben Stratton had always planned to come back to Castle Clare. He just never thought it would take him so long to make the journey. But it was six long years since he'd said goodbye to his home town, packed a modest bag and taken off with no real direction in mind – just the conviction that he had to get away. It had been the right decision, but so had coming home. He hoped.

How tiny the town looked now after the vast cities like Rome and Lima, and how lush the countryside seemed to him, how gentle its valleys and how verdant its woods. Yes, he could safely say that he'd missed Suffolk. As much as he'd wanted to get away from it, his return had been much longed for.

Of course, he was going to have to find a job as well as a place to live. His younger sister Georgia was putting him up on a futon bed in her spare room. It was luxury after some of the hovels he'd stayed in on his travels, that was for sure, but it was only a temporary measure. One could only live off the goodwill of a sibling for so long.

Dear Georgia, he thought as he walked through the tiny Victorian terrace she was renting on the outskirts of Castle Clare. She'd just left for university when he'd gone away. She'd been studying in Manchester and he'd told her not to come home during the holidays. Take a job, he'd told her. Stay with a friend, but don't come home. He'd made her swear that she wouldn't and she'd listened to him. They'd been close and she'd always looked up to her big brother. His word was golden. Thank goodness.

He walked to the dresser that Georgia had bought. The house had come partially furnished and she'd done her best to turn it into a home with a few modest purchases from eBay and the cheaper corners of local antique shops. She adored her dresser, filling it with all that female paraphernalia that Ben found baffling. Like why did you need a dozen mugs when there was only you in the house? And there were loads of jugs too – floral ones, spotty ones... He couldn't help but smile. Maybe his years as a traveller were telling on him and maybe it was time now for him to start buying furniture. And mugs.

There was one thing that particularly caught his eye on the dresser: a photo in a pretty glittery frame. He picked it up and looked at his and Georgia's smiling faces. It had been taken about seven years ago. The summer before Paul Caston arrived on the scene. Ben swallowed hard. How long ago those Paul-free days seemed before the shadow he cast had descended. But what could Ben have done about it? He'd been a student, studying English, and still living at home during the holidays when his mum had first brought Paul Caston into their home. Paul had been a few years older than Marion Stratton and he knew that she'd been easy to charm. Life hadn't been easy: she'd raised Ben and Georgia alone after their father had left them, flitting from relationship to relationship, never able to settle. Until Paul.

Ben groaned as he remembered the tyrant they had been forced to share their home with. When Ben had left Castle Clare, he'd hated abandoning his little sister, but he'd got in contact with several of her friends and made them promise to keep an eye on things and to make sure that, when she left for university, she never came home again.

Ben had had to go then. He'd been close to breaking point after Paul's constant bullying. He knew something bad would have happened if he hadn't left when he had. Everything was leading up to it, he could sense it. Only he hadn't meant to stay away for so long. That hadn't been the plan. But one country had led to another and one job followed on from the next, and Castle Clare and all the bad memories of Paul had seemed ever more distant.

He shook his head. He didn't want to think about that now. He'd promised himself that he wouldn't get sucked into a negative spiral of thought if he returned to Castle Clare. That wasn't what his return was about.

It was as he was replacing the photo on the shelf that Georgia bounced into the room, her dark curls bobbing around her face and her fake eyelashes making her look like a little doll. What was it with girls and fake eyelashes, he wondered? He didn't understand how they could be bothered with such things. Surely she was pretty enough?

'Want a cup of tea?' she asked.

'I'm good,' he said.

'What have you been up to today?'

He shrugged. 'Not much. Sleeping mostly.'

'Oh, Ben!'

'Hey, if you'd been travelling around the world for six years, *you'd* have a jolly good sleep when you finally made it home.'

'Oh, and that's the excuse you're going to trot out forever, is it? I can't empty the bin – I've been travelling around the world for six years. You make dinner, I've been travelling around the world –'

'Ha ha – very funny!'

She flopped down onto the sofa and he sat down beside her.

'Have you spoken to Mum yet?' she asked him.

Ben shook his head.

'Ben! You've got to ring her. Or – better still – go round.'

'I'm not ready for that.'

'No? And when will you be?'

'Maybe never.'

'Don't be like that. She's changed. She's not the woman she was when Paul was hanging around here.'

He shook his head. 'People don't change.'

Georgia gaped at him. 'You really believe that?'

'I really do.'

'So, all your travels and meeting people and experiences and foreign food and god only knows what else you ate or imbibed – all of that hasn't changed you just a teeny tiny bit?'

'Well, I've grown, obviously.'

'Yes, you have!' she said, poking his belly with a finger.

He frowned at her. 'I meant spiritually, emotionally.'

'And physically!'

'I keep myself fit.'

'I know you do. I was just teasing!' she told him. 'So, in all those years you've been away, you've stayed exactly the same Ben Stratton who left Castle Clare?'

'Well, I'm not *exactly* the same,' he admitted. 'I've got a couple of new scars and I've picked up a few new languages. I've learned some stuff along the way.'

'Exactly. And so's Mum.'

'What, Mum speaks Spanish and Italian now, does she?'

'That's not what I meant,' Georgia groaned. 'But she's learned some other stuff since you've been gone. She's learned that she's missed you more than anything in the world, Ben. You broke her heart when you left.'

'Rubbish. She wouldn't even have noticed I'd gone.'

'Oh, she noticed. She noticed every single day. She cried for a whole week when you left.'

Ben sighed. It surprised him how much his sister's words hurt him.

'Go and see her, Ben. You don't have to stay or say much. Just go and see her.'

'Does she know I'm back?'

'Of course she does.'

'You told her the minute I touched down, didn't you?'

'It would've been abnormal if I hadn't, wouldn't it?'

'I guess,' he confessed.

They sat in silence for a moment and then Georgia spoke again.

'You never visited once.'

The statement hung in the air a while before Ben responded.

'What would have been the point of that?'

'To say hello.'

'I'd left. What was the point in leaving if I was going to come back every five minutes?'

'Yes, but you didn't come back every five minutes. You didn't come back at all.'

'You could have come out to me,' he told her.

'Oh, yeah. I could have just hopped on a plane to South America with what I'm earning from the NHS.'

'You'd have loved South America, Georgie. The rivers, the waterfalls, the wildlife –'

'Don't change the subject. We're talking about you going to visit Mum.'

'No – *you're* talking about it. I'm doing my best not to.'

'Just say hello to her, Ben.'

'Say hello and leave?'

'If you need to. But go – and go soon.'

He held up his hand. 'Don't push me on this,' he warned her.

'Okay, okay,' she said, visibly backing down, 'but you really should think about it. Promise me you will.'

'I'm not going to make promises I can't keep,' he told her and then he saw the disappointment flicker in her eyes. 'I'll think about it.'

'That's all I ask.'

Bryony really couldn't understand how there was still such a big stigma about internet dating. Or maybe it was just a small town mentality. Maybe places like Castle Clare still believed that you should find a partner down the local pub or by being introduced to somebody – a friend of a neighbour, perhaps, or somebody you'd grown up with. That's why everybody had expected it to work out between her and Ben, wasn't it? Theirs had been a good old-fashioned love story. They'd met at school, they'd grown up together, they would get married and have children who would then go to the very same school that they had gone to. That's the way it worked in small towns. Life was simple and repeated itself over and over again. It was predictable, but oh-so comfortable in its predictability. Until one of you broke the cycle and upped and left.

Bryony clicked and scrolled. There were some pretty decent blokes on the Country Catches dating site like thirty-four-year-old Clive who was pictured holding a muddy Jack Russell Terrier and said he liked 'Ladies and Land Rovers'. He looked fun. Then there was the handsome Bradley who said he owned a yacht. Bryony bet it was more of a canoe, but he had a nice smile. Andrew looked fun too. Or he did until she read that he liked football and the girl he met had to love the one novel he'd ever read: *Tron*. Was that even a novel, Bryony wondered? Wasn't it a novelisation of quite a dull film? What a shame. And he had such a cute face too.

Her mother and Sam had both voiced their opinions about Bryony's dating agencies calling them dangerous and unnatural, but they were no such thing. Well, she had had her share of weird dates, she had to admit. Even when people put their photograph up online, you could still be taking a terrible gamble. Photos, she had soon found, could be years out of date or tampered with . Filters were used or flattering lighting and weird angles that would make people look much taller than they really were. But how else was she going to meet people? Castle Clare was a small town and she needed to widen her search because she couldn't help believing and hoping that there was somebody out there for her that could set her pulse racing like it did when she picked up a really good book.

Her mobile rang and she saw Colin's name flashing up on her screen. She instantly felt guilty for being on the dating site, but then she told herself that she had given things a good go with Colin. It wasn't her fault that their relationship just didn't seem to be working for her.

For a moment, she thought about ignoring his call, but that would have been mean and so she picked up.

'Hello,' she said, trying to sound more cheerful than she felt.

'Hi Bryony. This is Colin calling you later.'

'Pardon?'

'You told me to call you later.'

'Oh, I see!'

'What are you doing?'

'Oh, nothing,' she said, closing the browser on her laptop as if he was actually in the room with her.

'Fancy going out for a drink?'

'It's very late.'

'No it isn't.'

'I mean, I'm very tired. Would you mind if we didn't?'

'Of course not,' he said, but she could hear the disappointment in his voice.

She was always disappointing him, wasn't she? The sweet, kind man who made her cakes and did his very best to make her happy. She took a deep breath. She could either have an evening at home giving herself RSI from scrolling page after page of dating sites or she could stop moping and get up and go out.

'Okay,' she suddenly said. 'Let's go out.'

'Really?' He sounded positively shocked.

'Yes.'

'Great!'

She couldn't believe that she had made him so happy by just agreeing to go out for a drink with him.

'I'll pick you up in ten minutes, okay?'

Twenty minutes later, the two of them were in The Happy Hare. The pub was busy for a midweek evening and they were lucky to find a table in the corner where they took their drinks.

'A bit crowded, isn't it?' Colin said, taking a sip of his apple juice. Bryony had permitted herself a white wine, as she wasn't driving, and was just savouring its warming qualities when the pub door seemed to explode as two men came tumbling in.

'You idiot!' one of them called. 'I nearly got run over by that bike.'

'You shouldn't have tried keeping up with me,' the other one said. 'You know I'll beat you every time!'

They walked to the bar, panting slightly after the exertion of their run. Bryony shook her head. Why were men always showing off? Why did they need to be faster, fitter, better than each other? She watched them for a moment. They were laughing at something. The one nearest her was wearing dark jeans and a light shirt in defiance of the cool spring evening. His dark hair was too long and she could just make out a bit of a beard from where she was sitting. Bryony didn't like beards. They indicated laziness to her.

And then she recognised him. It was funny because she'd always assumed she'd know her Ben anywhere and at any time in their lives, in any room, any country, any situation. Only she hadn't.

But it was Ben. Her Ben.

He turned around from the bar and she gasped. He looked different and yet the same. The short dark beard made him look so much older than when she'd last seen him. She supposed that shaving wasn't a priority for someone who was travelling.

She swallowed hard, her focus doing a strange kind of contrazoom. Ben. Right there. After six years of being in some far-flung part of the globe, he was standing just feet away from her and there was a part of her – the twenty-two-year-old woman still somewhere inside her – who longed to shout across the room, to reach out to him.

Hey, Ben! It's me!

That part of her would have launched herself into his arms and kissed him, her fingers brushing across his beard as she teased him about it. But that part of her had long been replaced by another woman – the woman he'd left behind.

Colin placed his hand over hers.

'Bryony? Are you okay?'

She nodded, but didn't look at him. She couldn't drag her eyes away from Ben. She wasn't ready for this. She felt panicky – as if she was going to hyperventilate and need a paper bag to breathe into or some smelling salts to rouse her and she certainly wasn't that kind of woman. She refused to make any sort of scene.

They were bound to run into each other sooner or later, she knew that. She just hadn't banked on it being sooner.

'Bryony?'

Colin was saying something to her, but she wasn't hearing him properly because it was then that Ben saw her and their eyes locked.

'I've got to get out of here,' she told Colin and she was on her feet in an instant.

'Okay,' he said, looking around in a startled fashion as if she might have spotted a fire he hadn't yet seen.

'Right now!' she urged him, and they were out of the door of The Happy Hare before he could put his coat on or help her with her own.

CHAPTER 3

'Bryony Nightingale – come *here*!'

Ben Stratton looked up from his exercise book. He was stuck on the third comprehension question, which was asking him to imagine that he was one of the characters in the story they'd just read around the classroom and to write a short diary entry as that character. He'd been staring at his blank page for a good five minutes now and was glad of a distraction.

He watched as Bryony made her way to the front of the classroom and then looked at the thunderous expression on Mrs McKee's face. She was new to the school and all the pupils hated her because she was so strict and totally devoid of humour. Nothing made her laugh – not the joke dog poo in the desk drawer nor the whoopee cushion slipped onto her chair when Ed Friar was delivering books to her desk. Her stony face never shifted. There was never a sparkle to be seen in the dark eyes behind the black-rimmed glasses.

Bryony had reached the desk now and Mrs McKee thrust a book at her.

'What is the meaning of this?'

Ben saw Bryony's eyes widen as she looked at the page before her.

'I – erm – I don't...' Her voice petered out.

'Is it or is it *not* a rule that doodling in school books is *not* allowed?'

Bryony chewed her bottom lip and looked down at the floor as the old witch continued to cross-question her. Ben's breathing thickened and he could feel his hands clenching into fists.

'It was me, Miss,' he blurted, standing up.

Mrs McKee frowned. 'I beg your pardon?'

'I did it. I doodled in Bryony's book.'

Bryony shook her head in warning which Ben thought was really cute. She didn't want him to take the rap for her, but he was going to anyway.

'Come here,' Mrs McKee said with a twitch of a long bony finger.

Here we go, Ben thought, but he didn't regret his decision. He'd do anything for Bryony. She was his best friend. His *girlfriend*.

'So, Master Stratton,' Mrs McKee began, '*you* doodled this heart, did you? With your own initials inside it?'

A wave of laughter sounded from the rest of the class.

'SILENCE!' Mrs McKee cried.

Ben looked at the drawing in the back of Bryony's book. The heart was drawn in pink pen with a cupid's arrow in a lurid purple. His initials were smack bang in the middle of it. He swallowed hard.

'Yes,' he said.

'Yes, what?'

'It was me. I drew it.'

Mrs McKee's dark eyes narrowed at him in evil little slits. 'You honestly expect me to believe that?'

'I'm not lying. I drew it.'

'Why on earth would you draw a heart embellished with your own initials in Bryony's exercise book?'

Ben wasn't at all sure what the word "embellished" meant, but he thought he could wing it.

'I thought it would be funny,' he told her.

'Sit!'

Ben sat down in the chair at the side of Mrs McKee's desk. It was the greatest of all punishments to have to sit next to the crabby old teacher for the rest of the day.

She turned her attention to Bryony. 'Go back to your desk and take your book with you.'

Bryony did as she was told, but not before giving Ben a look which told of her deep gratitude towards him. Ben grinned back at her which earned him a rebuke from Mrs McKee.

Ben had to miss break-time and was kept back ten minutes at lunch. When he finally made it out into the playground, he saw Bryony sitting on a low wall swinging her legs as she read a book. It was one of the adventures of *The Famous Five*.

She looked up as he approached her and smiled. A few of his classmates laughed and pointed at him, calling him 'Love heart Ben', but he shrugged it off.

'You shouldn't have lied like that,' Bryony told him as he sat on the wall next to her.

'I wanted to.'

Bryony shook her head, but she was still smiling.

'I'll lend you my pink pen if you want to draw me some more

hearts,' she said.

'Very funny!'

She giggled and then handed him her book. 'Here.'

'What's this for?'

'To say thank you. I think you'll like it. It's the best *Famous Five* by far.'

'*Five Go to Smuggler's Top*,' Ben read.

'I've got another copy at home.'

'You've got *two* copies of the same book?'

'At least!'

'Your family's book crazy.'

'I know. It's great. You never get bored because there's always something to read. You should come over sometime.'

'Yeah?'

She nodded. 'You should come to Sunday lunch. Mum likes lots of people around the table and it's always something really tasty on Sundays.'

Ben frowned. 'Like what?'

'Like a roast with all the trimmings.'

'Trimmings?'

'Roast potatoes, parsnips, cauliflowers, cabbages, peas, carrots, onions —'

'You eat *all* that?'

'Not all at the same time!' Bryony said with a laugh.

'We usually have pizza or some kind of frozen pie with baked beans. My mum doesn't like cooking.'

'Then you should *definitely* come over.'

Ben remembered with fondness that first magical visit to Campion House for Sunday lunch. It was everything Bryony had promised and more. For one thing, he'd never seen so many people around a table, and then there was the immaculate silver cutlery and gleaming white plates. There were glass vases of flowers on the table, linen napkins inside silver rings and endless plates and bowls of food. He'd eaten so much that he felt quite sure he was going to burst. Eleanor Nightingale had hugged him and told him that he must come again which he had of course – over and over again. But that first visit had been particularly special.

His mum had dropped him off at Campion House with a dire

warning.

'You be nice now. Wash your hands and say please and thank you.'

'Yes, Mum.'

'The Nightingales are good people. Better than us. Don't you go breaking anything in there, you hear? That house is probably stacked full of priceless antiques and they'll be wanting your pocket money for a year at the very least if you do any damage.'

Ben had been terrified when he'd walked inside, his eyes darting around each room he walked into, tucking his elbows close to his body and barely breathing as he noted silver photo frames, china ornaments, beautiful mirrors and fascinating paintings. All horribly breakable if he got too close. But then there'd been the books. In bookcases, on shelves, stacked on tables, heaped on the floor – they were everywhere. Nice, safe books which looked as if they'd been handled for generations. You couldn't break a book, could you? Not unless you tried really hard. Books were safe even around him.

Bryony had taken him up to her room before lunch and he'd whistled when he'd seen the bookshelves in there. Most girls had rows and rows of toys and dolls, but not Bryony. She had books.

Ben had soon forgotten about the fear his mother had instilled in him. Being with Bryony again and talking about books had calmed him. He felt as if he'd found his natural home. In short, he felt like a Nightingale.

Ben gave a melancholy smile as he remembered that day. He hadn't thought about it for years, but it was still tucked away in that corner of his mind where happy memories were stored, ready to be relived at a moment's notice. And then he remembered something else. He still had the old faded copy of *Five Go to Smuggler's Top* and he hunted for it now.

His sister had been persuaded to retrieve a box of Ben's books from their mother's house when he'd told Georgia he was coming home. He'd missed his books. He had an e-reader loaded with novels and biographies and it was a fantastic lightweight device, which meant he could have a whole library about his person at any time whether he was in a city or up a mountain, but it wasn't the same as his books – his *real* books – books you could hold in your hand, which you could feel and hear when you turned the page. He missed their comfortable weight and how they looked on a bedside table.

The box of books was in the bedroom he was using at Georgia's and he got a penknife out of his jacket pocket and slit the tape, opening up the box and lifting out book after book, smiling as he recognised his old friends: the adventure novels, the spy stories, the memoirs of travellers and mountaineers, the atlases and travel guides to places he'd now been to.

And there it was: the Enid Blyton which Bryony had given him that day when she'd been sitting on the wall, swinging her bare legs as she'd been reading. It was faded with a cracked spine and had dog-eared pages just as a favourite book should have. But there was something else special about it and he opened it and looked at it now. It was a pink heart with a purple cupid's arrow through it and Ben's initials in the centre. He thought of when she'd given him the book. She'd asked to have it back for a moment and had turned.

'What are you doing?' he'd asked.

'You'll see.' She'd handed it back to him, her smile stretching from ear to ear.

But she hadn't been smiling at him in The Happy Hare the night before. Her eyes had been so full of pain and confusion that it had knocked the breath out of him and the speed at which she'd fled had hurt him so much.

And who had that guy been? Was she dating him? He didn't like the idea of that, he had to admit. But he couldn't expect her to have remained single all the years he'd been away. She would have been getting on with her life – dating men, letting them get close to her.

He shook his head. He couldn't bear to think about that.

Bryony Nightingale. How often he had thought of her as he'd journeyed from country to country? She'd never been far from his mind even after he'd stopped writing to her. He'd taken a photograph of her with him, keeping it close to him at all times. He even had it now and he took it out of his wallet to look at it. It was a photo which he had taken on a trip to Southwold. They'd walked down to the sea together and she'd gazed out at the horizon, her long dark hair blowing back in the breeze and the sun full on her face.

He'd had a few girlfriends as he'd worked his way across Europe and America, but that hadn't been until a full three years after leaving Castle Clare. He was no monk, after all, and yet his mind had always slipped back to Suffolk and to the girl he'd left behind. His best friend. His first love

'Bryony.' He spoke her name softly and, in an instant, he knew what he had to do.

Ben walked into the centre of Castle Clare, passing The George pub and Lottie's Antiques before entering Market Square and walking on towards Church Street. The place hadn't changed much. The three Nightingale bookshops were all looking resplendent with eye-catching displays in their beautiful bow windows. The bakers looked as if it had had a makeover. A new name too: Well Bread. Ben smirked. Very funny, he thought, peering in through the window, his mouth watering at the delights on offer.

It was then that he saw the man serving. It was the guy who'd been with Bryony in the pub. Was she going out with a baker? Ben frowned, a wave of jealousy hitting him as this stranger placed Viennese slices in a paper bag for a customer. He knew what he'd like to do with one of those Viennese slices. The thought of this man dating his Bryony was enough to make his nostrils steam.

Only she's not your *Bryony*, a little voice said – a voice he did his best to quash as he approached Bryony's bookshop.

He paused on the pavement, taking in the sunshine-yellow paint of the window frame and door. It was typical Bryony, he thought. She'd never been conservative when it came to colour. Even as a youngster, she'd always favoured rainbow-bright scarves and multi-coloured beads and bangles. Her accessories would often get her into trouble at high school and there was more than one occasion when her peacock-blue dangly earrings had been banned.

'I can't *live* in a grey world!' she'd protested to her form tutor as she pulled at her school jumper.

Her teacher, who'd worn grey even though she didn't have to, had looked completely baffled by this.

Ben grinned at the memory and, taking a deep breath, opened the shop door. A bell tinkled above his head and Bryony's voice came from a room behind the till.

'I'll be with you in a moment! Make yourself at home.'

Would she be saying that if she knew who it was, he wondered? Probably not.

He closed the door behind him and looked around. Eleanor Nightingale had just begun training Bryony to take over the shop when he'd left on his travels. She'd been so excited to be given so much responsibility and she was anxious not to let her family down. After all, Sam had done sterling work running the secondhand bookshop and Josh had been proving his worth in the independent which sold new titles. Bryony had a lot to live up to.

Well, Ben thought as he looked at the neatly stacked shelves, the colourful beanbags and rugs, the posters and the tiny chairs, she'd certainly achieved all she'd set out to. It was exactly the kind of shop Ben had expected her to run: warm, bright and welcoming. He could well imagine the children of Castle Clare flocking there in their hundreds.

'I've just had a delivery I couldn't resist opening,' Bryony said as she came out of the stock room, pushing her dark hair away from her face. It was loose, just the way Ben loved it, and it was all he could do not to race across the room and run his fingers through it.

The smile that had been on her face now vanished and Ben felt the same hollowness that he'd felt in the pub the night before.

'Hello, Bry,' he said, his voice barely above a whisper.

She didn't say anything, but continued to stare at him for a moment, colour rising in her cheeks.

'I saw you last night,' he continued, feeling like an idiot for saying something so inane. Of course he'd seen her, and she'd seen him seeing her which was why she'd left so quickly. 'Why didn't you come and talk to me?'

Her mouth opened as if she was about to say something but, instead, she turned away from him and went back into the stock room.

'Bryony?' He followed her, standing in the doorway and watching as she scooped up an armful of books. 'Do you want a hand with those?'

'No!'

It was the first word she'd directed at him and it felt like a bullet entering his chest.

'Talk to me,' he said. 'Please.'

She pushed passed him and placed the pile of books on the counter by the till and he honestly thought that she was going to keep her back to him and that he'd have to leave, but then she spoke.

'I don't know what to say to you.' Her voice wavered slightly as if she was on the verge of tears. 'Anything,' he told her. 'Say *any*thing to me.' He slowly approached her, stopping just short. 'Tell me that you've missed me or tell me I'm a prat. I won't mind.' He gave a little laugh, not at his humour but because he was nervous. He couldn't ever remember feeling so nervous in his life, not even when he'd been told to get out of the River Nile presto pronto because there'd been a crocodile attack less than two hours before, and not even when he'd encountered the world's largest spider in the South American jungle. He'd rather face a dozen Nile crocodiles and a thousand spiders than this appalling silence of Bryony's.

He swallowed hard, not knowing how to continue.

'I like your skirt,' he bumbled on. 'I've always loved red, blue, purple and pink together.'

Still nothing.

'You know, we're going to have to speak sooner or later so why not get it over and done with now? Bryony? *Please!*'

She turned to face him. 'I don't want to speak to you. I have nothing to say.'

He shook his head. 'I don't believe that. I can see all those words you want to fling at me just bubbling under the surface. Your eyes are practically on fire with hate for me. Go on – let me have it. You've been storing up for this very moment, haven't you? Well, I'm ready.'

She stared at him with those big brown eyes of hers which looked so full of emotion. His brilliant, bright, beautiful Bryony. How he wanted to reach out to her.

'You've got such a massive ego, haven't you?' she said, finding her voice at last. 'You think I've been doing nothing but pining for you since the moment you left? You can't imagine that I've been leading my own life without giving a second thought to you, can you?'

'Hey – that's not true.'

'No? Are you sure?'

'Bryony – you're not being fair.'

'What?' she cried. '*I'm* not being fair? After what you did to me?'

There was a dreadful pause as her question hung in the air between them. This wasn't going well, he thought. What on earth had made him think he could just walk into Bryony's shop after six years and expect her to want to speak to him? He'd been a fool to imagine that she'd be civil let alone friendly. But he couldn't help hoping that the connection that they'd once shared – that wonderful bond they'd had – would be remembered.

'Why did you come back, Ben? We'd got used you will being

away.'

The blunt statement was like a punch to his stomach. Was that how she really felt? He looked at the expression in her eyes and it was easy – so easy – to read the pain there.

'I just want to talk to you,' he said gently. 'I've missed you. I've missed you so much! And I insanely thought that you might want to talk to me or shout at me or ask me about my travels or tell me what's been going on with you. Six years is a long time not to speak to your best friend.'

'Best friends don't leave one another.'

And there it was. The accusation that had so wounded him when he'd left Castle Clare. Her opinion hadn't changed, had it? He had let her down in the worst possible way and there was no coming back from that in her eyes. But he couldn't give up because he believed in them and so he took a deep breath and continued.

'Who was that guy you were with in the pub?'

Her mouth dropped open at his bold question.

'What on earth has that got to do with you?'

'He didn't look like your sort.'

'My sort? How do you know I have a sort? You don't *know* me, Ben Stratton!'

'I did not so long ago and I don't think you've changed that much. Not really. And, if you have, then I want to know. I want to get to know you again. I missed you. I really missed you. You got the packages didn't you? The postcards, the books? I wanted you with me, Bryony. I waited for you, hoping you'd come out and join me.'

'You only waited two years.'

He frowned. 'Two years of writing to you is pretty good going, isn't it? I felt it was foolish to continue after I didn't hear from you. I didn't want to go on pestering you and pressurising you.'

'So, you gave up?'

'You're not being very fair here,' he told her. 'I didn't have one word of encouragement from you, Bryony. Not one. You had my details. Unless I was in the middle of nowhere, you knew how to get hold of me, but you didn't. Not once did you reach out and make contact.'

He could hear the anger and the pain in his voice and he really didn't want to get angry with her. That's not why he'd come to see her today. He didn't want to make hurtful accusations or push her even further away than she already was. Today was about saying hello and extending olive branches.

'Look,' he said, doing his best to calm down, 'I just want to talk to you. Perhaps we can go out sometime?' He paused, waiting for her response, her dark eyes holding his. 'What do you think? Could we go out? Get a drink or go for a meal or something?'

'I'm not going out with you.'

'Listen –'

'I want you to leave.'

'Bryony, please!' He reached a hand out towards her, but she turned her back on him and started shuffling books on the counter.

'Please leave.' Her voice was ice-cold and unrelenting.

'I'm not giving up,' he said, but he knew he was defeated today.

Ben left Bryony's shop feeling as if he'd just been kicked in the gut. She was the one he'd held in his heart all the way around the world. Hers had been the face he'd pictured each and every day whenever he'd seen something special he'd wanted to share with somebody.

Bry would love this, he'd think. Or *Bry would laugh at that.*

But she didn't want to see him. She didn't want to talk to him. She wanted nothing to do with him.

He was just about to head back to Georgia's when he saw Josh standing outside his shop, resting his chin in his hand as he examined his window display.

Ben sneaked up behind him.

'Ditch the encyclopaedia. It's *way* too big for that display.'

Josh turned around and a smile instantly engulfed his face.

'BEN!' he cried and the two of them slapped backs. 'Sam said you'd come home.'

'Yeah, a few days now.'

'And you didn't drop by to see me?'

'Hey – I was working my way around the Nightingale family. There's a lot of you!'

Josh laughed. 'And I guess you wanted to see a certain sister of mine?' He nodded across the road at the yellow-doored bookshop.

Ben sighed. 'It didn't go well, I'm afraid.'

Josh gave him a sympathetic look. 'Give it time. There's a lot of resentment there.'

'You don't say.'

'It's going to take a while for her to process it all.'

'She's had six years. I was kind of hoping she'd have mellowed towards me by now.'

'*Mellowed* – Bryony?'

Josh was right. Bryony just wasn't the sort of girl who'd mellow over time.

'So, what do I do now? Any suggestions from you as her brother?'

Josh looked serious for a moment – a look he inhabited well.

'Why don't you come over this Sunday?'

'Where?'

'Campion House, of course. Sunday lunch. Like the good old days.'

Ben looks surprised by the suggestion. 'Seriously?'

'*Seriously*! Mum and Dad – well, everyone – would love to see you.'

'Everyone? Are you sure?' He glanced back at Bryony's bookshop. 'She'll be fine.'

Ben frowned, uncertain of Josh's optimism and then something else occurred to him. 'I haven't got any wheels at the mo.'

'No worries – I'll pick you up.'

Ben grinned. Josh was certainly making it hard for him to say no.

'Where are you?' Josh asked him.

Ben told him the address.

'Great. I'll pick you up at midday. Give us plenty of time to catch up with everyone before lunch. Mum's going to have a thousand questions for you, I just know it.'

And there'll probably be one or two questions from Bryony as well, he thought. Like what the hell was he doing there? The likelihood of Bryony being happy to see him again was slim indeed, but he wasn't going to let that put him off.

CHAPTER 4

Josh picked Ben up at noon on Sunday to drive the short distance to Wintermarsh.

'You look smart,' he said as Ben got in the car.

'Don't sound so surprised. I can dress up when the occasion demands it.'

Josh laughed. 'Mum always likes us to wear proper shirts on Sundays. No tracksuit bottoms. No trainers. The funny thing is, she says she wants us to feel relaxed.'

'I think it's nice to make an effort.'

'Yeah, me too.'

They turned down the country lane from Castle Clare that would lead to Wintermarsh. It was a bright April morning with a blue sky dotted with happy white clouds and it almost felt warm enough to venture forth without a winter coat.

'They do know I'm coming, right?' Ben asked.

Josh shifted a little in the driver's seat. 'I've kind of left it as a surprise.'

'You haven't!'

'Mum loves surprises and there's always plenty of food, you know that.'

'It's not your mum I'm worried about.'

'Relax. Bryony will be fine,' Josh said as if reading his mind.

'It's easy for you to say.'

'And if she isn't, she's not going to cause a scene, is she? Not in front of everybody.'

'You sure about that?'

Josh gave a little shrug. 'It won't really matter if she does, will it?'

'You're not exactly making me feel comfortable here.'

'It'll be fine, trust me.'

Ben sighed. As much as he loved Josh's optimism, he couldn't help having misgivings all the same.

It wasn't long before they reached Campion House, pulling into the gravelled driveway in front of the elegant Georgian home. How he'd missed this place with its warm welcome, its squashy sofas and tea on tap, its dog walks round the fields and gentle conversation. It had been a perfect haven for him when he'd been growing up. His mother had gone through an alarming number of boyfriends and Ben and his sister had never known whom they would find at home. It was easier for them both to be elsewhere and Ben had so looked forward to his Sundays with the Nightingales.

'Is Bryony here yet?' Ben asked.

'Her car's not here, but she could have got a lift with Polly. That's her Land Rover. Wait till you meet Polly's new man. And Archie - you won't recognise him!'

They got out of the car and walked to the front door and went straight inside.

'Mum?' Josh called down the hallway, setting off a sudden volley of barks.

Ben watched as a large pointer and a pair of springer spaniels came charging towards them.

'Hardy the pointer and Brontë and Dickens the spaniels,' Josh said. 'Mum?'

'I'm coming, darling!'

Suddenly, Ben felt nervous about being there. What if Eleanor Nightingale wasn't happy to see him? What if Bryony had rung and told her mum about their awkward exchange in the bookshop earlier that week? It really wouldn't surprise Ben if Eleanor charged right back to the kitchen and came out with the steak knives. Or else set the dogs on him.

But he needn't have worried for, as soon as Eleanor saw him, she screamed in delight.

'Ben! My Ben!' she cried, tears instantly filling her eyes as she moved forward to embrace him.

'Mrs Nightingale!' Ben managed to choke up the words through the tight embrace.

'Eleanor! You can call me Eleanor!' She laughed and loosened her grip on him. 'What a wonderful surprise. I'd heard you were back.'

'I'm sorry you didn't know I was coming.'

'You don't need to apologise. I adore surprises!'

Josh gave Ben a knowing look.

'Well, it's kind of you to make me so welcome.'

There then followed a mad scrambling sort of welcome as heaps of Nightingales filled the hallway, clambering to get close to Ben.

First there was Polly who gave him a big kiss and teased him for having a beard.

'This is Jago,' she said and Ben shook the hand of a tall, good-looking man whose hair was even longer than his own.

'Archie won't recognise you, I'm afraid,' Polly said.

'I remember Ben!' Archie chirped up as he came forward.

'You can't possibly!' Polly laughed. 'You were tiny when Ben left. You probably remember the stories you've heard about him.'

'Stories, eh? All good I hope,' Ben said.

'Well, mostly!' Polly confessed.

The group migrated to the living room where Grandpa Joe was just getting up from an armchair to see what was going on.

'You remember Grandpa Joe?' Eleanor said.

'Of course I do. How are you?' Ben and Grandpa Joe hugged.

'I bet you've had a few adventures, my young man!'

'One or two.'

'And I expect you to tell me each and every one of them, you hear?'

'You're on!'

'Grandma Nell okay?' Ben asked Joe.

A tender look came into Joe's eyes. 'She's slowing down a little. Needs a bit of extra care these days. She'll join us for lunch. You'll get a chance to catch up then.'

Frank was next to come forward.

'How are you, sir?'

'None of this *sir* business,' Frank said. 'How are you, Ben?'

'I'm good.'

'You look well. I like the beard.'

'You do?' Ben said in surprise, stroking his face. 'My sister hates it. Actually, most women I meet hate it.'

'It makes you look –' Frank paused, 'like a real adventurer.'

Ben laughed. 'I'll take that!'

It was then that Sam stepped forward. Ben had already spoken to Sam on the phone, but it was great to see his old friend again and the two of them embraced.

'Hey, I want you to meet my girl.'

'I've been looking forward to it.'

'Callie, this is Ben. Ben – Callie.'

'It's really good to meet you at last,' Callie said.

'Likewise. Sam's told me a lot about you. You're a writer?'

'I am.'

'I'd love to talk to you about that sometime,' Ben said.

'You'd like to write?' Callie asked.

'Not fiction – nothing that ambitious – but I'd love to gather all the real stories from my travels. A kind of journal so I can remember everything. I'm worried about forgetting it all.'

'I'd be happy to help if I can,' Callie said.

'Thanks!' Ben said. 'That would be really great.'

'I'm afraid our Lara isn't here to say hello today. She had tickets for a concert last night,' Frank said. 'Some group all the students are crazy about and I'm guessing it was a late night.'

'I remember those,' Ben said.

'Listen,' Eleanor said, 'this is all absolutely wonderful, but has anybody thought what Bryony is going to make of – well – Ben being here?' She looked at him. 'I'm sorry. I hate to say this because it's so wonderful to see you and you are more than welcome to join us.'

'I don't want to cause any trouble,' Ben stated.

Eleanor nodded. 'I'm not sure Bryony's going to be too happy about –'

'What am I not going to be happy about?' Bryony asked. With all the noise in the crowded living room, nobody had heard the front door open and Bryony now stood looking at them from the doorway. 'Mum?'

'Bryony, come on in and see who's here,' her mother said. Ben watched as if in slow motion as the cheery smile which had been on Bryony's face vanished as quickly as the sun being swallowed up by a storm cloud. He knew what would follow and he wasn't a bit surprised when she bolted, the front door slamming behind her a second later.

'Oh, dear,' Eleanor said. 'I'll go after her.'

Bryony couldn't believe it. First her shop and now her family home. Was nowhere to be safe from Ben Stratton?

She knew she couldn't stay and that made her sad as well as angry. She couldn't remember the last time she'd had to miss a Sunday lunch with her family. They were a weekly touchstone for her and they'd got her through the rough times when Ben had first left. But now her family seemed to have taken his side, allowing him in when she'd made it perfectly clear over the years how she'd felt about him leaving.

She'd just opened her car door when her mother's voice called after her, as she'd known it would.

'Bryony?'

'I'm going home.'

Her mother's hand reached out and gently touched her shoulder. 'Can we talk about this?'

'There's nothing to say, Mum.'

'I beg to differ, darling.'

'Ben's here which means I can't be.'

'I know this is difficult for you.'

'Difficult? You have no idea! Why is he even here? Did you invite him? Did Sam?'

'Actually, he came with Josh.'

'Josh?'

Her mother nodded. 'I had no idea Ben was coming today.'

'But you're thrilled that he's here, aren't you?'

'Well, I can't deny that it's very good to see him.'

Bryony could feel tears rising now and she did her best to blink them away. 'I hope you all enjoy your Sunday lunch together!'

'Don't be like that, Bryony. We want you here.'

'I can't be here – with him.'

'Won't you at least try? I know this isn't easy for you, but you're going to run into him sooner or later. Castle Clare's a pretty small town. You can't avoid him forever. Wouldn't you rather get it all over and done with now – here at your home with your family all around you?'

'The family that's betrayed me?'

'Josh wasn't betraying you. He probably thought you'd got over Ben a long time ago. And it has been a long time, hasn't it, darling?' She paused, giving her a gentle smile. 'And you must remember that Ben was a friend to all of us, not just you. He practically grew up here – an honorary Nightingale, isn't that what you used to say? We've all missed him and I very much want him to stay for lunch. So, you can go back home and open a tin of soup to eat with your crackers because I know you won't have a fresh loaf of bread in, will you? Or, you *could* stay here and enjoy roast beef, Yorkshire puddings and all the trimmings and the rather wonderful treacle tart and home-made custard.'

Bryony inwardly cursed her mother for knowing her and her bare cupboards at home so well. Why should she sacrifice a family lunch just because Ben was there? It wasn't fair. If anyone should be running, it should be him. This was her family home, not his, and she was jolly well going to enjoy her Sunday as usual whether he was there or not.

'Well? What you want to do, darling?' her mother asked gently.

Twenty minutes later, Bryony was sat at the table with her family. It was customary at Campion House to sit the guest next to the person who'd invited them so Ben was placed next to Josh which meant that he was also next Bryony. She tried not to physically flinch as she sat down next to him. At least, she thought, she wasn't opposite him and so could avoid looking at him. She could do this. She just had to keep telling herself that she was an adult and that something like this wasn't going to faze her at all.

Grandma Nell didn't recognise Ben at first, narrowing her eyes at him as she sat down at the table.

'It's Ben,' Grandpa Joe told her.

'Bryony's Ben?'

Bryony rolled her eyes. 'He's not Bryony's Ben anymore,' Grandpa Joe corrected.

'Then whose Ben is he?' Nell asked.

'Nobody's,' Ben said. 'Yet.'

Bryony swallowed hard. It was almost too much to bear. Just what was her family thinking, forcing her to endure this torture?

Luckily, the food was served without delay and the family and their guests got on with the business of eating.

'I can't remember the last time I had a Yorkshire pudding,' Ben said. 'These are delicious, Mrs – erm – Eleanor.'

'Thank you, Ben. Do help yourself to more. There are plenty of them.'

He leaned forward towards the blue and white china bowl heaped with golden puddings, inadvertently knocking Bryony's elbow which sent her fork scratching across her plate.

'Sorry!' he blurted.

'It's okay,' she said, her mouth tight, willing the time to pass so she could return to the sanctuary of her home.

'What are your plans now, Ben?' Frank asked as he plunged the serving spoon into a bowl heaped with glazed carrots.

'I've just been offered a part-time teaching job in Ipswich.'

'What are you teaching?' Eleanor asked.

'English to foreign students and a bit of Spanish and Italian. I've also got some translation work through an agency. It's not much, but it's a start.'

'You should have said you were looking to teach,' Polly piped up. 'I could have asked around at my school in Bury.'

'Thanks,' Ben said with a nod.

'Let me know if you want me to ask. The pay's not astonishing, but the support team is really great and the students are lovely.'

'So, tell us about your travels, Ben,' Callie said from across the table. 'What were the most exciting places?'

It was so very hard for Bryony not to look at Ben at this moment for she too wanted to ask him that question. So many questions, in fact, but her pride was stopping her.

'I can honestly say that every single place was exciting because it was all new to me. I'd only ever known Castle Clare. We'd never been able to afford proper holidays growing up. We used to get a few days out to the coast if we were lucky, so it was even exciting just going to Gatwick.'

Everybody laughed. Everybody but Bryony.

'Seriously! Have you seen that place? It's enormous. They've got shops. There's even a Harrods there.'

Bryony had to will herself not to laugh. How easy it would have been to join in with everybody else and enjoy Ben's stories, and to reach out and place a hand on his arm and squeeze it gently.

'But – seriously – I loved it all. I think the first place I fell in love with was Rome. The scale of it. The endless streets with architectural wonders around every corner. It's like the world's largest film set. But it's so noisy. I think I had a permanent headache from the crowds and the traffic. Same in Sorrento and Naples – the motorbikes get everywhere.'

'I don't like motorbikes,' Grandma Nell said.

'Jago does,' Archie stated with pride.

'But I don't terrorise tourists with mine,' Jago said.

'Although you did have that run in with Antonia Jessop last week,' Polly reminded him.

'Ah, yes. The indomitable Miss Jessop!' Jago said with a chuckle.

'What does *that* mean?' Archie said, his nose wrinkling.

'Erm, it means she doesn't like motorbikes,' Jago told him.

'Or anything else much,' Polly added and there were a few knowing nods from around the table.

'Sorry, Ben, we interrupted you,' Jago said.

'It's okay,' he said.

'Tell us about South America,' Frank said. 'I'd love to see the plants there.'

Eleanor rolled her eyes. 'You'd turn Campion House into a rainforest if you ever went over there.'

'I am increasingly drawn to tropical plants,' Frank admitted.

'Whereas I like a traditional English garden,' Eleanor said.

'Well, I couldn't name any of the plants I saw, but the colours of the flowers along the Inca Trail were pretty spectacular. But I have to say that the best thing about travelling was the people I met and the stories I heard. It's very comforting to know that, in every corner of the world, there are good people willing to share their homes with you, their food and their experiences. I loved that.'

'You'll have to bring your photos over sometime,' Eleanor said. 'We'd love to see them.'

'We could have a slide show!' Grandma Nell said excitedly. 'Where's the projector?'

'You don't need a projector anymore, Mum,' Frank told her.

'What do you mean?'

'It's all digital now.'

She frowned at him and shook her head. 'Silly boy.'

Grandpa Joe reached out and patted her hand as Bryony silently cursed her mother for giving Ben an excuse for a return visit.

'I bet you had to eat some weird food along the way,' Josh said.

'I certainly did and you properly don't want to hear about it the dining table,' Ben warned them.

'I do!' Archie insisted.

'Yes, go on, Ben,' Sam encouraged.

'Well, I think the most surprising was a place we were staying in Peru. We were up in the mountains, sleeping in this tiny home where all these guinea pigs were just running around the floor.'

'Oh, I love guinea pigs!' Polly said.

'So do I,' Ben said, 'and I just assumed these were pets at first, but there were rather a lot of them and I suddenly realised that they were food. Rather like chickens wandering around.'

'You didn't eat a guinea pig?' Polly cried.

'It was that or go hungry,' Ben told her.

'Then you should have let your stomach rumble!'

'It would have also been an insult to our host. Rather like refusing to eat these fine Yorkshire puddings here.'

'Yes, but Yorkshire puddings aren't alive. They haven't been scampering around our front room,' Polly pointed out.

'True enough.'

'It's all part of the adventure of travelling, isn't it?' Frank said.

Eleanor shook her head. 'Not any travel we've ever done. Burnham Overy Staithe is about as exotic as we get these days.'

'Everyone should travel,' Ben said. 'If you don't see any of the world, how do you know how wonderful home is?'

'Some people just know,' Bryony said, feeling that Ben's barb was aimed at her.

'But it's healthy to get out and see other people, other places,' Ben went on, turning to look at her now.

'You can do that through books,' Bryony said.

'It's not the same though.'

'Some people prefer to stay at home,' she said, her eyes resolutely looking at her plate.

'Yes,' Eleanor interrupted as if coming to her daughter's rescue. 'Travel doesn't suit everyone. Now, let's see about some pudding. Everyone want some?'

There followed a chorus of approval at the suggestion and it wasn't long before they were all enjoying the delicious treacle tart and custard. Archie ate his in record time even by his own exacting standards, and seconds were dutifully handed around.

After all the plates, bowls and glasses had been cleared away, tea was served in the living room and the Nightingale family and their guests sprawled comfortably on the squashy sofas and armchairs heaped with pretty floral cushions.

'I miss the fire,' Polly said, nodding to the empty fireplace.

'We've not lit it for a few weeks now, have we?' Frank said to Eleanor.

'I've been tempted on a couple of evenings, I have to say.'

'I'm afraid I've had mine lit,' Callie said. 'Owl Cottage may be small, but it seems to be perpetually cold.'

'They're such cheerful things to have even if you don't necessarily need them,' Polly said.

'Do you have a fireplace at Lilac Row?' Callie asked.

'We do, but we've not used it yet,' Polly said.

'We're looking forward to it, though, come winter,' Jago said.

'Oh, who's talking about winter when we're just getting over the last one?' Eleanor cried. 'How I long for, warmer days.'

'Not long now,' Frank assured her. 'The earth's warming up nicely.' He finished his tea and got up and walked across to the sash window which overlooked the front driveway, peering up into the sky. 'Who's up for a dog walk?' he asked, clapping his hands together and startling Grandpa Joe who was dozing off behind the book review section of the Sunday paper.

Sam, Callie, Bryony, Polly, Jago and Archie were on their feet in an instant.

'Ben – like to join us?' Frank asked.

'Sure,' he said.

Bryony seethed inside. Was even the Nightingale ritual of a Sunday afternoon walk to be violated by this man?

There then followed a mad scramble for wellies, shoes and coats before everyone trooped out of the house and into the country lane, the two spaniels and the pointer on leads. The sky was a pearly blue and there were signs of spring everywhere with primroses and violets starring the banks along the lane and the sweet scent of bluebells filling the air as they entered a wood. But Bryony was much too focussed on Ben to take notice of the heavenly scene before her. He was walking with Sam and Callie and they seemed deep in conversation and so she took the opportunity to speak to Josh, sidling up next to him as he did his coat up.

'Hey, I want a word with you!'

'Oh, yeah?' he said, his tone betraying nothing of the guilt she felt he should be harbouring.

'You just don't think, Josh!' Bryony hissed.

'What are you talking about?'

'What am I talking about? *Ben*!' she said. 'What were you thinking of inviting him here?'

'It seemed like a good idea,' he told her. 'I thought you'd get to talking and –'

'And what? Miraculously work things out? That I'd forgive him for leaving me?'

'Well, yes!' Josh said.

Bryony thumped him in the arm.

'Ouch!' he cried, causing several heads to turn around. 'Anyway,' Josh continued in a whisper, 'don't forget that you broke up with him too. He asked you to go with him, remember?'

The pungent scent of wild garlic assailed them a moment later as Josh scooted ahead to avoid more aggravation, and Bryony tried to forget her woes and take pleasure in the beauty of the place. The three dogs gambolled through the woods and Archie did a surprisingly good impression of a cuckoo which must have given the one they could hear pause for thought.

How, in a group of ten people, Bryony happened to find herself next to Ben at a stile, she didn't know. It was the old rickety stile too which usually necessitated a helping hand.

'Careful over the stile!' Frank called as he always did. 'It's worse than ever. Slippery too.'

Bryony watched as Josh leaped over without any bother. Her father helped her mother over, then Sam helped Callie and Jago took Polly's hand and then Archie's. Which left her and Ben.

'Come on,' he said once he was on the other side.

'I can manage,' she told him without looking at him.

'It's pretty slippery.'

'I said, I can –' As soon as her foot hit the bottom plank of the stile, it skidded out from underneath her, sending her flying right into Ben.

'Woah there!' he said. 'You okay.'

She pushed him away and straightened her hair, catching his gaze as she righted herself. He was looking at her with such tenderness and concentration that she suddenly felt self-conscious.

'You all right, Bry?' Polly said, coming forward and reaching a hand towards her.

'I said I'm fine,' Bryony said. 'I don't know what all the fuss is about.'

Without looking at anybody else, Bryony strode ahead on the footpath, determined to be the first person back at Campion House. There, she would kick off her boots, kiss her grandparents goodbye and get in her car and drive home before anybody could stop her.

CHAPTER 5

By the time Bryony got home, she felt emotionally drained and she still couldn't help harbouring the thought that her family had betrayed her in the worst possible way. Welcoming Ben back into the Nightingale fold might have been a normal thing for them to do with an old family friend, but it couldn't possibly be the right thing to do because she'd never felt so uncomfortable in her life.

Sitting next to him at the dining table had been unbearable. Their arms had nudged and touched in an agonised sort of dance. Had he felt it too – that awful sense of unease? No, he'd told his jolly traveller's stories and stuffed his mouth full of her mother's food. He'd had a brilliant time, but it had been at her expense.

Bryony did what she did best when she was mad: she tidied. She moved around her small home like a whirling dervish, her colours flying as she scrubbed and dusted until she was not only emotionally drained but physically too. By that time, it was after five and she realised that she was hungry, probably because she'd only been able to eat half her lunch what with having Ben sitting next to her. As her mother had predicted, there was nothing to make a decent meal in her cupboards.

It was then that she remembered the little table of goods for sale outside the cottage across the road from her. Cuckoo Cottage, she thought it was called. It belonged to Flo Lohman who Bryony knew in passing. She'd been into the children's bookshop on a number of occasions. Bryony tried to think back now and recalled a thin, pale-looking boy had accompanied her. He'd been terribly shy and hadn't said a single word. Flo was also a part of the new book group which her brother Sam had set up. She remembered Sam talking fondly about her and laughing at the 'cake wars' that had ensued between her, Honey Digger and Antonia Jessop.

Popping her jacket on, Bryony left the house and headed towards Cuckoo Cottage, sighing in disappointment when she discovered that the table was empty of produce. She looked at the pretty pink home with its thatched roof and white-painted door and wondered if it was worth knocking. What did she have to lose?

As soon as she knocked, she heard a strangled call coming from inside.

'Coming!'

A moment later, Flo Lohman opened the door. She had pretty green eyes and a lovely smile which creased her face, but it was her shoulder-length white curls Bryony was staring at in bemusement.

'You – er – you have a feather in your hair,' Bryony managed at last.

Flo's hands flew to her hair. 'Usually do,' she said. 'Just had my head in the coop trying to find Hermia. She's very shy and often hides away there during the day.'

'I was just wondering if you had any eggs. There aren't any out for sale.'

'Ah! Very remiss of me. And I'm absolutely overrun with eggs too. Come on in and I'll gather some up for you. How many would you like?'

'Half a dozen would do very nicely.'

Flo nodded and led the way into her kitchen at the back of the house. It was a sweet little room with low beams and the sort of kitchen cabinets that had been cobbled together over many years with none of them really quite matching. Still, the overall picture was one of comfort and charm and Bryony instantly felt at home there. The place she was renting had one of those bland, fitted kitchens all in an off-white and it was anything but homely.

'Now, where did I put the egg boxes? They're here somewhere. I just got a new stack last week. Where are they?' Flo looked around the kitchen, bending and stretching and peering around corners and under tables.

'There!' Bryony said, pointing to a table to the left of a dresser which was laden with papers, envelopes and an assortment of jam jars.

'Ah, marvellous!' Flo said, grabbing one and popping six plump eggs inside. 'Fresh as a daisy these,' she told Bryony.

'What beautiful colours,' Bryony said. 'All so different.'

'Like the hens who laid them – Viola's are as pale as milk and Gertie's are nice and dark.'

'How much are they?'

Flo told her and Bryony paid her.

'Thank you. Bryony, isn't it?'

'Yes.'

Flo nodded. 'We've spoken only briefly, haven't we?'

'You've been in my shop a couple of times.'

'That's right. Lovely it is too. I brought my great-nephew with me.'

Ah, so that was the pale, young boy, Bryony thought.

'Not seen him for a while. I'd say he's due a visit if I know anything about my nephew.' She tutted and then peered closely at Bryony. 'Are you alright, my dear?'

Bryony felt surprised by the question. 'I'm okay.'

'Hmmmm, that's the worst impression of somebody who's okay that I've ever seen.'

Bryony's mouth dropped open to protest, but she found she couldn't say anything and then her eyes began to well with tears and, all of a sudden, she was crying, right there in Flo Lohman's kitchen with a box of eggs in her hands.

'Oh my dear girl. Come and sit down. I'll move that cat off the chair. Dusty knows he shouldn't be in here. Then I'll make us a nice cup of tea.'

Bryony let herself be led to a wooden chair at the kitchen table and sat down. Flo handed her a tissue and Bryony dried her eyes and blew her nose as Flo put the kettle on.

'Milk and sugar's on the table,' Flo told her. Bryony nodded, but decided to forgo her usual sugar when she saw a hen feather in the blue bowl.

'Thank you,' she said as Flo handed Bryony her tea.

'Sorry about the mug,' Flo said as she moved a heap of old newspapers from a chair and sat down next to her. 'It's one I made at an evening class.'

Bryony looked at the asymmetrical mug with the handle that was slightly too big and tried her hardest not to laugh. It was so very Flo, she thought: home-made, funny and very comforting.

'Tea,' Flo said, 'the universal cure-all.'

'I wish it was,' Bryony said.

'Man trouble, is it?' Flo boldly asked. 'You have that sort of weary look about you.'

'Do I?'

'Oh, yes,' Flo said. 'Unmistakable.' She took a huge slurp of tea. 'Want to talk about it? I'm a very good listener, you know.'

'Thanks, but I'm okay.'

Flo nodded, not looking convinced.

'So, this man trouble,' Flo began a moment later. 'Is it Colin the baker?'

Bryony frowned. 'How do you know about him?' she asked, although she really shouldn't have been surprised that that particular piece of gossip was out there.

'You're going out with him, aren't you?' Flo said, sounding baffled.

'Well, not really.'

'Oh, I'd heard –'

'Well, we're sort of going out I suppose,' Bryony said.

'You don't sound too sure, my dear,' Flo said. 'If you don't mind me saying.'

Bryony sighed. 'But it's not Colin that's the problem. I mean, the reason I'm crying.'

'You mean there's someone else?'

'You could say that.'

'Oh, my.'

'Exactly.'

'Is it Ben?'

'You know about Ben?'

'He was your childhood sweetheart, wasn't he? Or have I got his name wrong?'

'No, you haven't got his name wrong.'

'He's back, I hear.'

Bryony frowned and then laughed. 'You don't miss much, do you?'

'Well, my eyesight isn't what it used to be and my right foot seizes up with arthritis from time to time, but I'm still pretty hot when it comes to what's going on in Castle Clare.'

Bryony gave a wry laugh. 'Life in a small town.'

'Better than any gossip magazine,' Flo said.

'He was at my parents' today,' Bryony said.

'Ben?'

She nodded. 'Josh invited him. Can you believe it? And my parents were all over him. Everybody was. The long lost hero, he was, stuffing his face full of Yorkshire puddings at *my* family dining table whilst I was sitting there with my heart breaking all over again.'

'Oh, sweetheart!' Flo said, her hand moving across the table to hold Bryony's.

'I left after the dog walk which really made me mad because we were probably going to have hot chocolate afterwards.'

Flo shook her head. 'He sounds like a very cheeky chappie to me.'

'He is,' Bryony agreed. 'He's cheeky and insensitive and thoughtless –'

'And you're still in love with him?'

Bryony gasped. '*No!*'

'Then why is he riling you so much?'

'Because he thinks he can just breeze back into all our lives after having left us. You know he actually came into my shop? He expected me to talk to him too.'

'Well, let him.'

'Let him what?'

'Let him get on with it. You do what you do and let him get on with his Ben stuff. You can't stop him, but you *can* control your response to him. By getting up and leaving your parents' this afternoon, you gave him control. You showed him that he upset you. Is that what you wanted?'

'But I couldn't stay there a minute longer. I *had* to leave.'

Flo nodded. 'I know it must have been hard, but if he sees you're not bothered by him, he'll soon go away.'

Bryony took a sip of her tea, wishing there wasn't a hen feather in the sugar bowl.

'That is what you want, isn't it?' Flo asked. 'For him to go away?'

'Yes, of course it is. With any luck, he'll take his ugly beard and leave Castle Clare for the nearest jungle as soon as possible and things can go back to normal around here.'

'He's got a beard, has he?' Flo said with a chuckle.

'It's horrible.'

'Oh, I've always rather liked a beard. Makes a man…' she paused, '*manly.*'

Bryony examined Flo, taking in the dreamy look on her face. Perhaps she was remembering a bearded beau from her past, she thought.

'Have you ever been married, Flo?'

The dreamy expression on Flo's face vanished as she was brought back to the present.

'I've had my share of experiences, but marriage wasn't one of them,' she told Bryony. 'My brother, Robert, married. It wasn't a happy affair. Perhaps that put me off a bit. They had a son. Just the one. He's a bit of a handful if I'm honest. Mitch. He married a woman who did a runner after their son's first birthday party. The cake had just been cut. Can you imagine? It's him, my great-nephew, who I bring into your shop from time to time. He's a sweet boy. Painfully shy. It must be hard to grow up without your mother. I try to fill in a bit when I can, but I don't suppose I'm much of a substitute.'

'Oh, I bet he loves you. And I bet he loves coming here with all the animals,' Bryony said.

'Pity he's not a little bit older and stronger, though,' Flo said. 'He's only eight, you see, and he's small for his age, I could do with a bit of help around the place.' She shook her head. 'But I mustn't wish his little life away just so I can get a few chores done.'

'Doesn't your nephew help?' Bryony asked.

'Mitch?' Flo almost screamed. 'He's no help to anyone. He just drops his boy off and disappears. I've no idea what he's up to. He barely says a word when he does deign to come in. He just sort of skulks about a bit, grumbles something and then leaves. I notice he usually swings by before lunch and comes back after dinner so his boy gets fed twice. I don't mind. Don't get me wrong, now. But he never asks if that's okay. Never checks if I've got enough food in. I don't mind doing my bit and taking care of little Sonny, but I don't like being taken advantage of.'

'Of course not. Nobody does,' Bryony said. 'Sonny's a sweet name.'

'Yes, well, it beats his given name.'

'What's that?'

'That daft mother of his called him Jefferson. Imagine landing a little boy with a name like Jefferson and then doing a runner after the birthday cake.'

Bryony had to hide her smile at the scenario Flo painted.

'I don't think Jefferson is too bad a name. Not when you think of all the odd things kids get called these days. Did you know there's a Rainbow in Castle Clare?'

Flo almost spluttered into her tea. 'No!'

'She was in my shop just last week.'

'It's like something from the sixties.'

'And it suits her too. She's a fairy-like sort of girl.'

It was then that Bryony thought of something.

'Flo?' she said as she finished her tea. 'You mentioned needing a bit of help around the place.'

'Yes,' Flo said. 'The problem is I can't afford to pay very much. In fact, it would be handy if I could pay in eggs and cabbages and other produce.' She gave a laugh. 'I don't expect that would wash, though. Why? Do you have somebody in mind?'

'Yes – me.'

Flo frowned. 'But you've got your shop to run.'

'Only during the day and not on Sundays or Mondays and my cupboards and fridge are permanently bare.'

'But you wouldn't want to clean out hen coops and shovel up donkey poo, would you?'

'I would. I absolutely would.'

Flo looked puzzled by this.

'I need the exercise,' Bryony said, 'and I like you, Flo.'

Flo shook her head. 'There's something else going on here, isn't there?'

Bryony held her gaze for a moment and then sighed. 'I need a place to hide.'

'I see.'

'Do you?' Bryony asked.

'From this Ben, is it?'

Bryony nodded. 'He's already got to me at my shop and my family home and I wouldn't be surprised if someone gives him my address, but he doesn't know about this place.'

A small smile spread across Flo's face. 'So, this would be like a refuge. A hideaway!' she said excitedly.

'Yes!' Bryony said.

'Okay then, my dear. You're on!' Flo was on her feet and Bryony got up too.

'Thank you so much, Flo! You don't know how much this means to me.' She flung her arms around the old lady who giggled like a little girl.

'This will be our secret. A real adventure!' Flo said and Bryony nodded. Yes, she thought, Cuckoo Cottage would be the perfect Ben-free zone.

After Josh had dropped Ben off at his sister's house, he'd poured himself a glass of the cheap white wine Georgia had in her fridge and knocked it back. He shouldn't have listened to Josh. He'd been wrong to go to Campion House. It had been great to see everyone again. He'd been made so welcome, but it had come at a great price: he'd upset Bryony. She'd quietly slipped away some time after the dog walk. He hadn't seen her go and Eleanor had looked upset when she'd realised her daughter had gone.

'I'm sorry,' he'd told her. 'It's my fault. I shouldn't have come.'

'Nonsense,' Eleanor had said. 'You're always welcome in this house. You know that.'

And Ben did, but he also knew that Bryony would never welcome him there nor in her shop.

'Nor in Castle Clare,' he said to himself. Actually, she probably wished he hadn't come back to the UK at all. He bet she'd be happier if he'd found a friendly Amazonian tribe to live with. But he'd felt it was time to come back home. The truth was, he'd not only missed Bryony and his sister and friends; he'd missed the old town too, and he planned on staying. It was his hope – his dearest hope – that he could make peace with Bryony. Even if it didn't go any further, even if they couldn't go back to that special place they'd once shared, that warm and loving place where only the two of them existed, he'd feel as if he was making progress if she'd at least speak to him.

He poured himself a second glass of wine, remembering the time he and Bryony had drunk their first bottle of red together. They'd been seventeen and Bryony had sneaked it out of the dining room after a Christmas party. There'd been so many bottles left around the place that they'd felt sure one wouldn't be missed.

They'd drunk it in Bryony's bedroom, taking it in turn to swig from the bottle. It had been a horrible mistake. Ben had had to spend the night in Sam's room because he was totally incoherent and couldn't possibly drive home and Bryony had fallen asleep with all her clothes on. Ben had woken with a crashing hangover and Bryony had been sick all the next day. Luckily, Frank and Eleanor Nightingale had laughed it off, telling them that it was a lesson learned. Ben hadn't touched red wine since even during his stint at a vineyard in Umbria.

Drinking his glass of white wine now, he remembered the pale-faced Bryony from that day after the red wine.

'I'll never forgive you for this, Ben Stratton,' she'd told him.

'It was your idea!' he'd told her.

But she had forgiven him even though he didn't need forgiving and they'd even been able to laugh about it later on.

But she wasn't laughing now, was she? And she would probably never forgive him either.

CHAPTER 6

Cuckoo Cottage was exquisitely pretty with its Suffolk pink colour and its thatched roof, but what set it apart from its neighbours was its enormous garden at the back. Over the years, Flo had bought pockets of land from the neighbouring farmer, slowly extending her garden to accommodate her ever-expanding family of animals which included three threadbare stray cats, a large flock of free-ranging chickens who frequently made it into the kitchen, half a dozen vociferous geese, a little flock of ducks, a pair of pigs and a couple of retired donkeys.

That the little house was called Cuckoo Cottage wasn't lost on Flo who thought it a very apt name indeed. After all, she'd been called everything from eccentric to doolally on account of her animals. The recently arrived donkeys she'd acquired from an ancient major general, for example, had really caused a stir in the neighbourhood. The trouble was, once one got a name for rescuing things, people wouldn't leave you alone. The phone would be forever ringing with people saying, 'I've got this kitten that I simply can't find a home for,' or 'I know you love animals. Well, there's this snake…'

She'd had to say no to the snake. As much as she hated turning an animal away, she had to draw a line somewhere and legless reptiles was it. But she hadn't been able to say no to the pair of donkeys with their long sad faces and their oh-so-tickleable ears, and the poor major general simply hadn't been able to cope any longer. Not that Flo was a spring chicken. She was in her late sixties now and had all the usual aches and pains that accompany old age. It was funny, though, because she didn't feel old. Sometimes, when she glanced at her reflection in a mirror or a window, she'd do a double take. Just who was that barmy-looking woman with the wild white hair? Ah, her beautiful hair which had once gleamed a rich chestnut. She'd sigh and shrug her shoulders. Life was about more than hair, and pining about things that had been lost long ago wouldn't get the animals cleaned and fed now, would it?

It was Monday morning and, true to her word, Bryony had

turned up bright and early wearing a pair of jeans and a pair of purple wellies.

'Well, here I am,' she said, a very cheering smile on her face. 'Where do you want me?'

Flo had considered this very question the night before. The truth was, although she'd longed to have help for some time, she just wasn't used to it. She did things her own way and in her own time. Not all of the jobs got done, of course. There was only so much Flo could accomplish on her own, but she always muddled through. It would be strange having Bryony coming into her little world. What if she challenged the way she did things? What if they didn't get along together? Flo shook her head. Bryony seemed like a lovely young woman. Perhaps she wasn't used to physical work like Flo was, but she seemed keen to get stuck in.

'I thought the donkeys,' Flo said.

'You have donkeys?'

'You didn't know? I thought everybody within a mile radius could hear my two.'

Bryony shook her head.

'Well, come and meet them.'

Flo led the way to the back garden, filled with raised beds, old sheds, a couple of greenhouses and endless animal enclosures.

'The donkeys are my latest arrivals. Belle and Beau.'

'What fabulous names.'

'Yes, well, they're dear things. I'd always fancied keeping donkeys, but never had the space until last year when I had a little windfall and bought another bit of land out the back. Come and see.'

They walked to the end of the garden towards the field where the donkeys lived and there they were, standing together by the gate, waiting for their morning carrot which Flo duly gave them.

'They've caused me no end of bother since their arrival,' she confessed. 'Haven't you, darlings?' she said, giving them both a tickle behind their ears. 'You see the neighbour over there?' She nodded to her right. 'He plays the trumpet. I never really noticed it until I got the donkeys. I was sort of aware of it. It was sometimes quite nice to do my chores to a musical accompaniment, and he's very good, you know. But it sets the donkeys off.'

'How do you mean?' Bryony asked.

'Braying,' Flo explained. 'They seem to want to answer it back whenever they hear it. At first, I thought it was rather funny, but the uppity neighbour there,' she said, nodding to her left, 'Dr Skegby, well he becomes incandescent with rage and swears all sorts of nasty words over my hedge. Honestly, I never thought to hear such language from a retired GP.'

Flo could see that Bryony was doing her best not to laugh.

'Just wait until you hear it. Trumpet first, then donkeys then uppity Dr Skegby! It's a wonder I haven't been reported to the authorities.'

'Oh, Flo!'

'They've also proved excessively costly because I've had to have repairs done to the field they're in, as well as to the stable, and I'd no idea that donkeys' feet were so expensive. My savings aren't what they were, but we muddle through somehow. They're such wonderful creatures, you see. One can't help but smile when one looks at a little donkey with its woeful expression and those great long ears.'

'So you'd like me to clean their stable?' Bryony asked.

'Would you mind?'

'Not at all.'

'The equipment's over there and the muck heaps by the hedge. I'm hoping it will make good compost in due course. Nothing goes to waste here.'

Bryony hesitated for a moment. 'How do I get in?'

Flo opened the gate and gave Belle and Beau a little slap on their bottoms.

'Just push them to one side. You don't need to be afraid of them,' Flo said, and then added, 'you aren't *afraid* of them, are you?'

Bryony shook her head, but Flo thought that the young lady looked decidedly nervous. Flo had never been able to understand people who didn't automatically love and trust animals as much as she did, but realised that they did exist.

'If you'd rather clean out the hen coop –'

'No, no!' Bryony insisted. 'I'm good with the donkeys.' And she walked into the field.

Flo left her to it, but sneaked back later and was pleased to see that Bryony had a big smile on her face and was actually giving Beau a little scratch behind his ears.

It was little wonder that housework was such a very low priority with so many lives to take care of, Flo thought as she walked into the kitchen to make them both a cup of tea. The animals always came first, but she couldn't help wishing that things were a little tidier. Just the other week, she'd thought she'd lost the necklace that her mother had given her on her eighteenth birthday. It was a simple gold chain with a beautifully fashioned letter 'F' for Florence. It had turned up when she'd been hunting through one of her recipe folders. How it came to be there, goodness only knew.

The garden also seemed to run away with her. Some would call it wild, but Flo referred to it as voluptuous, which was a much nicer word and captured well the beauty and fecundity of everything from the fruit trees to the fat blooms in the flower beds. Everything was big and bountiful. Yes, Flo had a lot to be grateful for, she knew that, especially as summer was fast approaching and the evenings were getting longer. Summer was always so much easier and she loved nothing more than pottering around her garden with the animals as her companions.

Having made the tea, Flo took the two mugs outside. Bryony had finished in the donkey field and it looked as if she'd already cleaned out the hen coop and the ducks and goose enclosure too.

'You found the outside tap, then?' Flo said, handing her a mug.

'Oh, yes. But I startled a cat when I turned the hose on, and I think I saw another one under the hen coop.'

'That's okay. They don't worry the hens. Actually, the hens stand up to them.'

'How many cats have you got, Flo?'

'Just the three. Patches, Dusty and Threddy.'

'Freddy?'

'No, *Threddy*. Short for Threadbare.'

Bryony laughed and then sipped her tea.

'I say three,' Flo continued, 'but there are always others hanging around and I'm not sure if they've got proper homes or not. Now, I don't want to turn into one of these mad old cat ladies, but it's looking more and more likely, isn't it?'

'I've always thought of you more as a mad old hen lady,' Bryony said.

'Cats, hens, donkeys – doesn't matter to me. I might be deemed mad, but I couldn't be happier.'

'But how do you take care of all these animals on your own?'

'How? Because I want to,' Flo told her. 'They're my family.'

Bryony seemed to be thinking about this for a moment.

'What about real family, Flo?'

'There's just Mitch and Sonny these days.'

'You never wanted children yourself?' Bryony asked. 'I mean – sorry – I didn't mean to pry. I'm just, well, interested.'

'It's okay,' Flo assured her. 'I don't mind talking about it.' She took a deep breath, her mind flitting over the decades that had passed her by all too quickly. 'It never happened for me. That whole marriage and children thing. It would have been nice if it had happened. Then again, maybe it wouldn't have. Maybe I would have married a toe-rag.' Flo chuckled and Bryony laughed too.

'There's no way of knowing, is there?'

'Exactly. Maybe if I'd turned left instead of right one day, I'd be Lady Flo, living in a mansion somewhere with a butler and a Rolls Royce. Or maybe I'd be living in poverty after some toe-rag had duped me out of all my money. But what's the point in speculating? You can't live like that and I've had a good life and I don't live with regrets, Bryony, that's the main thing. I'm grateful for what I have.'

Bryony looked around the garden and Flo saw her taking it all in. The greenhouse was full of young plants waiting to be planted out, the geese were bathing and the hens were pecking happily at the corn she had sprinkled on the ground.

'Well, I think this is heaven,' Bryony said.

Flo smiled. 'I'm glad you think so. Not everyone does, you know. They take one look at this place and deem it a tip. They don't see the beauty or the joy. They just see the nettles and the chaos. But this is paradise to me.'

'And I can clear the nettles for you,' Bryony said, 'but I'd like to leave a little bit of the chaos because that's just you, I think.'

That made Flo laugh.

It was then that they heard a car horn sound.

'Is that for you?' Bryony asked.

'I'd better go and see,' Flo said, finishing her tea and heading towards the house.

There was only one person who sounded their car horn to get her attention. Mitch Lohman. Sure enough, as she walked around the cottage to the front garden, she saw Mitch's beaten-up old car sitting out in the road. Only when he saw her did he switch the engine off and get out of the car.

'You took your time,' he said.

'I was out the back with the animals.'

He gave a dismissive sort of laugh.

'You got Sonny with you?' Flo asked. 'Shouldn't he be at school?'

'He's not feeling so bright.'

'Oh, dear,' Flo said, going to the passenger door and opening it. 'How are you, my cherub?'

The little boy shrugged his bony shoulders as he got out of the car.

'Well, come inside and I'll find you some cookies.'

They both followed Flo.

Mitch, who was beanpole tall and as skinny as a rake, had to bend almost double so as not to knock himself out on the low door-frame of the old cottage.

'I can't stop,' he said. 'Just came to drop him off.' He slapped the boy in the middle of the back and nearly sent him flying. Flo instinctively held her arms out towards him and he walked into them. She stroked his chestnut hair. It was exactly the same colour as hers had once been, but it was a tad too long on him, the fringe dangling over his eyes. Perhaps she could give it a quick trim once Mitch had left. She'd done a pretty good job with Belle and Beau's tails when they'd first arrived. How hard could a little boy's hair be?

'I'll leave him with you, then,' Mitch said with a sniff.

'All day?'

'Gotta work, ain't I?' he said although he'd never satisfactorily explained what it was he did. He then bent down to whisper something in Sonny's ear. 'Got that? Don't you forget, now?'

Sonny stared at his father, but didn't say anything.

'I'll just grab his bag,' Mitch said, disappearing out to the car and coming back a moment later with a large sports bag. 'He's got all his school books and stuff in there in case he needs them.'

'But you'll be picking him up later?' Flo asked.

Mitch didn't answer, but turned around and headed towards the front door.

'Mitch?' Flo called after him but, by the time she'd reached the garden, he was driving away.

Flo closed the door on her nephew and returned to the kitchen, watching as Sonny ate his cookies. He didn't look ill to her, but maybe he was hiding it well or maybe he'd told his father a lie to get out of going to school. Hadn't kids always manufactured a quick tummy ache to get out of a lesson they hated? Or maybe he was being bullied, Flo thought in dismay. He was a delicate sort of child. She wouldn't be surprised to find out he had an enemy or two.

She pulled up a chair and sat down next to him.

'Okay?'

He nodded.

'Everything all right at school?'

He nodded again.

'No problems?'

He looked up at her. 'Like what?'

'I don't know,' Flo said, trying to sound casual. 'Like other kids.'

He shook his head.

'Good,' she said, hoping he was telling the truth. 'So, what do you want to do today? Because you don't look ill enough for bed.'

'I'm okay.'

'You are?'

'Yeah. Dad just said I should have the week off.'

'The *week*? Don't you mean the *day*?'

Sonny looked confused for a moment and Flo frowned. Why on earth would Mitch tell his son he should have a week off?

'So, you're feeling okay?'

He nodded.

'That's good. Well, maybe we shouldn't take you to school just in case, okay? Maybe we should do something fun. After all, it isn't every day I get to spend with my great-nephew, is it? Now, have yourself another cookie. I've just got to nip outside, okay?'

Flo left the house and soon found Bryony. She was wearing Flo's strongest gardening gloves and had made a good start on the nettles behind the hen coop.

'Everything okay?' Bryony called over, wiping her hands on the front of her jeans and coming to meet Flo.

'I'm not sure,' Flo said honestly. 'That was Mitch. He's dropped Sonny off.'

'Is he okay?'

'Yes, I think so, but Mitch told me that Sonny wasn't feeling well, but he seems alright to me.' Flo shook her head. 'I can't help thinking Mitch is up to something. Isn't that awful? To be so suspicious of your own family? But that's just the way it is with him. I simply don't trust him.'

'Maybe Sonny was feeling unwell at home, but made a recovery as soon as he saw you?'

Flo smiled. 'Maybe.'

'*I* feel better for being here,' Bryony told her.

Flo reached out and gave her arm a squeeze. 'And I feel better for having you here.'

'Would you rather I skip off now and leave you to it with Sonny here?'

'Whatever you want to do, my dear. Although I might take him into town later and have a browse around.'

'Well, I'll just pull a few more of these nettles up and then I'll get going.'

'Thank you, my dear. You've been a great help. Do take a couple of boxes of eggs and a nice fat cabbage with you. I've got some cookies wrapped up for you too.'

'Oh, thanks, Flo! I'll come again later in the week, okay?'

Flo left her to it and returned to her great-nephew who was finishing a cookie.

'Right!' she said, startling him as she clapped her hands. 'Let's have a day out!'

Flo couldn't remember a more splendid day. She and Sonny had driven into Castle Clare, climbed to the very top of the castle and looked out over the town below. They'd had sandwiches and ice lollies from the supermarket, had poked around the antiques shops trying on silly old hats and had even made a good effort in the garden together, watering the greenhouse and collecting eggs. It had certainly put colour in the young boy's cheeks, but he was still looking anxious which made Flo feel ill at ease.

'Sonny, dear,' she said after they'd eaten tea and had washed and dried all the dishes, 'did your dad say anything about picking you up?'

Sonny shook his head.

'Did he tell you if he was going anywhere or what he was doing?'

Again, Sonny shook his head.

'No, of course he wouldn't,' Flo said, silently cursing her nephew. 'Well, listen, let's make some hot chocolate, eh? And, whilst you're drinking it, I'll make up the spare bed for you. You'd like that, wouldn't you? You can stay the night.'

'Can Threddy sleep in my room?' Sonny asked.

Flo smiled. Sonny really adored that old cat of hers. 'Of course he can. You'll find he makes a pretty good hot water bottle, that cat. But we'll have to find you something to wear.'

'I've got my pyjamas,' Sonny said.

'You have?' Flo said in surprise. 'Well, good.' She smiled at him whilst silently wondering just what her nephew was up to.

When Tuesday morning dawned, Mitch still hadn't shown up and there was no answer whenever Flo tried his mobile. She was seriously beginning to wonder if Sonny was there for the whole week like he'd suggested the day before.

They ate their breakfast together, collecting the first of the eggs and Flo watched the clock tick round.

'I suppose we'd better take you to school,' she said at last and Sonny nodded as if he'd been expecting it. Luckily, Mitch and Sonny lived within the catchment area for the school in Castle Clare so that made life easy for Flo.

'I don't suppose you've got a uniform in that bag of yours, have you?'

'Yes.'

'Yes? You mean you *have* got a uniform in there?'

He nodded and Flo scratched her head. 'Let me take a look in there.'

Sonny looked panicky for a moment, but said nothing as Flo opened the bag and looked inside. There, she found a few items of clothing including Sonny's school uniform and his packed lunch box which she hastily filled with a rather haphazard sandwich and a banana.

'You'd better get into this,' she said, pulling the uniform out. 'I'll take you to school.' She bit her lip. 'What time do you get out?'

'Half-past three,' he told her.

Flo took a quick look at her calendar and cursed. She'd got an appointment with her podiatrist and it had taken her an absolute age to get one too because there were an awful lot of feet needing attention in the Castle Clare area, it would seem.

'Oh, dear,' she said, and then she thought of something and picked up the phone.

'Bryony?'

'Flo?'

'I've got a huge favour to ask you.'

CHAPTER 7

Flo Lohman wasn't in the habit of breaking into people's houses, but the circumstances warranted it, she told herself. After she'd dropped Sonny off at school, she'd called Mitch yet again but there was still no answer and she knew that he hadn't tried to contact her because she'd made sure her mobile was on and that the land-line hadn't been pulled out by Dusty who like to play with the cable.

Sure enough, the spare key was where it always was – under the gnome with the missing right arm – and she let herself inside, grimacing at the state of the place. She couldn't remember the last time she'd visited. Mitch always came to hers with Sonny rather than her going to his and now she felt guilty. Perhaps she should lend a hand here. Then again, wasn't she struggling just to keep her own place running? She hadn't hired Bryony just so she could spend time tidying up Mitch's place.

She felt anxious about breaking into her nephew's home and wondered if she could be arrested for such a thing.

'I was looking for clothes for Sonny,' she'd tell the officer if it came to it, and she honestly was, but she was momentarily waylaid by what she found in the living room. At first, she could only make out odd shapes because it was so dark in there. She walked towards the window and dared to pull back the curtain and gasped at what she saw. The room was stuffed full of things. *Old* things. Things like candlesticks and lamp bases, silver photo frames and pretty glasses. There was even a suit of armour in the corner. Flo shook her head in confusion. Was Mitch in the antiques business now? Funny he'd never mentioned it.

Her gaze landed on a little table in the middle of the room where there were heaps of pound coins and fifty-pence pieces. She wasn't sure how many there were, but it looked like the best part of one hundred pounds. She shook her head and moved on, taking in a collection of mirrors and a shelf full of figurines.

Climbing the stairs, she turned left into Sonny's room and caught her breath. Like the living room, it was dark because the curtains hadn't been opened and it was also full of antiques. Other than a football poster and a sticker album on the bedside table, it would have been impossible to tell it was a young boy's bedroom. Was the rest of the house similarly stuffed, she wondered, walking back out onto the landing and poking her head into the next room? Yes, it was. There were antiques everywhere apart from the bathroom, she was relieved to notice.

Returning to Sonny's room, she picked up an empty carrier bag from the floor and started to fill it with clothes from a drawer. She was just folding up a little jumper when she heard the front door open and close. Her whole body froze in panic. She might have gone through the scenario of what she'd do if the police caught her, but she hadn't reckoned on Mitch catching her. There was only one way to handle this, she thought – face on – so she boldly walked downstairs and into the living room.

'What the hell are you doing here?' Mitch shouted as soon as he saw her.

'Mitch, I –'

'How did you get in here?'

'The key.'

'What key?'

'Under the gnome.'

He swore and she was just about to chastise him, but realised she was in no position to take the higher ground.

'Mitch, love, what are all these things?'

'What business is that of yours?' he snapped.

'I just wondered –'

'I'm a trader. On eBay, okay?'

'eBay? Where's that?'

'It's not a *where*, stupid. It's a website.'

'Oh,' Flo said. She'd never got the hang of the whole internet business. The modern world had passed her by. She'd only got her first mobile phone last year.

'What's in that bag?' Mitch said, his face full of suspicion.

'Some clothes for Sonny.'

'I gave him some.'

'Not enough,' she said, squaring up to him now and remembering how mad she was at his treatment of his son. 'Not if you're going to leave him for god only knows how long.'

'I'm busy, Flo. I haven't got time for this,' he said, shuffling around the living room, picking up random objects.

'You haven't got time for your son either, have you?'

'That's right.'

Flo felt stung by this admission and wanted to lash out at him, but it wouldn't do any good, she knew that.

'So, he's staying with me, then?'

'Looks like it.'

Flo could feel tears threatening to spill as she thought about the poor boy whose mother had walked out on him and whose father didn't want him in his life.

'Fine!' she said.

'Good!' Mitch replied, not bothering to look up.

'I'll let myself out.'

'Like you let yourself in?' Mitch retorted.

Flo chose to ignore him and made a quick exit.

The classroom Ben had been assigned in the school on the outskirts of Ipswich wasn't the worst he'd taught in, but it was definitely on the shabby side with its rickety desks, patchy paintwork and windows that constantly jammed at just the wrong height. Still the pupils were great, the hours good and the pay – well – he could manage on it for now.

Ben had never planned to be a teacher, but had found he had a natural aptitude for it when he was working abroad and had since gained qualifications to teach. It certainly beat some of the waiting jobs he'd had or the dish-washing job in the centre of Naples with the irate Italian chef who used to throw saucepans at his staff.

He'd just finished his last class for the day and had walked to his car for the drive to Castle Clare. He'd been thinking about it all day. Discovering that Bryony's shop was closed on a Monday after a fruitless trip into town, he'd determined to revisit the next day. Today. Right now.

He'd tried to formulate some kind of plan and had even pulled out his A4 notepad to write some ideas down, but the page had remained blank. The truth was he didn't know what to say to Bryony, especially not after the Sunday lunch fiasco. He'd been relying on his old charming self – his cheeky chappie sense of humour – to win her over, but cracking a joke wasn't going to get him out of this fix. He knew that now.

Just talk to her, he told himself. Heart to heart. Tell her how you're feeling. Women like to know that kind of stuff. They want contrition, they want to see those tears in your eyes. He looked at his reflection in the rear-view mirror. Oh, he'd cried over Bryony. He'd never admit it to anybody, but there'd been tears when he'd left the UK. He hadn't been able to believe that she wouldn't come with him. He could understand her anxiety. After all, she had a wonderful family whom she loved. That couldn't be easy to give up. But hadn't she also loved him? Hadn't she wanted to be with him more than her family? Obviously not.

But how he'd done his best to persuade her to come to him. He'd never shown his fear that she might not join him. Instead, he'd sent book after book, picked up on his travels, and postcard after postcard, full of his love.

She's probably burned the lot, he thought to himself.

Before he knew it, Ben had arrived at Castle Clare and managed to find a coveted parking space in the market square, which was surprising because the school had just finished for the day. He walked the short distance to the yellow-painted shop and paused. He still had no idea what he was going to say and the irony of being lost for words in a bookshop wasn't lost on him. He just hoped that it would be easier to be with her this time. She'd had a little while to get used to him being back and had also had a chance to calm down after he'd barged in on her Sunday lunch. Maybe she'd be more receptive this time.

Taking a deep breath, Ben entered the shop, the little bell tinkling above his head. At first, Bryony didn't turn around because she was focussed on a small boy in a school uniform. He noticed that she had her hand on his shoulder and they were laughing together.

'Oh, you're so clever. I'm so proud of you,' she told him and Ben swallowed hard as the boy looked up at her with adoration in his eyes.

Nobody had told him Bryony had had a child. He wasn't very good when it came to estimating a child's age, but it seemed as if Bryony hadn't wasted any time once he'd left Castle Clare. Ben looked at the kid. He had chestnut hair. He cast his mind back to the baker fellow he'd seen Bryony with in the pub that night – did he have chestnut hair? He couldn't remember. Anyway, what did it matter who the father was? The only issue was that it wasn't Ben. His

Bryony hadn't waited for him. She'd moved on the minute he'd left her and had made a life for herself.

Bryony looked up when the shop bell rang the second time and saw Ben leaving. She hadn't been aware he'd come in at all; she'd been so focussed on Sonny and his response to the book she'd chosen for him. He really was a bright lad, but it was obvious that he was totally lacking in confidence and that he could do with a lot more encouragement when it came to reading.

But what had Ben been doing in her shop? Hadn't she given him a clear enough message already? Before she had time to dwell on that, the shop door opened again and in came Flo.

'Oh, Bryony,' she cried. 'Thank you so much for picking Sonny up for me.' She came forward and kissed his cheek. 'You okay, monkey?'

He nodded.

'He's been an angel,' Bryony said. 'He's helped me unpack some new arrivals and we've been reading together, haven't we? He's very good, you know.'

'Is he?' Flo looked surprised by this declaration.

'But he needs to *keep* reading,' Bryony asserted.

'I'll take him to the library before we go home.'

Bryony nodded.

'Oh, and buy him plenty of books too!' Flo added, making Bryony smile.

'That sounds like a good idea. It's important for him to have his own books – ones he can return to rather than ones which have to *be* returned.'

'Got you!' Flo said and then she noticed Bryony looking wistfully out of the shop window. 'What is, dear?'

She sighed. 'Something strange just happened.'

'What?'

'Ben came into the shop.'

'What did he say?'

'Nothing. He left before I realised his was here.'

'Is he the good-looking guy with the dark hair and beard I passed on my way?'

'I don't like beards,' Bryony stated.

'He's very handsome,' Flo said. 'From what I saw.'

'Why would he come in here only to leave without saying

anything? Don't you think that's strange?'

Flo looked confused for a moment, but then clapped a hand over her mouth. 'You don't think –'

'What?' Bryony asked.

'He saw you with Sonny, didn't he?'

'I guess.'

'You don't think he thought he was your son, do you?'

Bryony frowned, but then let out a laugh. 'You think?'

'It's possible, isn't it?'

Bryony nodded and then smiled. 'I think I'll have to borrow Sonny more often,' she told Flo. 'It seems he's the best possible Ben deterrent there is.'

'For goodness' sake, will you stop pacing?' Georgia told Ben. 'What is *wrong* with you?'

'I went to see Bryony,' he began.

'Oh, Ben! You've got to give up on her. She doesn't want to know.'

'I can't just give up. I have a feeling about this. We're meant to be together.'

'I think it's only you who feels that way.'

He shook his head. 'No, no. I carried that woman in my heart right around the world. She's a part of me.'

'So what did she say to you this time?'

'Nothing.'

'She ignored you?'

'No.' Ben raked a hand through his hair. 'I didn't talk to her because she was with her son.'

'Bryony has a son? I didn't know that.'

'No, neither did I,' Ben said, visualising the young boy once again.

'How do you know it was her son?'

'What do you mean?'

'I mean, she didn't introduce him to you, did she?'

'No.'

'Then maybe it wasn't her son at all. Maybe a parent had left him in the bookshop for a moment.'

'Maybe,' Ben conceded.

'Anyway, what does it matter if she does have a kid? People do, you know. Although I hadn't heard she'd had a boy. Mind you, I've only been back in Castle Clare myself for the last year so it's possible I've missed the news and I don't really mix with the Nightingales. Not after what you did to Bryony.'

'Gee, thanks for the support.'

'You're welcome!'

'Surely Sam or Josh would've mentioned her having a kid to me.'

'I don't see why,' Georgia said. 'It's not that big a deal, is it?'

'I just never imagined it. All those years away and she was settling down and making a family.' He swore under his breath. 'I should never have left.'

'You had to leave.'

He flopped down on the sofa next to her. 'Yeah. Yeah, I did.'

'But you're back now and you have to build a new life for yourself here. Possibly without Bryony.'

'But she's not married.'

'What?'

'She's got a kid, but she's not married.'

'What difference does that make these days?'

'I'm just saying that the father couldn't have counted for much.'

'Maybe it was a one-night stand with some hunky musician she met after a gig in London or something.'

Ben glared at his sister. 'What?'

'Could happen. The father could be anyone – a random stranger, a summer fling, a sperm donor.'

'Georgia!'

'I'm just saying. Women do that, you know, if they want a baby but don't want all the hassle of a man.'

He frowned. Would Bryony really have done something like that? He didn't think so. She'd never seemed like the one-night stand sort of person either, but then he couldn't really claim to know her anymore, could he? Although he strongly believed that people didn't change that much. Not fundamentally. You could be damaged and wounded by life, you could have your heart broken and learn from lessons you'd rather never have had, but the core of you never really changed.

'You've got to make a decision to stop thinking about her. To move on. I thought you'd forgotten about her years ago,' Georgia told him. 'I didn't know you were still hoping to get back with her.'

He gave a little shrug. 'What can I say? She got to me good and proper and coming back home made me realise just how much. I didn't think it was going to be easy, but I never thought it was going to be this hard.'

'I'd move on,' Georgia said. 'Move on and forget her.'

Ben sighed. 'I don't think I can.'

It was later that evening when Ben's phone went. He looked at the screen and saw the name. He'd been waiting for this call and answered without delay.

'Hey,' he said. 'You okay?' He paused. 'You found the place alright? That's good. No, I've not had a chance yet, but I will now. I know and I will, I promise. I'm here for you. I told you that, okay? Alright. Get a good night's sleep and we'll talk in the morning.'

He hung up. Just when he'd thought life couldn't possibly get any more complicated, Aria had arrived in England.

CHAPTER 8

There were several sets of footprints in the muddy lane which led out of Castle Clare into the fields beyond: a large pair, a medium-sized pair, a small pair and an excited set of dog paws. They belonged to Jago, Polly, Archie and Dickens.

It was a bright and breezy April afternoon and it was lovely to take time out to spend together. Polly Prior, née Nightingale, and her son, Archie, had recently moved into Lilac Row with Jago Solomon. As much as she'd loved her home at Church Green, in the village of Great Tallington, she'd had no qualms about leaving it. Although she didn't believe that her husband, Sean, would ever turn up on her doorstep again, she just wasn't willing to take the chance. Besides, she had fallen madly in love with Jago and couldn't wait to start her new life with him. Archie adored him too. Even Dickens the spaniel loved him, trotting happily alongside him whenever they had a family walk.

There'd been a bit of gossip about the arrangement, of course. Polly wasn't immune to the conversations that had been had in Castle Clare.

'She's still married, isn't she?' she'd heard one customer ask another when she'd been in Bryony's stock room.

'Hasn't been with that guitar fella five minutes before moving in with him. And he's at least ten years younger than her. *Shocking!*' another customer had said when she'd been working in Sam's shop and had left the main room for a moment in search of a book.

But these silly women didn't wound Polly as much as she'd thought they might. They could think what they wanted. She didn't care because she'd found a good, gentle man whom she loved with all her heart.

Holding hands after jumping over a stile, she looked up at him and smiled.

'We really should make a list,' she told him.

'What for?'

'A list for Lilac Row. You know, for all the jobs that need doing.'

'All in hand,' he said.

'Oh, you've made a list already?'

71

'Don't need to. It's all up here,' he said, tapping his forehead.

'Okay,' she said incredulously, 'and what's on this list?'

A slow smile spread across his face. 'Number one, kiss Polly. Number two, hug Polly. Number three, kiss Polly some more.' He leaned towards her and did just that, causing her to giggle.

'I was thinking more along the lines of buying a new carpet for the living room and replacing the taps in the bathroom,' she said.

Jago groaned. 'Polly the practical.'

'Get used to it.'

'Mum's always got lists,' Archie said, stopping to let them catch up with him. 'She even makes them for me. I don't ask her to, but she does anyway.'

Jago laughed at that.

'And then there's the garden,' Polly went on. 'We shouldn't need to buy too many plants. Mum said that Dad's splitting perennials like there's no tomorrow and he's got heaps of herb cuttings on the go too.'

'Okay. I didn't understand a word of that,' Jago said.

Polly grinned. 'You will soon enough if you hang around with me and my dad.'

'Mum's plant crazy!' Archie said. 'She makes me grow them on my bedroom windowsill.'

'It's good to teach the importance of growing and nurturing things,' she said, 'and it's a lot of fun too when you can eat what you've grown.'

'That's the bit I like best,' Archie said.

They continued their walk through a small wood with Dickens the spaniel sticking his nose in the newly emerging bracken.

'You look thoughtful,' Jago said after a few minutes. 'You okay?'

She nodded. 'I'm worried about Bryony.'

'You mean with Ben being back?'

'I don't think any of us really thought he was coming back. He'd been away for so long and it's taken all this time for Bryony to move on,' Polly said.

'You really think she *has* moved on? I mean, she was pretty annoyed that Ben was there on Sunday.'

'Well, she's been dating Colin the baker, but I'm not convinced she's really into him,' Polly said, clipping the lead on to Dickens as they walked through a field of sheep. 'And there's something else.'

'What?'

'I feel really bad for welcoming Ben back with open arms. I could see how uncomfortable Bryony was about it all, but I was really pleased to see him.'

'He was your friend too, wasn't he?' Jago pointed out.

'Yes, of course. We all kind of grew up together.'

'Then don't feel guilty for having been pleased to see him.'

Polly chewed her lip, thinking of how awkward it must have been for her sister.

'What do you think will happen?' Jago asked. 'Do you think Ben's going to fight to get her back?'

Polly thought about this before answering. 'I was watching him at the dining table and there was softness in his eyes every time he looked at Bryony,' she told Jago. 'You know, I don't think he's ever got over her.'

'That's going to be a problem,' Jago said. 'I mean, if she's got over him.'

'I'm not totally sure she has though.'

'So, what's keeping them apart? I mean if they haven't got over each other and they still adore one another?'

'Bryony's pride? Her resentment at him leaving her? I don't think she can ever forgive him for that. It was a terrible time. She was miserable for months, *years*. Nothing seemed to be able to shake her out of her mood. Taking over the children's bookshop helped, but I don't think she's ever really healed. It was a long time before she dated again and each and every date has been rather half-hearted in my opinion. I feel sorry for the men she goes out with.'

'What about Colin?' Jago asked.

'She's never brought him to Sunday lunch.'

'And that's the litmus test, is it?'

'It kind of is in our family.'

'I remember when you first took me there.'

'I'm sorry it was so awkward,' Polly said with a little smile.

'I guess it was my fault for dating Bryony,' Jago said. 'You know, when she went out with me, I never got the feeling she was still hung up about somebody else.'

'No, you wouldn't,' Polly told him. 'She's very good at hiding things.'

Jago nodded. 'I hope she finds some kind of peace soon. It

sounds like she deserves it.'

'Oh, she does,' Polly said, 'but I don't think it's on its way anytime soon.'

Bryony's hands hovered over the keyboard of her computer. The shop was quiet. It had been all day. Colin had been in twice with little treats and she'd told him off twice. Really, her waistline didn't stand a chance at this rate. She'd always been on the curvy side and didn't want those curves getting any more pronounced just because a baker had a crush on her.

She really should do something about that. Both Polly and Sam had told her that she mustn't string Colin along and she knew she wasn't being fair to him because she was still looking at dating websites. But there was a part of her that couldn't help thinking that having Colin around – as well as Sonny – would be the best possible deterrent when it came to Ben, and Colin was a sweet guy. Okay, so he didn't read much, but nobody really did when compared to the Nightingales. Her family had set her up for perpetual disappointment when it came to meeting men because nobody could possibly have such an interest in books as them.

Ben did, a little voice said.

Yes, she acknowledged somewhat grudgingly. Ben had loved books almost as much as her family. She thought back to the books they'd shared and swapped as youngsters – that pure joy of talking about a story with a fellow addict, of exchanging thoughts about your favourite characters, analysing the most exciting scenes together and imagining yourselves in the world of the book you'd been reading. And Ben had read his way around the world too, hadn't he? Not only had he sent her foreign editions of the greatest love stories, but he'd told her of the books he was reading too. Travel memoirs, mostly, and autobiographies. He was following in the footsteps of some of his heroes, guided up mountain passes and down into verdant valleys as he read their innermost thoughts set down years – sometimes centuries – before.

Ben *got* books. It was plain and simple. Colin didn't. Well, he liked cookbooks, but he didn't even have many of those. He preferred to use a big old family scrapbook of recipes scrawled in bad handwriting in faded ink and stained with odd blobs from busy kitchens.

If only Colin could be more like Ben, and Ben more like Colin, she thought. If only she could blend the two and give Ben Colin's home-loving instinct so that he'd never want to leave Castle Clare. Colin would never leave the county. He'd once told Bryony that he'd had a day trip to Great Yarmouth and couldn't wait to get back home. She'd laughed, but she'd completely understood the sentiment because she felt it too. She was happiest when she was at home, surrounded by her books, her home, her family and friends.

But staying at home and leading a small life was proving difficult when it came to relationships. There were just so few men about or, at least, so few decent men who came into her life. Which was why she was still messing about on dating websites. She'd found a new one recently called Country Catches aimed at those living in rural communities. It was a fun site although she was still finding her way around it.

She did a search, choosing men under forty within a twenty-mile radius, and entering keywords to see if any matches came up. *Men, books, reading, countryside.*

Eleven matches came up and she scanned them, discounting a couple immediately who'd clearly lied about their age and were at least fifty. Her eyes settled on one image and she gasped because she'd been instantly drawn to the handsome face with its soft dark eyes and kind smile. Until she'd realised who it was.

Ben! Ben Stratton had registered on the dating website. Bryony gasped. What business had he barging back into her life if he was trying to date other women? Why, the cheek! How dare he?

Still, she couldn't resist clicking on the profile.

Hi, I'm Ben. I'm Suffolk born and bred, but have spent the last few years travelling and reading my way around the world. Think Bear Grylls with a backpack full of books.

Very cute, Bryony thought. It was just the kind of profile she'd go for too if it wasn't bloomin' Ben Stratton. She read on.

But I'm back home now and looking to settle down with the right woman.

Bryony frowned. That didn't sound very much like something Ben would say. Maybe he'd had help writing it, though.

I like a woman with a sense of humour.

What a cliché, Bryony thought.

Someone who enjoys reading and talking about books. Who likes romantic walks in the country and cosy chats by the fire, perhaps with a dog at her feet.

Bryony rolled her eyes. He was really going for it, wasn't he?

I am kind and honest. I love to have a laugh and I like good conversation.

Bryony swallowed hard, acknowledging that there was a little part of her that envied the future woman who would enjoy conversations by the fireside with her Ben.

She hit the home page of the website, not wishing to read any more of Ben's profile. It was then that she saw a little symbol in the top menu which she hadn't noticed before and she clicked on it now.

'Oh, wow!' she cried as it revealed all the people who had clicked on her profile in the last few days. She grinned. She'd had quite a bit of interest by the look of it, including from a very cute science teacher called Arnie. For a moment, she wondered about clicking the "Ask me a question" button, but then realised that he hadn't asked her one. Had he read her profile and decided she wasn't for him? Or maybe her photo had put him off. Maybe science teachers didn't like bohemian bookshop owners. Still, it was nice to have been noticed by him and maybe he'd return to her page in the future.

Bryony suddenly gasped as realisation dawned.

'Oh, no. Oh, *please* no!'

She could feel a deep blush of mortification creep over her face. If she could see who'd looked at her profile, then Ben would be able to see that she'd looked at his, wouldn't he?

Ben had had a tiring day's teaching. Some lessons, he thought, seemed to make no real progress at all. They were just repeating what he'd thought he'd made clear in a previous lesson. He found that frustrating because he was the sort who liked to be moving forward and covering new ground. It had been like that on his travels too – once he felt he'd seen a place, his feet would itch to move on to the next. Of course, there'd been times when he'd had to take work and that meant staying in one place for a bit, but he was always happiest when on the move with a new adventure on the horizon. Until now.

He was crossing the car park and checking his messages on his phone when he saw one from a company he didn't recognise.

'What the blazes?' He shook his head. No, that couldn't be right.

It wasn't until he got home that he realised what had happened.

'Georgia?' he called as he entered the hallway. She'd be home now from her job as a physiotherapist.

Sure enough, he found her in the living room, her feet up on the sofa.

'Hey, Ben.'

'Hey,' he said. 'I got an email today welcoming me to a dating service.'

'Did you?' Georgia said, not looking up from the magazine she was reading.

'Yes, I did,' he said curtly. 'Wouldn't happen to know anything about that, would you?'

'Me?' she said innocently.

'Yes, *you*!'

She didn't answer for a moment.

'Georgia?'

At last she looked up, waiting a moment as if gauging his mood. 'Promise you won't shout at me.'

'What have you done?' he asked.

'Promise first.'

'What have you *done*?'

She sighed. 'Okay. I signed you up to that dating website.'

'I *knew* it!' Ben shouted. 'What on earth did you do that for?'

'Because you need to meet people, Ben. You've done nothing but skulk around since you got back and it's driving me mad.'

'Driving you mad? But I'm at work most of the time. How am I driving you mad?'

'I mean, you're always going on about Bryony. I think it's time you met some other girls.'

Ben grabbed the laptop from the coffee table and logged on to the website, his eyes doubling in size as he read his profile.

'Oh, my god! Did you *really* write this? I sound like a dork!'

'No you don't. You sound really hot and cool.'

'Can you be both hot and cool?'

'Totally.'

Ben sighed. 'This is so bad.'

'Look! It's a really great site, Ben. There are loads of gorgeous girls on there.'

He swore. 'I can't believe you really did this, Georgia.'

'You might be thanking me in a minute.'

'You think?'

'Oh, yeah! Guess who's on there?'

'Who?'

'Your Bryony,' Georgia said. 'I signed you up so you could meet other women, but seeing she's on there, and she's looked at your page, I think you should message her.'

'Wait – how do you know she's looked at my page?'

'It's a new feature. Like a secret spy. You can see exactly who's been looking at your profile.'

Ben watched as his sister moved forward and hit a little button on the menu bar.

'Look – hundreds of women have been ogling you. Well, eight.'

'*Eight?*' Ben couldn't help feeling a little wounded at the low figure.

'It's early days,' Georgia reassured him.

'Take it down,' he told her.

'What?'

'Delete it. I want nothing to do with it.'

'Oh, come on, Ben! Give it a chance.'

'I don't want to date other women.'

'Just Bryony?'

He didn't answer.

'Well, if that's the case, you should so message her!' Georgia told him.

Ben frowned. 'That's a really bad idea.'

'Why? She's on there and you're on there. Why shouldn't you send her a quick hello. You don't have to say much. Just make contact. You said yourself that talking to her face to face wasn't working out. Maybe this platform could be the way forward. I mean, if you really can't live without her.'

'I don't know,' he said, scratching his chin.

'What harm can it do? So she might ignore you. But she might not. You might be able to charm her with your words. Send her some poetry and stuff. You two used to like that sort of thing, didn't you?'

Ben wanted to flash her another retort, but realised that she might actually be on to something. She was right – trying to talk to Bryony hadn't worked, but *writing* to her might just break down her defences. Provided he chose the right words, of course. But wasn't that the very thing they had in common – the written word. He thought about the love and joy he'd filled his postcards with as he'd been travelling. She might never have written back, but he knew she would have read them just as she'd read any messages he sent her now.

'I'll leave you to it,' Georgia said with a knowing wink. 'You can thank me later.'

'Yeah, we'll see about that,' he said as she left the room.

For a long time, Ben sat staring at the laptop and his profile on the dating site. He might have tried to sound cross with his sister but, deep down, Ben couldn't help feeling just a little bit excited by the prospect of writing to his first love.

CHAPTER 9

It was strange to be back in London, Ben thought the next day, crossing the concourse of Liverpool Street Station and heading for the underground. He'd spent a few days there at the beginning of his travels. As a Suffolk boy, London had been a destination on school trips and he remembered visiting the Natural History Museum and the National Portrait Gallery. The gallery was the one that had got him really excited because it had contained so many portraits of the writers he was beginning to appreciate.

He and Bryony had been fourteen years' old and were meant to be filling out a questionnaire about the Tudors and then tracking down some boring politicians, but they'd naturally gravitated towards the writers, staring up at the haunting faces of the three Brontë sisters and marvelling at the luminescent skin of Lord Byron.

'I want to be a writer,' Ben had declared that day.

'Do you?' Bryony had looked surprised by this.

'I want to write great adventure stories.'

She'd wrinkled her nose. 'Write a love story.'

'Men don't write love stories!'

Bryony had gasped. 'What do you think Shakespeare was writing? And Byron here? Some of the greatest love stories were told by men.'

'Yeah, but I don't want to write all that soppy stuff.'

She'd laughed and it had been such a joyous sound. He could still hear it echoing in his memory.

Coming out of the tube, Ben blinked in the brilliant sunshine, waiting to cross the busy road. He was meeting Aria at Trafalgar Square, just in front of the steps of the National Gallery. Everybody could find that, he'd thought, and she'd had a few days staying with a friend in London and had, hopefully, got her bearings.

He spotted her straight away. She was looking out into the square, her dark hair blowing about her face in the April breeze. She was a pretty young woman. He'd noticed her as soon as she'd walked into his classroom in the little school in Florence, Italy, where he'd taught for a while, but they'd only ever been friends. Still, he couldn't help acknowledging once again just how much like Bryony she looked with her dark hair and wistful eyes. That's what had drawn him to her in Italy. It had been like having a little bit of Bryony with him for a while.

Then she'd started arriving late to class. Her work wasn't completed on time and she was struggling with her concentration. Ben had been concerned and had taken her to one side.

'Aria – is anything the matter?'

And the whole story had come blurting out along with the tears. Ben hadn't interrupted, but he'd known there and then that he'd become involved because the story Aria told him was one that Ben knew well as he'd experienced it himself first-hand. In fact, he'd confided it to her a few days before when she'd asked him what had brought him to Italy. It had been strangely comforting to confess it all to a relative stranger.

'Ben!' Aria cried as she saw him approach, her eyes glittering with joy at seeing him.

They embraced.

'How are you?' he asked.

'I'm worried. I still haven't heard anything. I've left so many messages on his phone. Why doesn't he ring me back? Where can he be?'

'I'm here now so we can find him together, okay?'

'You really think we'll find him?'

'I really do,' Ben said with more certainty than he felt.

'Thank you,' she said. 'I couldn't do this without you. My friends here – they don't know. I couldn't tell them. It's too, too –' she seemed to be struggling to find the right word, '*horrible*.'

'I know,' Ben told her. 'I know.' He gave her a little hug.

'I'm okay,' she said, pulling away from him after a moment. 'Let's go, yes?'

Ben nodded. '*Andiamo*,' he said, and the two of them headed towards the tube.

Flo Lohman was getting used to having her great-nephew in her home. She had to admit that it was nice to have company even though he didn't say a lot. He was slowly coming out of his shell, though, but he spent more time talking to her animals than he did to her. Flo had noticed that about people in general over the years. The shy, the awkward, the grieving and the wounded would naturally gravitate towards an animal – something which could be fussed and pampered, something you could talk to but which would demand very little from you in return. Animals were such easy companions, she thought, which was perhaps one of the reasons she chose to surround herself with them.

It had been three days since Mitch had dropped his son at Cuckoo Cottage and he'd made no noises about when he might be picking him up again. Flo still hadn't got over the rude outburst at his house and sending Sonny back to that place was the last thing on her mind. Still, she couldn't help wondering how long Mitch was expecting her to keep him for.

She looked at him as he sat happily on the kitchen floor petting Dusty the cat. He didn't seem to mind the mess and she loved him for that. He blended right in to life at the cottage.

'Piece of cake, Sonny dear?' she asked him, having made a chocolate cake for him whilst he'd been at school. With a constant supply of eggs, it was very easy to indulge in the sweeter things in life and impossible not to when you had a great-nephew to spoil.

'Yes,' he said.

'We say, "Yes please", remember?'

'Yes please,' he said meekly.

That was another thing. Mitch appeared not to have taught his son the manners of polite society. It wasn't that Sonny was rude – he just hadn't been taught 'please' and 'thank you' and that could come across as impolite to other people.

Flo took out two pink and white china plates from a cupboard and then opened the cutlery drawer.

'Sonny, dear?' she said a moment later. 'Have you seen that nice cake slicer?'

He looked up at her and shook his head.

'No, of course not,' she said. 'I must have mislaid it again.' She tutted, annoyed with herself and her seemingly growing absent-mindedness. The cake slicer was a pretty one made of real silver. It had belonged to her maternal grandmother and Flo remembered trips to her neat little home where the cake slicer would be brought out to divide her glorious Victoria sponges and lemon cakes.

Perhaps she'd put it in the dishwasher by mistake, she thought, opening it up. No – no sign of it there. She looked at Sonny again. A young lad wouldn't go off with a cake slicer, would he? A small knife, maybe. Boys and knives were more natural companions weren't they? But she couldn't envisage him tramping through the local countryside with a cake slicer in his pocket. She shook her head. It would no doubt turn up. In the meantime, a regular knife would have to do the job.

'Come and wash your hands at the sink,' she said. 'There's a towel over there to dry them. It's very important to clean oneself after touching animals and before eating. Remember that and you won't go far wrong.'

A moment later they were sat at the table together and Flo served two generous slices of the chocolate cake. Sonny smiled and Flo's heart swelled with love. It was obvious that the little boy wasn't spoiled enough and that was a crime in her eyes. She had a lot of time to make up for and silently cursed herself for letting so many years go by without stepping in.

'Sonny, dear – what kind of food does your father give you to eat?'

Sonny looked confused by this question for a moment, but managed an answer. 'Orange.'

Flo frowned. 'What do you mean, *orange*?'

'Baked beans, tomato soup, pasta with sauce. It's all orange.'

'Oh, I see,' Flo said. 'So mostly tinned food?'

'I guess.'

'No fresh? No vegetables or salad?'

'He doesn't like salad.'

'But you do, don't you?'

He shrugged. 'It's okay.'

'It's important to get your greens, you know. You're a growing lad. I grow a lot of vegetables here – all organic and fresh as can be so you get all of the goodness. I'm told my produce is the best around. I sell a bit of it out the front.'

He looked up at that.

'You've seen that before, haven't you? Lots of people do it around here. Lots of gardeners, you see, and we always end up growing too much stuff so we sell a bit of it. There's an honesty box. I don't charge much, but it's something.'

'What's an honesty box?' Sonny asked.

'It's where people put their money when they buy something. You see, it's not like a shop where there's someone waiting to take your money. You rely on people being honest and leaving you the money for the goods they take. It might be eggs or vegetables or flowers. I've sold all those from my little table out the front. It's a lovely thing to do – much fresher than the supermarkets too.'

Sonny had gone quiet. Perhaps little boys weren't interested in that sort of thing, Flo surmised and then an idea occurred to her.

'How about we find a little corner of the garden where you can grow your own produce?' she suggested. 'I've got plenty of seed packets and we're not too late to grow a number of things. If you're successful, you can either eat what you've grown or sell it.'

'Sell it for money?' he asked, wide-eyed.

'Absolutely! Priced fairly, of course. Everything's fair and square at Cuckoo Cottage.' She smiled at him. 'What do you think? We could make a start after you've finished your cake.'

Sonny nodded, but still didn't look convinced. However Flo wasn't deterred. Sonny was biologically connected to her and she felt sure that his instinct for gardening would awaken as soon as he got his hands in the soil and started to grow things.

Ben had a headache brewing as he rushed across the concourse to catch the train home. It had been a long day in London. Long and fruitless. He'd lost track of the number of people they'd spoken to and the places they'd visited, and he'd left Aria with a pale, tear-stained face, promising to do the whole thing again as soon as he could. He wanted to help, of course he did, but a part of him wondered what he'd got himself involved with that day in the classroom when Aria had told him about her family.

'He's a *pig*!' she'd shouted through angry tears once the classroom was empty and it was just the two of them there.

'Who's a pig?' Ben had asked, wondering if one of the young men in the class had been paying Aria unwanted attention when they should have been concentrating on their verbs.

'Sergio,' she'd said. 'He pigs around the house all day in his underwear.'

Ben hadn't had the heart to tell her that you didn't really say "pigs around". Actually, he'd quite liked it.

'Who's Sergio?' he'd asked her gently as she blew her nose.

'My mama's new boyfriend.'

Ben had swallowed hard. It was because of his own mother's new boyfriend that he'd left home in such a hurry. It was because of that vile man that he'd had to leave his beautiful Bryony.

'Mama doesn't see how cruel he is, but *I* see it!' she cried. 'My brother, Dario, sees it. He hates the pig.'

'Is he living with you?'

'He comes and goes. I wish he'd just go.' Her eyes filled with tears again.

'Aria,' Ben began, 'has he hurt you?'

She looked up at him with those dark eyes of hers, like wounds in her face, and Ben held his breath as he awaited her answer.

'No,' she said. 'But he fights with Dario.'

'What, physically?'

'No.' She paused. 'Not yet, but I can feel it coming.'

Ben nodded. He knew exactly how that felt and it wasn't a nice feeling.

Now, as he boarded his train with only a minute to spare, he could feel his pulse accelerate at the thought of Paul Caston. Being with Aria had brought it all to the forefront of his mind. There was no getting away from it, he realised. Even after all these years, and the distance he'd tried to put between him and the memories of that time, they were still there, threatening to spill at any given moment as painful and as raw as ever.

He glanced out of the train window at the dark city landscape, the blocks of flats, the Olympic Park, the station platforms, but he didn't really see any of them because he was thinking of the day he'd made his mind up to leave. He hadn't been able to stay a moment longer, he'd known that, and the decision had been easy to make. He'd never told Bryony the truth. He hadn't wanted to pollute her sweetness with the foulness of Paul Caston and it had hurt him so much when he hadn't been able to truly explain to her why he was leaving. He'd said he had the travel bug and that he was desperate to see the places he'd read about for years although that was true enough. But Bryony seemed to know that that wasn't enough to take him away from her.

He sighed. He wanted to close his eyes, but he couldn't help pulling his phone out and visiting the Country Catches website. And there she was – his Bryony. He would never think of her as anything but his. No matter if she was involved with somebody else or had a child, she would always be *his* Bryony.

The photograph on her profile showed her with her dark hair held back with a sweep of blue and gold scarf. He'd always preferred it loose and unadorned, but he knew she liked to dress it up and she did look beautiful. She was pictured in her bookshop in front of the main fiction shelves, the coloured spines vying with her flamboyant outfit for attention, and a part of him grimaced at the thought of other people ogling her. How could she have put her picture up on such a place? Anybody could be out there masquerading as some nice country gent, posting any old picture of a handsome guy posing with a Labrador or in a library. But she'd see through that, wouldn't she? God, he hoped so. He hoped she always arranged to meet new men in public places too like a nice crowded pub. The thought of her being lured anywhere else was almost too much and he wondered if he should warn her of the dangers out there. He felt so very protective of her, just as he did with Aria. The world, he knew, was filled with prats and perverts and he'd met more than his share of them.

Ben's fingers itched to write to Bryony, but he wasn't sure what he wanted to say. Well, he did.

I love you. I love you. I love you.

That's what he wanted to write in his heart of hearts, but it would probably scare her off if he did. But there was something about the agony of the day he'd just been through that he needed to counteract with her sweetness. He needed to reach out to her and so he took a deep breath, settled himself back in his seat and sent a message.

Bryony made herself a large omelette using two of the eggs Flo had given her. They really were the tastiest eggs she'd ever had and the yolks were as bright a yellow as her shop front.

After eating and tidying away her dishes, she settled down at her computer. It had been easy to avoid the website at the shop. She couldn't help wondering if Ben had realised that she'd looked at his profile and if he'd responded in any way. And had he looked at hers today? She hated to admit it, but she desperately wanted to know and, every time she'd passed her computer, her eyes had been dragged towards it.

So here she was, logging in against her better judgement. She really should just abandon that particular website altogether, but her curiosity had definitely got the better of her and, before she could stop it, she had reached her personal page. Sure enough, there were half a dozen messages – two from the website company trying to sell her their latest upgrade which she deleted, and three from potential suitors which she would read in due course. But it was the sixth message which caught her eye because it was from Ben.

She took a few deep, settling breaths before opening it.

It was short, unfunny and totally clichéd.

Come here often? Ben had written.

She shook her head as she read it over and over again, and then she did something that he hadn't been able to make her do in a long time. She smiled.

CHAPTER 10

Flo Lohman was walking around the garden, checking on her livestock and noticing the new flowers which had opened and the areas of the garden which still needed attention, even though Bryony had put many hours into it.

She smiled as she thought about the company she had these days. It wasn't so long ago that she'd been struggling on her own. She'd got by, that was true, but getting by was never much fun, was it? Now she had Bryony visiting whenever she could spare a few hours and she had Sonny too. What a surprise that had been, she thought. As each day passed, it looked more and more likely that Sonny wouldn't be going home anytime soon. She was quite relieved about that having seen her nephew's house. She knew that Mitch was busy with his work, but it looked as if he didn't spend any time trying to make a decent home for his son and that was wrong.

As Sonny slowly began to open up more, he gave her little insights into life with his father – like the countless times he'd gone to school having had a chocolate bar for breakfast, or the number of times he hadn't had money for trips or the right books or clothes for sport. Flo might never have had children herself, but a boy of eight shouldn't be expected to remember such things as having his PE kit or his Maths homework book.

There was also something so intensely solemn about the boy too. He couldn't be carrying the weight of sadness from his mother's desertion because he'd been so young when she'd run out on him and he must have been used to it just being him and his dad, and yet he still seemed to feel that loss. Or maybe it was something else, Flo reasoned. It was so hard to know how to find out. Would a vague question like, "What's wrong?" yield anything other than a shrug of his thin shoulders? Flo doubted it. Maybe he was just one of those quiet, thoughtful boys, or maybe he was just at an awkward stage? Flo shook her head and bent to pull a dandelion out of one of the vegetable beds, throwing it to the hens a moment later.

Suddenly, there was a blast of tinny music from her neighbour. Why he had to play the trumpet by an open window, Flo couldn't fathom. She rolled her eyes, knowing what was coming next and, sure enough, Belle and Beau began braying, their unhappy donkey honks filling the air. She could only hope that grumpy Dr Skegby wasn't around to complain.

It was as she approached the hedge that she noticed something very strange indeed. It looked like a big white hand had popped through the hedge and its long bony fingers seemed to be searching for something. She frowned and then blinked, wondering if she was seeing things and, when she looked again, it had gone.

It wasn't until later that she pieced together what it was she'd seen. One of her best layers, Hermia, was happily clucking as she made her way to the hen feeder – a clear sign that she had just laid an egg in the hedge. Flo smiled, thinking that her eggs were truly free-range, and that's when she saw a hand pop through the hedge. It was the same long-fingered hand that she'd spotted before and she watched, spellbound, as it searched around, patting the earth on Flo's side of the hedge, until it fastened around Hermia's freshly laid egg. Ah, so *that* was its motive, Flo thought, and that's why she had been shorter on eggs than normal recently. They were being stolen from her.

Looking around the garden, Flo spotted an old hoe leaning up against a shed and grabbed it, giving the hand a firm tap with the back of it a moment later.

'What the hell?' a voice cried from the other side of the hedge. It was Dr Skegby, her neighbour.

'What do you think you're doing?' Flo shouted. She might not be able to see him, but he couldn't deny being there.

'What does it look like I'm doing?'

'Stealing – that's what!'

'Yeah?'

'Yes!'

'It's not stealing. It's compensation for the racket those flaming donkeys make.'

Flo could feel her colouring rise at his appalling explanation. 'You have no right to steal my eggs. I could call the police and get you arrested.'

'Yeah? Well, I could call the police and get *you* arrested for grievous bodily harm, and then give the environmental health a ring about the noise your donkeys make. They'd be carted away in a heartbeat and turned into glue.'

Flo gasped. 'Why, you nasty old man! You keep your hands away from my eggs, you hear me?'

'You batty old woman! You keep it quiet, you hear me?'

'Oh, I hear you alright. You're louder than any donkey!'

She heard him curse. He really did have a shocking vocabulary for a retired GP.

With tears of anger blurring her eyes, Flo stormed into her cottage and shut the back door behind her, glad to be out of the garden and away from that horrible man. How dare he, she thought? How dare that obnoxious man make her feel like that and in her own garden too? What sort of a person found it in their hearts to complain about a pair of donkeys living out their retirement? It wasn't even as though they brayed every single day – they only did it to excess when her other neighbour played his trumpet. Perhaps she could have a quiet word with him and explain the situation.

She grabbed the kettle and put it on. A cup of tea should go some way to restoring her spirits after such an upsetting encounter, and maybe a biscuit. Just a little one.

She walked across to the dresser and stopped, noticing that the copper plate she kept there had gone. Hadn't it been there that morning? No, she couldn't say for sure. Gosh, she was getting so forgetful these days, it was kind of worrying. But where on earth could a copper plate have got to? She'd always kept it on the old dresser and it had looked so at home there, shining warmly against the dark oak.

It was then that Dusty the cat came into the room with half a dead rabbit hanging out of his mouth and the mystery of the missing copper plate was forgotten.

Later, when it was time to pick Sonny up from school, she thought about asking him if he'd seen the plate, but decided against it. He had enough to cope with without adding her scattiness into the mix. It would turn up, no doubt, along with the cake knife.

When they got home, Flo was surprised to find an envelope on her front doormat with her name scrawled on it in pencil along with the words, "For Sonny's food". She opened it up and found an old ten pound note. Ten pounds indeed, she thought, shaking her head. Well it was something at least when she hadn't expected anything out of her nephew at all.

'What's that?' Sonny asked.

'Just a message from your dad,' she told him. 'He says he misses you and that he wants me to give you a big kiss from him.' She leant down and planted a big smacker on the boy's pale cheek. He looked so surprised that Flo immediately knew she'd overshot with her lie because the boy didn't believe it even for a second.

The nightmares had begun again. Ben hadn't experienced them for years. It had taken long, hard months to purge Paul Caston from his subconscious and it rattled Ben now that Paul had found his way back.

It was always the same. Ben was in the front room in the tiny terraced home he'd shared with his mum and sister when the sound of the front door slamming shut startled them out of their wits.

'Be kind,' his mother would say and Ben would look baffled by her request. 'You know what he's like when he's had a few. He says things he regrets.'

Says things he regrets. Ben laughed now at that. His mother just hadn't been able to see the true man behind the honeyed words and the gifts he'd bought her. But there'd been no honied words to Ben.

It had started small at first. There'd been a few jibes like what was a hulking great lad of twenty-two doing still living with his mother? Ben supposed Paul had felt threatened by not being the only man in the house or else jealous of Ben's presence there. But when Ben refused to make Paul's life easy by moving out, the jibes had turned to insults. The charming facade had slipped and the true monster had emerged. Of course, Ben's mother didn't see that side of Paul because he was clever. He'd wait until she was out of the room or out of the house.

The first time Paul had laid a hand on Ben, he'd been so shocked that he hadn't been able to respond. There'd just been this dark look in Paul's eyes as he'd got hold of Ben's arm and twisted it like the very worst school bully.

'Me and your mother don't want you here,' he'd whispered as he'd twisted. 'You need to move on, son.'

Then came the punch in the face that had chipped a front tooth, made his nose bleed and had given him a black eye. He told his mum he'd fallen off his friend's motorbike and she'd believed him. He'd left shortly after that knowing that, if he didn't, he and Paul would end up killing each other.

It was the punch he always dreamed of. That colossal punch was the thing to wake him in the middle of the night. God, would it never leave him? That awful sick feeling he got whenever he thought of Paul Caston and those dark days.

He knew that Aria's hunt for her brother had stirred it all up again, but it pained him that he hadn't long forgotten all those feelings from the past – they had merely lain dormant, ready to rise at any given moment.

The first tender light of morning had peeped under the curtains and Ben decided to get up. He really didn't want to fall asleep again and risk another nightmare. He tiptoed across the landing so as not to disturb Georgia and went into the bathroom which was filled with rows of feminine beauty products.

He splashed his face with cold water and looked at his reflection in the mirror. He still looked like a traveller with his overlong hair and beard. Maybe he should shave. He stroked his face with tentative fingers. He'd forgotten what a clean-shaven Ben looked like. Naked, probably. He would feel horribly exposed without his beard. Growing it had been a metamorphic moment for Ben. It was like he'd crossed from boyhood to manhood, as if he was shaking off his small-town roots and becoming a man of the world.

Giving his face another stroke, he decided to leave the beard. His armour would live to see him through another day.

After a quick breakfast of scrambled eggs and toast, he couldn't resist logging onto the dating website. He knew he was probably setting himself up for disappointment, but he just couldn't help himself. He had to see if Bryony had responded to his message.

A moment later he found out and swore that his heart started to do the foxtrot inside his chest because she'd replied. It was just one word to his question: *Come here often?* But it was a word that filled Ben with hope.

Maybe.

That's all she'd written. *Maybe.* But, to Ben, it meant that *maybe* they had a future.

'When did you plant all these nettles, Flo?' Bryony teased as she put on a pair of strong leather gloves and began pulling for all she was worth.

'I don't know where they come from,' Flo said. 'There are whole armies of them. I don't mind a few. I'm all for a bit of biodiversity and they're good for the wildlife. I also make a bit of nettle soup each spring, but enough is enough.'

'Yes, this is war,' Bryony said, pulling a whopper out by its root.

'Oh, well done!' Flo cheered.

Bryony beamed with pride. Her dad would be proud of her. It was funny, but she'd never really shown an interest in gardening until recently. Her father had tried to encourage her, of course, but it had always been Polly who'd helped him out, diving into the borders with a big grin on her face. Bryony had been much more at home with arranging the flowers in vases with her mother or preparing the produce from the greenhouse and raised beds. She could appreciate what could be achieved in a garden, but she'd never taken an active part in curating it all.

'How did I manage without you?' Flo asked.

'You managed just fine,' Bryony told her, ever impressed with how Flo took care of so many animals and so much land all by herself.

It was as Flo was bending forward to pick up an ancient pair of secateurs, which had been revealed by Bryony's clearing of the land, that she noticed Flo's hands for the first time.

'Flo – your poor hands!' she couldn't help exclaiming.

Flo looked startled by her cry and looked down at her hands as if seeing them for the first time.

'Oh, it's nothing. Just a few cuts and bruises,' she said, self-consciously wiping them on her skirt.

'What do you use on them?' Bryony asked.

'Use?'

'To take care of them after gardening and – well – everything else you do.'

Flo took a moment to answer. 'Erm, a bit of beeswax in the winter.'

'Is that all?'

'It's good stuff, beeswax,' Flo said. 'I know I should use gloves. I have stacks of them, but they always seem to be in a different place from me and I think to myself, well, I'll just do this little bit of gardening and, before you know it, there's another cut to add to the collection.'

'They must be so sore!' Bryony said.

'No, no. My hands are used to being knocked about.'

'Well, I think they deserve a treat.'

'What do you mean?'

'You just wait and see. I'm going to give them a whole new look!'

A quarter of an hour later, having nipped home and returned, Bryony and Flo were sitting at Flo's kitchen table, a row of colourful bottles standing in front of them.

'Well, I never! Look at that pink. What a shocker! And gold. Ooooh, and that purple – it's all swirly and glittery.'

'Yes, I like that on my toes,' Bryony confessed. 'It makes them look as if they're dancing even when they're still.'

'How delightful,' Flo said. 'But it's really not me. Just look at my horrible stubby nails.'

'They will look gorgeous. Just give them to me and I'll turn you into a princess.'

Bryony began her work. First, she soaked Flo's hands in a bowl of warm water scented with orange essential oil. A lovely calming aroma filled the room and Bryony was delighted by the look of joy and calm on Flo's face. It was obvious that Flo wasn't used to being pampered, which was a terrible shame because she worked so hard.

After soaking, Bryony treated Flo to a hand massage, using almond oil. She then began to file Flo's nails into shape.

'Don't you ever file them, Flo?'

'Not really. I occasionally hack them off when they get too long.'

Bryony did her best not to laugh. She wouldn't be surprised if Flo used the ancient pair of shears she'd seen in one of the garden sheds.

'Hands are so important,' Bryony said. 'We must take care of them.'

Sonny, who was home from school and sitting in the old chair by the kitchen fire, looked up from reading a book, but didn't look interested in what was happening at the kitchen table.

'There, I've done my best to shape them,' Bryony said a few minutes later.

Flo inspected her nails. 'Why, they're lovely.'

'Now comes the fun bit – the colour.'

Flo looked at the candy-coloured bottles which stood before her.

'This one, I think,' she said, picking a pearly pink. 'It reminds me of my favourite peony.'

'It'll look really pretty on you,' Bryony promised, undoing the bottle.

Flo watched her every move. 'I don't often just sit, you know. There's always too much to do.'

Bryony wasn't surprised by this confession. 'But you read, don't you?'

'Oh, yes. I've been reading for the next book club.'

'Which book is it?'

'H E Bates's *The Darling Buds of May.*'

'Lovely!'

'Yes, everyone agreed it was the natural choice for a book club meeting in May and it's also nice and light – and short – after Hardy's *Far From the Madding Crowd.*'

'Yes, a much jollier read,' Bryony said.

'Exactly.'

'Sonny's reminding me a little of Cedric Charlton actually. You know the stuffy civil servant who ends up staying with the Larkins?'

'Well, it's definitely like Pop's farmyard here with all your animals.'

Flo gave a chuckle and then whispered so Sonny couldn't hear. 'If only Mitch was more like Pop Larkin.'

'What was your father like, Flo?' Bryony asked after applying a slick coat of peony-pink to Flo's left thumb.

'*My* father? Gosh, I haven't spoken about him for years. He died when I was seventeen. Dreadful road accident. He was cycling down a lane when a car came round the bend on the wrong side of the road.'

'That's awful!'

'Yes. He was a good man too. Loved life. Loved the countryside. I think I get my great love of the outdoors from him. He worked in an office, but always cycled there whatever the weather. It was his way of making sure he got a few good lungfuls of fresh air a day.'

'I like that,' Bryony said. 'It must have been hard growing up without him. I can't imagine my dad not being there.'

'Well, I was practically grown up when we lost him.'

'But you always need your dad, don't you?'

Flo nodded. 'I often think of him when I'm in the garden. I have some of his treasured tools. He was never happier than when wielding a fork or spade and making plans for a new vegetable bed.'

'Sounds a lot like my dad.'

Bryony continued to paint Flo's nails, her attention focussed on doing the very best job that she could.

'There we are,' Bryony announced after a few minutes. 'All done!'

Flo gasped as she looked down at her hands.

'They're lovely,' she announced in awe. 'I've never had my nails done before. I mean, I've seen those nail bars around the place, but they're not for people like me with my grubby little hands and stubby nails. They're for those young princess-types.'

'Well, *you* look like a princess now, Flo,' Bryony assured her.

Sonny looked over the top of his book.

'I can do yours next if you want,' Bryony teased.

He returned to his book and Bryony and Flo laughed.

It was the next day when Bryony called round at Campion House after work. She sat in her car looking at the friendly facade of the home she'd grown up in. How she loved the place and how lucky she felt to be able to come back whenever she wanted. Not everybody had that, she realised. So many of her friends had grown up with single parents or were children of divorce. Bryony could only imagine how that must feel, shuddering at the thought of that ever happening to her parents. She just couldn't imagine it, thank goodness. Frank and Eleanor had a good, strong marriage. It was the sort that Bryony hoped to have for herself one day, but the right man was proving elusive.

Getting out of the car, she knocked on the door and waited. Her mother answered, her rich chestnut hair swept up in a messy bun.

'Hello, sweetheart.'

'Okay if I come in?'

'Of course!' Her mother said. 'I've just been dusting the books.'

'Do you want a hand?'

'No, no. Nearly finished. I've been at it for days.'

Bryony could imagine. The Nightingale's private collection of books was vast and was distributed around the entire house.

'I found an old love letter from your father in the copy of *Tess of the D'Urbervilles* he bought for me when we first met.'

'I hope his letter was more uplifting than the book,' Bryony said.

'Oh, it was!' her mother said. 'You know how your father feels about Hardy. He was quite shocked when I told him I hadn't read any and he ended up sending me his complete works. I still haven't read *The Trumpet-Major.*'

Bryony laughed. 'Where is Dad?'

'He's in the garden.'

'Of course! I want to talk to him about something.'

'Put a pair of wellies on. It was wet in the night.'

Bryony made her way to the utility room to find a pair of wellies and was immediately assaulted by Brontë the spaniel and Hardy the pointer. She bent down to fuss them and got two wet noses in her face.

'Grandpa and Grandma around?' she asked, pulling a pair of red wellies on.

'No, they've gone to aquarobics.'

Bryony nodded. 'I'll just pop out and see Dad then.'

'Shall I put the kettle on?' her mother asked.

'Lovely.'

Leaving the house, Bryony made her way into the garden, wondering which corner her father was occupied in. After an unsuccessful tour of the greenhouse and sheds, she found him down by the pond and watched him for a moment as he dragged a broken branch out from the water.

'Hello, daughter,' he said as he saw her.

'Hi, Dad!'

'This is a nice surprise. What brings you to my corner of the world?' he asked, wrapping her in a big hug.

She grinned. 'You're going to laugh when I tell you.'

'Am I?'

'Yes. I've started gardening.'

'At your new place?'

'No!' she said, thinking of the tiny paved courtyard at the back of her terraced house. 'At Flo Lohman's. I'm helping her out in the garden and I'm really enjoying it.'

'That's good.'

'Yeah, it is,' she confessed. 'Why haven't I done it before?'

Frank shrugged. 'I guess there are those who are born gardeners – like me. Your gran used to tell me that I'd crawl out of the house to get into the garden when I was a baby.'

'You didn't!'

'She'd catch me in the vegetable patch, pounding at the soil with my fists.'

'You're making that up!'

'Ask her.'

Bryony laughed. 'No, I believe you. It sounds just like you. But I didn't do that, did I?'

'Nope. It was always Polly who showed an interest in the garden. She'd follow me around, toddling into the shrubs and grabbing fistfuls of flowers. Sam went through a phase too, but didn't really keep it up. You were always more interested in the fruit and flowers once they were picked.'

'Yes, I know,' Bryony said.

'I used to love watching you and your mother arranging displays for the dining room. You had such a great eye for colour. Like your clothes – you were never afraid to play with combinations. Polly always preferred the greenery, but you loved the bold, bright colours – the dahlias, the zinnias.'

Bryony smiled. 'I'd like to learn more. I'm helping Flo with all the weeding and maintenance, but I want to learn more about sowing and planting. Will you teach me?'

Her father's face lit up. She knew she couldn't have made him happier if she'd tried.

'Come with me,' he said and she knew where they were going – to the greenhouse.

There then followed a happy half an hour whilst her father took her through everything he was growing. It was quite impressive. Gardening, she realised, was a lot more than just wielding a fork – it took a great deal of planning. Planning and optimism. Her father didn't shield his failures from her. Not every seed germinated and not every seedling made it to adulthood. There were so many variables and every year was different with what the weather threw at you and the myriad pests around.

'It sounds like a kind of blood sport,' Bryony said.

Her father nodded. 'It can be a battle sometimes but, if you grow plenty, you'll see the rewards and nothing – absolutely nothing – beats picking something you've grown to eat.'

Bryony couldn't help recalling the years of teasing her father had endured at the hands of his children whenever he presented a plate or bowl full of home-grown produce. Of course, they loved it and everything would be wolfed down, but who could resist teasing a man who handled a cabbage as if it were a newborn baby?

'I just remembered,' Bryony said, 'Mum put the kettle on.'

'Let's get inside then,' her father said.

They left the greenhouse, careful to close the door behind them. Rabbits had been known to hop in and help themselves to salad.

They were half way back to the house when her father stopped walking and cleared his throat.

'How do you feel about him being back?' he asked. Bryony didn't need to clarify who he was talking about because it could only be one person.

She gave a little shrug. 'I don't know.'

'You don't know?' He didn't sound convinced by her answer.

'What do you want me to say?'

'The truth – whatever it is.' He held her gaze and she knew that anything but complete honesty was out of the question.

'I feel...' she paused and tried again, 'I feel mad and sad and baffled. All at once.'

Her father nodded. 'I'm not surprised. I didn't think he'd ever come home.'

'I wish he hadn't.'

'Well, there's not a lot you can do about it. He looks like he's here to stay so you'll have to work something out between the two of you.'

'Why?'

'Because this is a small town, Bry, and the sort of feelings you're carrying around aren't healthy. You've got to get things out in the open and move on.'

'I wasn't the one who messed things up between us. It's not fair that –'

'It doesn't matter what's fair,' her father interrupted. 'You've still got to sort it out. Ben's a good chap and he wants to talk to you.'

'What's he said? Nobody's told me what happened after I left on Sunday.'

'Nothing happened.'

'Dad?'

She saw him frown. 'He told us – he told *me* – that he wants you back.'

'When?'

'He asked to see the garden.'

'He knows that's your weak spot.'

'No, he was genuinely interested.'

'Dad, he was just trying to get to me through you, wasn't he?'

A little smirk lifted the corners of his mouth. 'Possibly.'

'So, what did he say?'

'It doesn't matter because I wouldn't do it anyway.'

'Wouldn't do what?'

'Secretly set up a meeting between the two of you.'

Bryony's jaw slackened. 'He asked you to do that?'

'He really wants to talk to you, darling.'

'Yeah? Well, I don't want to talk to him.'

'You've made that very clear.'

'Good.'

'Don't you believe in second chances?' her father asked her.

'No I don't.'

'Elizabeth and Darcy did.'

'Don't bring Jane Austen into this.'

He smiled as they continued to walk back to the house. 'If your mother hadn't given me a second chance, none of you would be here today.'

'What do you mean?' Bryony asked.

'Did I ever tell you about the time your mother played a trick on me?'

'What trick?' Bryony asked.

'After I stood her up.'

'You stood Mum up?'

'By accident. We had a date all planned – cinema, a meal and I kind of forgot. It was such a glorious day, you see, and I lost track of time in the garden.'

'Oh, Dad!'

'I know. She's never let me forget it.'

'So what did she do?'

'She wrote me a letter.'

'You guys were so old-fashioned,' she teased.

'It was the days before texting and emails, you see.'

'What did the letter say?'

He grinned. 'It was beautiful – she knows how to turn a phrase, your mother. It was full of poetry and love and,' he stopped.

'What?'

'Lies.'

'Lies? What do you mean?'

'I mean, your mother played a horrible trick on me. She led me right up the garden path.'

'I thought you liked garden paths.'

'Very funny,' he said. 'Well, I didn't like this one. She told me to meet her at this little country pub in the middle of nowhere. She said it was special, with secret corners where lovers could meet. There was a river too where she said we could walk. I couldn't believe my luck. I had all these romantic ideas –'

'Which you'd better keep to yourself, Dad.'

'Yes. I suppose I had.'

'And what happened?'

'She wasn't there. She'd stood me up!'

Bryony laughed. 'I think you deserved it after standing her up.'

'I know. But I couldn't believe she'd think to do something like that.'

'Yes, it's quite cunning, isn't it? I didn't think Mum had that in her.'

'Never cross your mother,' her father warned, shaking his head and smiling at the memory.

It was then that something occurred to Bryony. She could write to Ben via the dating website. She was her mother's daughter, wasn't she? And, like her, she'd always been able to turn a pretty phrase.

Slowly, a plan began to form in her mind and she smiled.

CHAPTER 11

How did such a short train journey cost so much money Ben wondered as he got off the train at Liverpool Street Station for the second time in a week? He objected to paying it, but what choice did he have? He'd just have to try and find a few more hours' teaching a week. After all, he'd made a promise to Aria and he wanted to help her and that meant coming into London.

He caught the tube, getting off at Covent Garden and taking the lift up to street level. He was meeting Aria at a cafe off the main piazza. It was an Italian place which Aria had insisted upon because she needed a proper cup of coffee.

He saw her sitting inside by a window and waved, joining her and ordering an espresso.

'You look pale,' he told her. 'Are you eating properly?'

'I don't like your English food.'

'But you're staying with Italians.'

'They eat rubbish. It's horrible. All pot noodles and stuff from tins.'

Ben grimaced, remembering his own student days. 'Have you had a word with the owner here?'

She nodded. 'He's not heard anything.'

'There are still plenty of others to try,' Ben said encouragingly.

'We can't go around all the Italian cafes and restaurants in London, Ben,' she cried.

'We're not – just the ones you have some connection to.'

'But what if he's avoiding those? What if he's trying to hide from us?'

'Would he really think you'd come after him?'

She nodded. 'He knows I will.'

Ben sighed. Aria and her brother were so close. He knew how that was with his own sister Georgia. He'd hated leaving her when he'd gone travelling, but he'd done his utmost to protect her. Now, Aria was doing the same – she was looking out for her little brother.

'Let's have a look at your list,' he told her as his coffee arrived. He sipped it as she opened her handbag and brought out an A4 sheet of paper with a long list of names and addresses on it.

'It sure would be easier if he just rang you,' Ben observed.

'I check my phone every twenty minutes. He's not returned any of my messages.'

'But you're sure he's here in London?'

She nodded. 'He always dreamed of coming to London.'

Ben grinned. He'd felt the same way about Rome. It was funny – that need to be somewhere different, somewhere one perceived to be slightly exotic.

'Well, there are a couple of addresses within striking distance of here,' he pointed out.

'Which ones?'

'There's a restaurant just a couple of streets away and then this address here.'

She looked at the name he was pointing to.

'Paulo's,' she said.

'Who's he?'

'I don't know,' Aria said. 'It was a name I found scribbled on a notebook when I was going through his things. I don't know if it means anything or nothing.'

'Okay, we'll check it out,' he said. 'It's probably another restaurant. Ready to go?'

Aria looked at him with a quizzical expression on her face.

'What?' he asked.

'I was just wondering why you have a – what's the word? *Barbe*,' she said in Italian, stroking her face.

'Beard,' Ben translated for her, his hand flying to his own face.

'Yes. Why do you have one?' she asked him with a frown. 'You'd look best without it.'

'Better,' Ben said, automatically correcting her. 'You'd look *better* without it.'

'Better, best,' she shrugged. 'It needs to go.'

He smiled. What was it with women and his beard?

They left the cafe and walked out into the main piazza of Covent Garden. The sun was shining down on the crowds and it was hard not to become caught up in the energy of the scene, but Ben knew that he wasn't there to enjoy the London experience. They had serious business to attend to.

He glanced at Aria. She looked so anxious. He wouldn't be surprised if she hadn't been sleeping well. She had that drawn look about her.

'It'll be all right,' he told her and she nodded, but he was worried about saying such things when he had no real idea about what was going to happen. London was a huge place and there were countless corners where Dario could be hiding. He might not even be in London at all, or the UK for that matter. Ben didn't voice his doubts to Aria, though, because that wouldn't do any good. They had some leads and that was enough for now.

The Italian restaurant on the list wasn't hard to find. It was a small, family-run affair with a deliciously simple menu of oven-fired pizza without all the nonsense of thick crusts or tropical toppings.

Ben followed Aria inside and hung back as she broke into Italian, reaching inside her handbag for the photo of Dario she was carrying with her. The waiter shook his head, but Aria wasn't giving up and he called through to the kitchen. A burly man with long dark hair came out and glanced at the photo and said something Ben didn't quite understand. His accent was thick, probably from the south, he guessed but, by the look on Aria's face, he hadn't seen anything of Dario.

'Grazia,' Aria said and the two of them left.

Ben reached out to touch her shoulder and she sighed. 'Lots more still to try,' he told her.

'I know.' She delved into her bag and brought out her phone, checking it for messages. There were none.

'This Paulo's place is only a few streets away. A ten-minute walk at the most.'

'Good.'

They marched on in silence, passing shops, offices and restaurants. One really only got to know the scale of a city when one was on foot, Ben thought, remembering the time he'd spent in some of the European capitals. He'd walked miles, soaking in the sites, locking it all away for the time he knew he'd come home. You could always tell the tourists from the locals wherever you were in the world, he thought, watching a couple strolling casually ahead of them, stopping to point at the buildings. Tourists saw things which locals had stopped seeing years ago; their fresh eyes noticed the original Georgian shop fronts, the pediments and the boot scrapers whilst the locals saw nothing but the time passing and the fact that they were late for their next appointment.

But Aria was a tourist of sorts and she didn't seem to be taking any joy in the beauty of her surroundings. His heart went out to her as he wondered, once again, what she must be going through.

They found the street they were looking for. It was pretty much like the others they'd walked down with a mixture of boutiques, cafes and restaurants.

'What number was it?' Ben asked.

'*Venti-sei*,' Aria said.

'Twenty-seven,' Ben translated. 'It's the cafe over there. Look.'

They crossed the road, stopping outside the tiny cafe. There were two small tables on the pavement outside and a pretty red and white awning, but Aria hesitated at the door.

'Want me to go first?' Ben asked.

She nodded and he opened the door. There were a few customers in for late lunch and they soon caught the eye of a member of staff. He was tall with the dark hair and olive-coloured skin typical of an Italian and he seemed to clock Aria right away. Before Ben realised what was happening, Aria had charged out of the cafe, the door slamming behind her. Ben turned to the Italian.

'Aria?' the Italian whispered, a frown darkening his face, but he didn't move. He then muttered something else in Italian which Ben couldn't quite make out so he left the cafe in pursuit of Aria.

She was running down the street and he had a job catching up with her.

'Aria – stop!' he cried.

Had she heard him? He didn't think so because she kept on running.

'ARIA!' he shouted louder this time and she was finally forced to stop at the end of the road. 'What's going on?' She was breathing hard, her dark eyes startled. 'What is it? Who was that guy?'

'Nobody.'

'But he knew you.'

She shook her head and mumbled something in Italian as she always did when she was stressed. Ben could only pick up bits and pieces of it, but he thought he heard her say something about mistaken identity.

'But he knew your name. He called after you. Who was he?'

She started to walk away from him. Ben turned back to see if the Italian might be following them, but there was no sign of him.

'Listen to me,' he said, catching up with her again and placing a hand on her shoulder. She flinched at his touch and he saw a hardness in her eyes which he'd never seen before. It startled him for a moment, but then he continued. 'I can't help you unless I know what's going on.'

'What are you saying? Are you threatening me? You don't want to help me?'

'Of course I want to help you. But I need to understand what just happened. Who was that guy back there? He clearly knew you. Is he a friend of Dario's? Why didn't you talk to him? He might know where your brother is.'

'He won't know,' she snapped.

'No? Are you going to tell me why he won't know?'

Her gaze darted about uneasily.

'I'm here to help you, Aria,' he said, his voice softer now, reassuring. 'Please tell me.'

She bit her lip. 'He's a friend of Dario's,' she said at last.

'Okay,' Ben said. That was a start at least.

'But Dario won't have been in touch with him. I wish I'd known.'

'Known what?'

'That it was *that* Paulo.'

'Which Paulo?'

'The one who hates me.'

'Why would he hate you?'

Her eyes avoided contact with his. 'I don't want to talk about it.'

Ben sighed. 'That's not really helpful.'

'I'm too tired,' she said. 'I want to go back to the flat now.'

'You're kidding me, right? I've travelled all the way into London and you want to give up for the day?' She walked away from him and he could see that he was fighting a losing battle. 'Aria!' He shook his head in annoyance. 'Call me, okay?'

Ben hung around Covent Garden for a bit, but he really didn't see the point in staying in London. He journeyed back to Liverpool Street Station and, as soon as he found a seat on the train, he closed his eyes, allowing the gentle movement to quieten his mind. Even though it had been cut short, it had been a stressful day. Aria's unexplained departure and her unwillingness to talk to him about what was going on had angered him. Then he felt guilty about being angry but, still, he couldn't help feeling mad at her cutting him loose like that. It made him wonder how much he actually knew about this woman and whether she'd been telling him the truth.

By the time he got home, his mood had softened and he made himself a cup of tea and checked his email before logging on to the Country Catches dating website on his sister's laptop. His face soon creased with a smile of gigantic proportions. There was a message from Bryony.

How are you?

It was only three words but that question mark opened up a whole world of possibilities. She was opening a dialogue with him, wasn't she? You didn't ask somebody you hated how they were, did you? She could so easily have ignored him, but she'd chosen not to. She'd engaged with him. And there was only one thing to do with a question and that was to answer it.

I'm good. Better than good. Just been into London.

He stopped typing. How much should he say? He didn't want to sound too keen and yet he was champing at the bit to get a proper conversation under way.

He deleted the *Just been into London*. After all, it probably wasn't wise to mention the young and beautiful Aria at this tenuous point.

Been thinking about you.

He looked at those four innocent words. They were the truth, but should he send them? He deleted them. Goodness, this was harder than he'd thought. He'd been desperate to talk to Bryony for ages but, now that the time had come, he had no idea what to say.

So what did he have so far?

I'm good. Better than good.

Did that sound too smug? She might think it did so he deleted it and was left with nothing.

'Come on!' he cajoled himself. 'What do you want to say to her?'

He sat looking at the empty message box. What a depressing sight it was. For a moment, he thought back to the postcards he'd written to Bryony from around the world, each one full of his humour and love. It had been so easy to write to her because he'd had so much to say, but words had deserted him now and so he wrote the only thing that seemed to matter – matching her three words with three of his own.

I miss you.

Bryony cursed herself for not closing up the shop on time because it gave Colin a chance to catch her. The last few days she'd been sneaking away early, but he was on to her now and was standing by the fantasy shelves waiting for her.

She knew she was being spectacularly unfair to this man. He'd been so patient with her when she'd given him so very little in terms of encouragement. She cast a glance at him now. His sweet face was slightly red from his day in the bakery. He'd just finished the catering for a corporate event, a new venture for his company, and he looked tired. She sighed to herself. The truth was her head was full of Ben at the moment so there was very little room to think about Colin.

Ever since her father had told her about her mother's little trick, she hadn't been able to stop thinking about how she could do something similar. She knew that it was mean and childish and it was totally beneath her, she knew all that, and she could hear the voices of her family admonishing her, but she just couldn't help it. Nobody knew how Ben Stratton had made her feel. They only had an inkling. But she'd felt such pain at what she'd seen as his betrayal that she had felt physically ill with it.

She knew that, for the most part, her family expected her to be over it by now. It had been an unfortunate incident, something to pick herself up from and move on. But she had carried that pain deep inside her all those years. It had tainted everything she'd done and every thought she'd had. Everything had always come back to Ben because he was the person in the world whom she'd loved the most. Loved and trusted.

She'd opened the dating website on her work computer and saw the very moment that Ben's message arrived, but she'd been delaying opening it, hoping that Colin would leave first, but he seemed adamant on waiting for her.

'Bryony?' he said now, as if reminding her he was there. 'You shutting up yet? It's pretty late.'

'I've just got to place this last order,' she lied, opening Ben's message.

She blinked when she read it.

I miss you.

It wasn't what she'd been expecting. She'd imagined some witty reply, some smug message to try and make her laugh, but those three simple words caught her completely off guard and her lips parted as she read them again.

'There's a dance at Torrington Barn Village Hall at the weekend,'

Colin said from the other side of the shop. 'I can get us tickets. It's a local band. They're really good.'

She looked up from the computer. 'Oh, Colin – that's not really me,' she told him.

'You don't have to actually dance,' he said. 'We can just sit and listen to the music together.'

'I think I'll give it a miss,' she said with what she hoped was an apologetic smile.

He sighed. 'Well, what do you want to do, Bryony? Because I'm at a loss here.'

She was a little taken aback at his tone. She'd never heard him angry before.

'What do you mean?'

He frowned. 'I mean, sometimes, I'm not really sure why you keep going out with me.'

She looked at him, her heart full of regret at what she was doing to this poor man. She should tell him. She knew in her heart that it would be the right thing to do and yet she couldn't bring herself to do it because a plan was quickly beginning to form in her mind – a plan which very much included Colin.

'I'm sorry,' she told him. 'I'd love to go to the dance.'

'You would?' He looked genuinely surprised by her turnaround.

'I would. Thank you for asking me.'

He beamed her a smile. 'It'll be a great evening. I'm sure we'll have fun.'

'Me too,' she said. 'I think it's going to be a really fun night. Just let me place this order and then I can shut up the shop.'

He nodded, looking pleased.

Her fingers danced over the keyboards and, once she'd finished, she read the message over before pressing send, a naughty little smile playing over her lips. Oh, yes, the night of the dance was going to be fun alright.

CHAPTER 12

Ben had lost all track of time. He wasn't sure how long he'd been sitting looking at the screen of his tablet when Georgia came in.

'What's the matter with you? Your eyes are all agog!'

'Look at this for me, will you?' he said, scooting across the sofa to make room for her.

'What is it?'

'That dating website.'

'I *knew* it was a good idea,' she said. 'It was, wasn't it?'

'I think you might have been right – read that.'

'Is it from who I think it is?'

'Well, of course it is. Just read it!'

'Okay, okay.'

Ben read it through for the hundredth time as his sister read it for the first.

'Tell me what it says,' he said after a moment.

'I think you know what it says.'

'Tell me anyway. I want to make sure I've got it right.'

'She's asking you out.'

'Yeah?'

'That what it looks like. I've heard about this dance too. It's meant to be quite good.'

'I don't really dance,' Ben announced.

'I wouldn't let that stop you from going,' Georgia said.

'I won't. I'm not.'

'How did this happen so quickly?' Georgia asked.

'What do you mean?'

'I mean, one minute she wasn't talking to you and the next she's telling you to meet her at this dance.'

Ben shrugged. 'Maybe she's forgiven me.'

Georgia frowned. 'That quickly?'

'Well, she's had a few years.'

'Yeah, but you said she was icy cold to you when you tried to talk to her. I don't get this sudden U-turn.'

'What are you saying?'

'I'm saying you should proceed with caution, little brother.'

'Hey, I'm your *big* brother.'

'Maybe, but that doesn't mean you know what you're doing when it comes to women.'

'Oh, really?'

'Really.' Georgia got up from the sofa. 'I just think you should be careful. You're acting like she's proposed to you or something.'

'No I'm not.'

'Yes you are – you've got a silly grin on your face as if you've won the lottery.'

He tutted at her. She was being ridiculous. 'This is better than the lottery.'

'Not if she's fooling around.'

'Why would she be fooling around?'

'Because you broke her heart?'

'Ah, there is that,' Ben acceded. 'But I think this is pretty genuine.'

'You only think that because that's what you want to think.'

'So you think I should ignore it?'

Georgia sighed. 'Just be careful, okay?'

He nodded and started typing.

'What are you doing?' she asked him.

'Sending a reply.'

'Not now. Not tonight. You don't want to look too keen, do you?'

'Hey, didn't you just say that it's wrong to play games?' Ben asked..

'Not exactly, but I think it would be wrong to let her get the upper hand so easily, don't you?'

Ben thought about this for a moment. He'd waited years to see Bryony again, to get close to her and tell her how he felt. Surely a day or two more wasn't going to hurt. Still, he couldn't help acknowledging how frustrating it was to wait. There was nothing he wanted more than to hold her in his arms. He ached with longing for her. She was the only woman he had ever really loved. He'd tried to switch his feelings off so many times in the past. After he'd stopped writing to her from abroad, he'd done his best to move on, but it simply hadn't worked. There was nobody else for him, he was quite convinced of that, and he knew his sister had come to understand that too. When he'd first arrived home, she'd been horrified to hear that he was still in love with Bryony and had encouraged him to move on, but she'd soon realised that that was hopeless. It was good to have her support, even though she was telling him to slow down.

'Ben?' Georgia prompted him now, motioning to his tablet.

Ben sighed. 'I'll wait,' he said through gritted teeth.

Bryony was completely stumped. She'd genuinely thought that Ben would reply within the hour if not sooner. Wasn't this what he wanted? She was inviting him back into her life. The least he could do was respond.

She shook her head. She was probably getting herself worked up over nothing. After all, she'd only just sent the message. She'd check again later.

Looking out of the window of her terrace, she noticed what a beautiful evening it was. The spring sunshine had encouraged a bright row of tulips to open in her tiny front garden and the sky was the softest of blues. It was far too lovely an evening to spend inside brooding, she thought.

Quickly, Bryony changed her clothes and walked the short distance to Cuckoo Cottage, knocking on the door of the pink house a few minutes later.

'Hello, my dear,' Flo said when she answered.

'I hope you don't mind me just turning up.'

'Of course not. You're always welcome here. Come on in. Sonny's just doing his homework.'

They walked through to the back of the house and Bryony saw Sonny hard at work at the kitchen table. He looked up when she came in and gave the tiniest of smiles.

'It's Maths so I'm trying to avoid him questioning me,' Flo said. 'I used to hate Maths as a kid. Hate it now as an adult too.'

Bryony laughed. 'Figures are sent to try us. I'm lucky that my dad still handles the books for my shop. I'd hate to be in charge of that. I mean, I have offered to do it because it's not really fair that Dad does it, but I think he can see I don't really enjoy it.'

'You're very lucky to have him.'

'I know,' Bryony said, thinking of the support her father gave her. 'I've been telling him about me coming here.'

'Oh yes?'

'He's thrilled that I'm showing an interest in gardening and I've been wondering if I could help you with the actual growing side of things. I mean, once we get all the wild areas under control.'

'Well, that would be marvellous,' Flo said. 'Let me grab my jacket and we can have a poke around in the sheds. 'You be okay, Sonny?'

The boy looked up and nodded and the two women left the house together, crossing the garden towards the shed.

'I'll just move these tools,' Flo said, shifting an old fork and spade which had been leaning against the door. Bryony hadn't been inside the shed and she had to admit to being surprised when Flo opened the door. From the state of the garden, she'd expected the shed to be a dark, damp, spidery sort of a place, but it was surprisingly light and tidy. A potting bench flanked one side and rows of terracotta and plastic pots were stacked underneath.

'Flo, this is lovely,' she told her.

'My little heaven,' she said. 'I'd rather be in here potting up my plants than doing any sort of housework. It's especially nice when it's raining. It makes a delicious sound on the corrugated iron roof. It's like a dozen Fred Astaires dancing up there.'

Bryony laughed.

'Now, let me see. This is what we want.' Flo picked up a large rusty tin and placed it on the bench before opening it. It was full of seed packets and old brown envelopes with handwritten notes on them.

'I think of this as one of my tins of dreams.'

Bryony smiled. 'What are they all?'

'There are all sorts of things in here. Salads, vegetables, herbs. Take a look. There are dates on the back. I fear some of them might be long expired and we might be too late to plant others. I've already got a few things on the go – some tomatoes and salad which I started off in the house in March – but I never have time to do as much as I want.'

Bryony grabbed a handful of packets and started reading. It was like entering another world where a different language was used. If it hadn't been for the photos of some of the plants on the packets, she wouldn't have had a clue as to what they were.

'Costoluto fiorentina,' Bryony read. 'What's this? It sounds like an Italian princess.'

'That's a beautiful big ribbed tomato. I'm growing those already.'

'Rainbow chard – Dad grows that.'

'Keep that packet out. I've got one row on the go, but we can definitely plant another.'

Bryony selected some more packets – some cabbages, kale and squashes which she liked the sound of. It was all very exciting.

'This squash,' she said to Flo as she held up a packet, 'it just says "sunburst". What's it like?'

'It's a kind of patty pan – a scalloped-edge squash. A bright yellow one.'

'Sounds fabulous. We've got to plant that!'

'How about flowers?' Flo asked. 'Do you like flowers?'

'What woman doesn't?'

'Then try that tin there,' she said, nodding towards a tin on one of the shelves on the other side of the shed which was suitably decorated with painted flowers.

'It's like Christmas,' Bryony said, opening it.

'Better than Christmas,' Flo said. 'Christmas only lasts for one day, but flowers are gifts which last for months.'

'Oh, sunflowers! We've got to have those,' Bryony cried.

'Absolutely. A garden isn't complete without a few yellow giants.'

'Zinnias,' Bryony read from another packet.

'Most definitely. Those are giant zinnias – wonderful to pick for the house. I'm hopeless at floral displays but they're so easy to plonk into a vase.'

'What's this one?' Bryony asked. She'd picked up a brown envelope with handwriting on.

'Phacelia – good for the bees. Bees are especially attracted to blues and purples.'

'And heartsease. Didn't Shakespeare mention it?'

'I don't know about that,' Flo confessed, 'but they look nice in a hanging basket.'

'I'll keep it out then.'

'I tell you, Bryony, there is nothing better than picking your own vegetables from your garden. To grow something you can eat, well, that's the most basic of human needs, isn't it?'

'Dad says that too,' Bryony told her. 'I once asked him what was more important – his plants or his books, and he went really red in the face and told me it was impossible for him to choose. It would be like trying to choose between breathing and swallowing.'

'You just wait until you harvest your first,' Flo paused. 'What have you chosen?' She picked up some of the packets Bryony had selected.

'Nothing will taste as good as these because you'll know what's gone into it. You'll have cleared and manured the land. You'll have selected the seed and planted it, nurtured it, weeded around it and protected it from the birds and butterflies. And then there'll be the flowers. When you're out gathering armfuls of blooms, well, if you're not smiling then...' Flo's words petered out and she looked lost in a wistful daydream.

It was then that Bryony heard the strangest sound.

'What's that?' she asked, straining to hear.

'Oh, Lord!' Flo said. 'It's my neighbour and his trumpet again.'

Bryony grinned, guessing what was coming next. Sure enough, a moment later, the donkeys, Belle and Beau, started braying, filling the evening air with their disapproval.

Flo shook her head. 'With any luck, it won't last long.'

The two women returned to their work, spending a happy hour filling trays and pots with compost, planting seeds and writing labels. It was a wonderfully repetitive job that was all consuming and, when they'd finished, Bryony realised that she hadn't once thought about Ben during that time. No wonder her father was always so calm, she thought. Gardening was really good for the soul.

'It's getting dark,' Flo said at last. 'We'll finish these another day.'

Bryony was loathe to leave the little shed, but consoled herself with the knowledge that she could come back very soon.

It was as she was walking down the little path back to the house that she screamed.

'Flo! There's a hand in the hedge!'

As quick as a bolt of lightning, Flo grabbed the hoe that was leaning up against the shed.

'Get out of my hedge!' she shouted, thwacking the hand with the hoe.

'You crazy old woman!' a voice came from the other side as the bony hand withdrew.

'You leave my eggs alone, you hear me?'

They waited a moment, making quite sure that the hand wasn't going to return, and then they walked back to the house.

'What was all that about?' Bryony asked.

'Dr Skegby – he keeps stealing my eggs. Says he has a right to them because of the noise the donkeys make.'

'That's outrageous!'

'He's always been a miserable sod.'

Bryony bit back a grin because Flo didn't look amused.

'Hey, where's Sonny?' Bryony asked. The boy was no longer sitting at the kitchen table, but his Maths book was still open.

'Sonny?' Flo called through the house.

A loud clattering sound came from the living room and they ran through to find Sonny crouched in the fireplace. He'd knocked over the old copper kettle which stood there and his hair was covered in cobweb.

'What are you doing, Sonny?' Flo asked.

He looked startled for a moment, but then shrugged. 'I wanted to see up the chimney.'

'That horrible, spidery place? I wouldn't go sticking your nose up there if I were you.'

'He's a boy, Flo – he's bound to stick his nose in horrible places,' Bryony observed.

'Did you finish your homework?' Flo asked him.

'Sort of.'

'Sort of?'

'I got stuck at the end.'

'Oh, well, it won't break the world if you miss one or two questions. Let's make some tea.'

Bryony joined them and they talked about the books they were all reading. Flo was still enjoying *The Darling Buds of May* and was looking forward to the book club meeting when they'd be discussing it. Bryony was reading Dodie Smith's *I Capture the Castle* because she was in the mood to relive the pain of first love, and Sonny was reading *The Twits* and took great delight in showing them all the illustrations.

'Did you know Roald Dahl scribbled down his idea for *The Twits* in a notebook? He wrote, "Do something against beards."'

Flo giggled. 'Well, there are beards and there are beards. Take your Ben's beard.'

'He's not *my* Ben,' Bryony quickly said.

'His beard is quite handsome,' Flo declared.

Bryony wrinkled her nose. 'How can you say that?'

'Well, he wouldn't lose his dinner in it, would he?' Flo said.

'I would hope not.'

'Auntie Flo?' Sonny said. 'Can I grow a beard?'

'Maybe when you're older,' Flo told him.

'Oh, please don't, Sonny. Girls don't like beards.'

'Why do you want to grow one?' Flo asked her great-nephew.

'To hide things in,' he said.

'Like what?'

'My Maths homework.'

Bryony and Flo laughed.

'Ah!' Flo suddenly said, 'that reminds me. Bryony, dear, would you be able to take Sonny to school in the morning? I've got an appointment in Bury that I can't get out of.'

'Sure,' Bryony said. 'I'll pick him up. What time?'

'Twenty past eight should do it. You don't mind? I know it's a bit earlier than you open your shop.'

'That's okay,' Bryony said. 'It'll give me a chance to clear out the stock room ahead of opening. It's a job I keep putting off.'

'I owe you,' Flo said.

'Not at all. I'm glad to be able to help.'

When Bryony got back from Flo's, she logged straight on to the Country Catches website. Sure enough, there was a message from Ben. Her fingers hovered over it for a moment, wondering what he'd written. There was only one way to find out. She clicked open.

Hello Bryony. I was so pleased to get your message. Pleased and perplexed.

She frowned. Did he suspect something? Had she come on too strong?

You did ask me out on a date, right? I mean to that dance? I didn't know you liked dancing. Remember that sixth form one when we sneaked out and sat under the stars? You said Mr Darcy didn't approve of dancing and neither did you. You were always quoting Darcy and Elizabeth back then.

Bryony smiled, cursing Ben for his memory.

If you want to go dancing then I'd be a very happy partner. But can we meet to talk first? I feel there's so much we need to talk about. Ben. X.

She swallowed hard. She didn't want to talk to Ben. That wasn't part of the plan. She reread his message, noticing the big kiss at the end. This was all moving way too quickly for her. She'd thought she was in charge of the pace of things, but Ben seemed to have taken the reins.

Her fingers poised over the keyboard ready to type her reply. There were two things you could do with a question: answer it or ignore it.

I had such a big crush on Mr Darcy, didn't I? I suppose I still do, along with many other fictional heroes, of course. B.

She pressed send. It was the coward's way out, she knew that, and he'd probably just ask to meet up again, but she'd handle that if and when it happened.

Flo was waiting by the front door with Sonny when Bryony pulled up in her car the next morning.

'All ready?' Bryony called from her open window.

Flo nodded and patted Sonny on his shoulder and Bryony watched as he struggled towards the car with his bag.

'Hi Sonny,' she said as he opened the back door and climbed in.

'Hi,' he said in that quiet way of his.

'Looking forward to school?' Bryony asked, turning round to smile at him.

'Suppose.'

'What lessons have you got today?'

'Maths.'

'Ah, the dreaded Maths homework due in?'

'Yes.'

'Good luck with that.'

She pulled out and drove the short distance to Castle Clare.

'Is it always so busy?' she asked as they reached the centre of town a couple of minutes later. Never having done the school run before, she didn't envy her sister Polly the morning rush. Indeed she could see her sister up ahead with young Archie who was in the year below Sonny. Now that Polly was living in town, she was able to walk Archie to school so that saved the problem of parking at least.

Bryony, though, had to park a short distance away from the school.

'I'm afraid this is as close as I can get,' she told Sonny. 'I'll walk with you to the gate.'

''sokay,' he said.

'It's no bother.' She got out of the car and opened his door for him, watching as he hauled his massive bag out after him. He walked ahead of her on the pavement and she couldn't help noticing the strange angle at which he was leaning, his bag obviously weighing him down.

'Here, let me carry that,' Bryony said. 'It looks way too heavy for you.'

He shook his head. 'I can do it.'

'I'm sure you can, but your arm might double in length in the process.' Bryony reached forward and took the bag from him. 'Heavens! What on earth have you got in here – an entire football team?'

Sonny didn't seem to appreciate her humour.

'Sweetheart, I don't think you need to be carrying all this around. Are you sure you haven't packed more books and kit than you need?' The boy didn't answer her and Bryony frowned. 'I'm sure we can sort it out,' she said, placing the bag on the ground for a moment and unzipping it.

'Don't!' Sonny cried, but it was too late.

Bryony stared at the contents of the bag in alarm. This was no ordinary school bag. She'd expected to find a tennis racket or a small mountain of books, but what she saw was a pair of silver candlesticks, a large framed print of a Labrador, a bronze figurine and a pink ceramic piggy bank that must surely be full by the weight of the bag.

'Sonny!' she exclaimed, swallowing hard as she looked up at him. 'Why are these things in your bag?'

His face had turned to an unearthly colour.

'Do these all belong to your aunt?'

He didn't answer her, but she could tell from his expression that they did. Where else would he have got them from?

'Oh, Sonny!' she exclaimed. 'What are you doing with all these things?' Bryony picked up the pink piggy bank and shook it. It rattled with coins. She put it back and picked up a silver candlestick. 'I don't understand – what were you going to do with all this because it looks like you've stolen them.'

He looked down at the ground and Bryony thought she saw his bottom lip quiver.

'I think we need to talk to your aunt about this, don't you? We should get you home.'

'I mustn't miss school,' he said.

'You're not going to school this morning,' Bryony said. 'You're coming home with me and we're waiting until Auntie Flo gets home to sort this out.'

'Please don't tell her!' he cried, his eyes filling with tears. 'I was made to do it.'

Bryony frowned. 'Someone made you take these things?'

'I can't miss school. He'll be waiting.'

'Who'll be waiting? Sonny, what's going on?' She moved closer to him, placing her hands on his little shoulders and then it all came pouring out in a torrent of tears and sobs. Bryony listened, her mouth open in shock at what she was hearing.

When he'd finished, she ushered him into the car, keeping the bag which she placed in the boot of the car. She then walked to the school and explained to one of the teachers that Sonny wasn't feeling well. And then she rang Flo's mobile.

'Bryony? Is everything alright?'

'I'm bringing Sonny home from school,' she told Flo.

'Oh, dear? Is he ill?'

'Not exactly.'

'Then what's the matter?'

'He's got something he needs to talk to you about.'

'Oh!' Flo said. 'Well, I'll be home as quickly as I can.'

'Don't worry and rush. I'll keep him at mine in the meantime,' Bryony said.

As soon as they got back to her house, Bryony poured Sonny some orange juice and watched as he sat on the sofa, his face miserable.

'It wasn't your fault, Sonny,' Bryony assured him, but you should have told Auntie Flo. She would have been able to help.'

The little boy didn't say anything and Bryony decided not to torture him anymore with her opinions She was sure he'd have enough to cope with once Flo knew what was going on.

'Listen, I've got to make a phone call. Why don't you choose yourself a book from that box over there?' She pointed to a box of books she'd been sorting through for the charity shop.

Sonny got up off the sofa and tentatively looked through the titles, choosing a boys' adventure with a lurid green cover.

Bryony left the room and called her sister.

'Polly? Can you get in to open the shop this morning? I'm afraid I've got to take care of something here.'

'Everything okay?' Polly asked her.

'It will be. I'll fill you in later, alright?'

Bryony hung up and took a deep breath. Well, that was another thing taken care of. It was the next part of the day she wasn't looking forward to, but she knew it had to be done even though it was bound to break Flo's heart when she heard what had been going on.

CHAPTER 13

Flo rang Bryony's mobile once she was back from Bury St Edmunds and Bryony and Sonny made the short journey to Cuckoo Cottage. Ordinarily Bryony would have walked, but Sonny's bag was so heavy that walking wasn't ideal.

An anxious Flo was hovering in the front garden when they pulled up by the kerb.

'Now what's going on here?' she asked her great-nephew as he got out of the car. Bryony joined him a moment later having retrieved his school bag from the boot.

'We'd better go inside,' she told Flo, her stomach churning for the older woman at the news she had to impart.

Once they were all seated in the living room, Flo looked across at her great-nephew who was looking very awkward in the old armchair next to the fireplace.

'Sonny, dear?' she began. 'What's the matter?'

He didn't answer. Instead he looked to Bryony.

'You tell her,' he said.

'I think you should, Sonny,' Bryony told him. 'Just tell her what you told me.'

Flo was looking deeply worried by this stage.

'She'll be mad at me,' Sonny said. 'She'll hate me.'

Flo gasped. 'I won't hate you, monkey! I could *never* hate you! Just tell me what's going on. I won't be able to help if you don't tell me.'

He swallowed hard, looking so awkward with his hands hidden under his legs.

'I took things,' he began.

'What do you mean?' Flo asked.

'Silver things. Jewellery. Some money.'

Flo looked baffled by this confession and gave a nervous sort of laugh. 'What?'

'He's telling you the truth, Flo,' Bryony assured her. 'His school bag is full of things from the house.'

'What things?'

Sonny's gaze was fixed on his shoes.

'A pair of silver candlesticks, a framed print, a bronze figurine and a piggy bank,' Bryony said.

'My piggy bank?'

Bryony nodded.

Flo took a moment to absorb this information. The school bag was sitting on the floor in front of them and she stared at it as if it were a malevolent thing and then she looked back at Sonny.

'Did you take my cake knife, Sonny?'

Sonny nodded.

Flo's mouth dropped open. 'But what did you want with a cake knife? I don't understand.'

'Tell her, Sonny,' Bryony said, resting a hand on his thin arm.

He looked up. 'He made me do it.'

'Who?' Flo asked.

'Dad.'

There was a pause.

'Mitch?' Flo said. 'Mitch asked you to steal things? But why?'

Sonny didn't answer, but he didn't need to because realisation seemed to dawn on Flo and she looked at Bryony.

'When I went to his house, it was full of things. Old things. He's been selling stuff. I guess online.'

'Like eBay?' Bryony asked.

'He says eBay is safer,' Sonny piped up.

'Less risky,' Bryony added. 'I guess buyers don't ask so many questions about how sellers came by their goods.'

'But how were you getting the goods to your father, Sonny?'

Bryony swallowed hard. Flo wasn't going to like this.

'At school,' Sonny said.

'How do you mean?'

'At lunchtime. He'd wait by the hedge at the back of the playing field. There's a gap there. I'd pass the bag to him.'

Flo shook her head in disbelief. Bryony had never seen her look so pale.

'My own nephew,' she whispered. 'How could he do this to me? And to use the school for his crime!' Suddenly she cupped her hands over her mouth. 'He *planted* Sonny here. He planned this from the start. And here was I thinking he was just a bit busy at work. I thought I was helping him, but he was just using me.'

'Oh, Flo!' Bryony said in sympathy, moving closer to her on the sofa and resting a hand on her shoulder.

'I can't believe it. My own nephew *stealing* from me. Plotting and stealing!' Flo suddenly cried out. 'The fireplace! Sonny – what were you doing in the fireplace yesterday?'

The little boy's bottom lip quivered.

'He told you, didn't he? He told you about the secret hiding place. Oh my god! Whatever did I tell him that for?'

'What is it, Flo?' Bryony asked.

'There's a loose brick.' She stood up and crossed the room, her head disappearing up the chimney. 'I told him about it once. Oh, how stupid was I to trust him?'

'You weren't to know, Flo,' Bryony said.

'I *should've* known!' Flo said. 'He's always been a no good...' her voice petered out. She obviously didn't want to bad mouth Sonny's father in front of him.

Bryony stood up. 'Can I help?'

'It's alright, my dear. It's still there,' Flo said, her head appearing from out of the fireplace again.

'What is it?' Bryony asked. 'Sorry – it's none of my business.'

'It's okay, my dear. It's just a bit of jewellery I inherited from my mother. It's not much, a couple of nice rings and an old watch. The secondhand value would be so little, but they mean a lot to me.' Suddenly, there were tears in Flo's eyes. 'I can't bear to think of them gone. To imagine them up for sale on eBay. My mother's precious things!'

Bryony moved forward, putting an arm around Flo and guiding her back to the sofa.

'They're safe,' she told her.

Flo took a minute, her hand diving into the pocket of her dress for a hanky. She dabbed her eyes and blew her nose.

'Has he done this before, Sonny?' she asked once the hanky had done its business. 'I mean, has he got you to stay in somebody's house so you could steal things from them?'

Sonny shook his head.

'At least that's something,' Bryony said.

'Have you stolen for him before?' Flo asked. 'Like in a shop?'

Sonny's eyes looked huge and full of anxiety. It was as if the truth was on the tip of his tongue and he was desperate to unburden himself, but he was also afraid to.

'You've got to tell me, Sonny. Now's the time for the truth.'

Sonny gazed down at the floor. 'He told me to once,' he confessed after a pause. 'In Castle Clare. But I got scared.'

Flo nodded. 'You did the right thing.'

'He got mad at me.'

Flo frowned. 'He's never hurt you, has he?'

'He shouted at me and pushed me into my room when we got home.'

Flo puffed out an angry breath.

'But we still take from boxes,' Sonny went on.

'Boxes?' Flo asked.

'Them boxes and jars and things. Like yours,' he said pointing out of the window into the front garden.

'You mean *honesty* boxes?'

Sonny nodded again.

'We do that on Sundays. That's the best day, Dad says. The jars are sometimes full of coins. If they're not, he gets me to take the eggs or other things. He told me to take some sprouts once even though I don't like them.'

Flo gasped at this new revelation from her great-nephew. 'But you know that's wrong, don't you? People like me put out a little bit of garden produce for a few pence. We do that in good faith that our trust won't be abused. The honesty box is sacred, Sonny. *Sacred!*'

Bryony rested a hand on Flo's. She could see that the boy was looking frightened.

'I've got my neighbour stealing eggs from the hedge and my own nephew and great-nephew stealing from my house!'

'It's going to stop,' Bryony assured her. 'Now that we know what's happening.'

'Yes,' Flo said, nodding. 'It's going to stop.'

They all took a minute to calm down and process what had been said.

'What are you going to do, Flo?' Bryony asked at last.

She shook her head, looking completely dazed. 'I can't ring the police, can I? I can't report my own nephew.'

'Well, you could. He is stealing from you and using a minor to do his dirty work,' Bryony pointed out.

Flo rested her head in her hands. 'I can't,' she whispered. 'I just can't. He's my nephew.'

'Then we'll think of something else.'

'He'll be mad,' Sonny said.

'What's that?' Flo asked, looking up.

'When I'm not there today.'

'He's right,' Bryony said. 'He'll be expecting Sonny at school.'

'I'll ring him,' Flo said, on her feet in an instant. 'I'll tell him Sonny couldn't come to school today. He won't suspect anything.'

They watched as Flo crossed the room, picking up the phone from a side table and dialling the number.

'Mitch?' she said a moment later, her voice light and friendly. She really was a very good actress, Bryony decided. 'Sonny's off school today. Tummy bug. No. No. He should be back in tomorrow. Yes, tomorrow. No, I'm quite sure. I think he just needs extra rest today. Toodle pip.'

She hung up.

'What did he say?' Bryony asked.

'Not a lot. Didn't even send Sonny his love.' Flo walked across to her nephew and bent to kiss his forehead.

'Do you think he'll be waiting for you tomorrow, Sonny?' Bryony asked.

Sonny shrugged. 'I guess.'

'He seemed to want my assurance that Sonny would be back at school then,' Flo said.

'Does he come every day?' Bryony asked Sonny.

'No. Not every day.'

'How many times have you done this for him?'

'I've lost count,' he said honestly.

Flo bent down and delved into Sonny's school bag, bringing out the pink piggy bank which she placed on the coffee table and then the print of the Labrador. The two silver candlesticks and the bronze figurine were next and she took them to the mantelpiece with shaking hands. Bryony's heart ached for her.

'Did you really think I wouldn't miss them?' she asked Sonny.

Sonny's eyes filled with tears again.

'He was just doing what his father told him to,' Bryony reminded her.

'I know,' Flo agreed. 'Did he ask you to get particular things?'

Sonny nodded.

'You know, now I come to think of it, the time before last when he was here, he was having a good nose around. Eyeing my things up. He was doing a secret inventory, wasn't he? Then he decided to plant Sonny here to take them all.'

'He took pictures,' Sonny said. 'On his phone.'

'Of my things?'

'Yes. He showed me. Told me where things were.'

Flo's mouth was a perfect O-shape of shock. 'And here I was thinking I was just getting a bit forgetful with where things were.'

Just then something seemed to catch Flo's eye and she crossed the room.

Bryony tried to see what she was doing and grimaced as Flo handed something to her.

'What is it?' she asked.

'A cheap ornament I bought from the back of one of those catalogues that fall out of magazines.'

Bryony turned the colourful figurine of Betty Boop over in her hands.

'What are you planning to do with it?'

'Put it in Sonny's bag,' Flo said. 'That'll teach Mitch a lesson, won't it?'

'I don't know,' Bryony said honestly. 'It'll probably just make him mad.'

'Yes, but wouldn't you love to see his face when he takes it out of the bag? Serve him right, the no-good rascal!'

'I'm not sure. I think we should probably put the candlesticks back in.'

Flo gasped. 'They were my aunt's,' she said.

'And we'll get them back before anything happens to them,' Bryony said. 'Here, I'll take a photo of them on the mantelpiece and then we'll have proof that they're from here.'

'I can't believe this is happening,' Flo said, shaking her head. 'It's like CSI Castle Clare around here.'

'I'm so sorry this has happened to you,' Bryony said.

'I'm sorry too,' Sonny suddenly piped up from his chair. 'Am I in trouble?' His big eyes were swimming with tears once again and Flo bent down to hug him.

'You're not in trouble, darling, but I do wish you'd told me what was going on. Your dad was wrong to put you in that position. He should never have asked you to do something like that. It was selfish and stupid of him.'

Bryony watched as Flo and Sonny embraced. It was a moving scene and Bryony felt the threat of tears herself as she watched them.

Finally, Flo broke away and mopped her eyes again.

'Right, what's next?' she asked.

Bryony took a deep breath. 'I suppose we have to ask ourselves what we want from this. Do we want to catch him red-handed with your candlesticks? Do we want the police involved?'

'I don't want to go to prison!' Sonny suddenly cried.

'You're not going to prison,' Flo assured him. '*Nobody's* going to prison.'

'But it might be a good idea to catch him on camera all the same,' Bryony said. 'If you don't want to hand the photos over to anyone, you can at least let him know that you've got them. That'll surely stop him from stealing from you again.'

'How would this photo business work exactly?' Flo asked.

'We could go to the school at lunchtime and wait for him. There's a line of trees the other side of the playing fields. There'll be plenty of coverage for us whilst we wait for the drop.'

'The drop?' Flo cried. 'I feel like I'm in the middle of a nasty crime film. One of those that you catch late in the evening by accident and that give you nightmares.'

'He might see you,' Sonny said, his face anxious.

'Yes, what if he sees us?' Flo asked.

'We'll just have to make sure that he doesn't,' Bryony said. 'He doesn't know me, anyway.'

'And I could wear a disguise!' Flo cried.

'Can I wear a disguise?' Sonny asked.

'No, silly! You don't need one,' Flo told him. 'You'll just wear your school uniform and go about things as you'd normally do. We don't want your dad to suspect anything, do we?'

'Are you going to arrest him?'

'No, we're just going to watch,' Flo said.

Sonny seemed to take all this in and Bryony and Flo went over their plan, deciding to get to the school ahead of the lunchtime break in order to get into position.

'Okay, I think we've covered everything, haven't we? We're all ready for tomorrow?' Bryony asked.

'You bet,' Flo said. 'I want my cake knife back!'

Bryony drove into Castle Clare and relieved Polly from her duties in the bookshop. She didn't tell her sister exactly what was going on because she thought it best to keep the whole secret mission quiet for the time being.

By the time she got home later that day, she felt absolutely exhausted. She kicked off her boots and made herself some tea and then flopped onto the sofa, closing her eyes for a moment. What a day it had been. Bryony wondered what would have happened if she hadn't opened Sonny's bag and found all of Flo's things inside it. How long would Mitch have gone on stealing from his aunt? Would he have emptied her entire house? Did he really think he could have got away with it?

The more Bryony thought about it, the more her heart ached for her new friend. How could somebody in your own family deceive you like that? Mitch Lohman must be a unique kind of person to do that to his own aunt. A part of her wanted to ring the police right now and report him, but what good would that do? This was Flo's call and Bryony had to support her friend and the decisions she made about how she wanted to handle things.

Getting up, she went upstairs and switched her computer on. The chaos of the day had meant that she hadn't had time to check in at Country Catches, but she did now and found a message from Ben.

What a day I've had, he began. *I made it all the way to class and realised I'd forgotten the worksheets I'd spent all night preparing! I had to totally wing it. I don't think anyone noticed.*

Bryony bit back a smile because she could imagine Ben improvising. Growing up, he'd always been good at getting himself out of trouble.

PS: I'd really love to meet up and talk to you. B x

She sighed. He wasn't going to give up, was he? Well, she'd just have to go on ignoring his request and talk to him about something else.

It was then that something strange happened. Before Bryony could stop herself, she found she was telling Ben her entire day. It was so easy, she thought, to fall into the old routine with him.

So you think you've had a hectic day, do you? she began. *You should have had my day! I dropped Flo's great-nephew at school this morning and, when I went to pick up his bag, I thought it was a bit on the heavy side so I took a look inside it and you'll never guess what I found in there: a pair of silver candlesticks and other things from Flo's home. I think I was in shock for a moment because he's such a shy little boy. I just couldn't wrap my head around it. And then I realised I had to tell Flo and she's one of the sweetest people ever. I knew it was going to break her heart.*

Bryony went on to tell him about Flo's reaction and how Sonny had been stealing for his father. She hadn't meant to write so much to Ben and she cursed herself as soon as she'd hit the send button. But she had to admit that she'd felt safe telling him about the whole Flo, Sonny and Mitch story. She'd *always* felt safe with Ben. She'd been able to tell him anything and that had been one of the things she'd missed so much when he'd gone. He'd taken away such an important part of her daily routine. Not only had she lost her boyfriend, but she'd lost her best friend too – the friend she'd call not only if something out of the ordinary happened, but if something completely *ordinary* occurred like running out of bread when all she wanted in the world was a slice of toast with seedless raspberry jam. Or that time when she'd got hiccups and couldn't answer the shop phone without cracking up. He'd run right round to hold the fort for her until the hiccups had gone.

When Ben had left, she'd felt utterly bereft. Of course, she had a great big family she could have shared all the silly moments of her day with, but it wasn't the same. Everybody had that one person in their life they were connected to in that very special way and, for Bryony, it had been Ben.

She swallowed hard as a thousand memories came swimming to the surface. She couldn't allow herself to become engulfed and she certainly couldn't allow herself to fall back into that easy relationship with him, however much it seemed natural to her and however much she craved it. That wasn't part of her plan, she told herself. And so she shut her computer down before she was tempted to write anything else. She had a big day tomorrow.

CHAPTER 14

Bryony wasn't the only one with a big day ahead; Ben had one too only he didn't realise it when he woke up.

His head was still spinning from the message he'd received from Bryony. He was thrilled that she was confiding in him, but it baffled him that she didn't want to meet up with him. Still, he didn't want to push things. If writing was her preferred medium and she was comfortable with talking to him that way then he wasn't going to push things.

Of course, he'd replied as soon as he'd got her message.

I can't believe what you just told me! I hope Flo's alright and you too. I can just imagine the shock. Mitch sounds like a modern day Fagin, using Sonny for his own gains. Are you okay? Let me know if you want to talk. B x

It was a strange time with the women in his life and communication, he thought. Aria had sent him a text after their disastrous day in London and it was full of remorse and apology, ending with the words, *I need your help.* In truth, he was glad to hear from her again.

Of course, he texted back.

They were going to meet up in Cambridge of all places. Apparently Aria had a lead from someone she'd tracked down in a little corner shop in Ruislip. Dario, it seemed, had been working there for a while, but had moved on to Cambridge. Ben, who knew Cambridge well from his days there as a student with Bryony, assured Aria that he'd help. She didn't have an address and she felt anxious that her limited English would only get her so far. Ben wanted to tell her that her English was better than a lot of English people's, but he realised that it might be her confidence that let her down and so they arranged a day and a time to meet at the train station.

He hoped this would be it for Aria. She sounded desperate to be back home and to take her brother with her, but what if that wasn't what he wanted? So far, their time together had only focussed on finding Dario, but what would happen when they did? Was Aria prepared for that? What if Dario didn't want to be found? What if he was mad with his sister? Ben suspected that part of the reason Aria wanted him with her was in case of trouble – he would provide emotional support as well as back up.

The more he thought about it, the more he realised that Dario might be angry at being found. When Ben had left Castle Clare, the last thing he'd wanted was his family to come chasing after him. He'd said his goodbyes to Georgia and told her to keep safe. He'd needed time and space not just to calm down, but to make sense of what had happened. He would not have appreciated his sister flying across the world to bring him home. Well, maybe Dario felt like that. Ben would have to warn Aria although he was sure she must suspect that.

One of the great regrets of Ben's life was not telling Bryony about what had happened the summer he'd left. He had a feeling that she'd have been more understanding if he had told her. Perhaps the great rift that had developed between them would never have happened, but he hadn't been able to. He'd wanted to protect her from the darkness of his life. He didn't want her tainted with it. Was that wrong? He didn't think so. Of course, she'd had no idea that he'd been hiding anything. She'd just thought he'd had itchy feet and that his wanderlust was more important than their relationship. Oh, how wrong she was.

Taking a deep breath, he read though the latest message from her again. It seemed strange that they were still using the dating site for their communication instead of swapping email addresses, but it was working well so far.

Hi Bryony, he began. *I can't believe Mitch treats his son and his aunt like that. It sounds like you had quite a day! If you need to talk about it, let me know. I'm just a phone call or a quick drive away.*

He gave her his number. Well, he had to try, didn't he?

I was thinking of you today.

That was an understatement, he thought, because she filled his every waking hour and he was betting that she knew that too.

I found that old book of love poems your Grandpa Joe gave us. Remember? The one with the red rose pressed into its pages at the Robert Burns' poem? You used to get me to read it to you all the time and we'd try and imagine the person who had placed the rose inside the book.

Ben thought back to it now. How exciting it had been to find that special flower within the pages. Grandpa Joe swore he hadn't known it was in there. He'd bought the book as part of a job lot from a dealer. And how they'd loved speculating about its history. Had the book belonged to a woman whose lover had given her the rose? Or had it belonged to a romantic man who'd placed a rose within its pages to remind him of the woman he loved? Books were so special, he thought. You never knew what you'd discover within their pages.

Bryony had loved him reading out the Shakespeare sonnets. She'd adored the language. Ben was less keen on it, but he'd loved how languid the rhythm had made Bryony. She'd virtually melted in his arms. Shakespeare was a genius; he knew the true power of iambic pentameter.

Perhaps we could read some of the poems again, he wrote, thinking of the way she'd snuggled in his arms as he'd read to her.

He shook his head. He was being much too forward and so deleted the line.

We used to read so much together, didn't we? Two bookworms. We never went anywhere without at least a couple of books between us. Remember that awful geography school trip to Wroxham? We were meant to be doing some study on traffic – counting cars coming into town. Anyway, it was really boring and so we made up a load of statistics and sneaked off down the river and read Coot Club. Do you remember?

Ben smiled as he recalled the day together with the line which had inspired them to sneak away. "They had left all the noise and bustle of Wroxham behind them". Ben had read that out to Bryony who'd been a little reluctant to just bunk off in case they got caught, but he'd managed to persuade her.

'We'll find a quite spot on the river – just the two of us,' he'd said.

There'd been a lot of kissing that day. Probably more kissing than reading. And he'd never been able to think of Arthur Ransome without also remembering Bryony's sweet lips.

He left his message to her there, hoping that she too would remember and maybe suggest meeting up. He could only hope.

The last thing Bryony had on her mind was meeting up with Ben. She had something far more pressing to think about and she had to admit to being a tad nervous about it. She'd never done anything like this in her life. Spying, for goodness' sake. It felt so horribly wrong, but stealing was wrong too and Mitch had crossed a line when he'd stolen from Flo. Bryony was determined to support her friend and put a stop to this dreadful business. Still she'd have to make sure she had her phone to hand in case they needed to ring the police in a hurry.

She'd tied her hair back so that it wouldn't blow about in the wind and give her away and she had chosen her very darkest clothes. She didn't have any black in her wardrobe so had had to make do with a very dark green in the hope that it would blend into the foliage they would be hiding in.

She'd got her camera which had a pretty good lens on it for close-ups. Mitch Lohman didn't stand a chance, she'd thought as she'd left the house for her morning stint in the shop before her lunchtime rendezvous with Flo.

Now, closing her shop, Bryony walked towards the school, turning into the lane which led to the community playing fields. Flanking the lane was the row of trees which Bryony had thought would make a good cover and she made her way over to them now.

She was the first to make it to the allocated place. It was cold for the end of April, but there was a bit of sunshine around. The kind of day, Bryony thought, that you wished you'd worn an extra layer – no matter how many layers you were wearing. Still she consoled herself that they shouldn't be outside for too long. Mitch surely wouldn't want to hang around in a public place with a bag of stolen goods.

She waited anxiously peering up the lane by the school, hoping Flo hadn't backed out, and was relieved when she saw her friend. Flo was wearing a wig of curly red hair and a pair of Jackie Kennedy-style sunglasses that obliterated half her face.

'How do I look?' she asked Bryony as scooted behind the tree.

'Like someone who's about to crack a case wide open!' Bryony told her.

'Good. That was exactly the look I was going for.'

'Castle Clare's own Miss Marple.'

Flo gave a little giggle and Bryony checked her watch. It shouldn't be long now, she thought, hearing the happy chatter of children being let out for their lunch break.

'We should get a good view from here,' Bryony said, nodding towards the hedge opposite where Sonny had said his father met him to take whatever he'd managed to steal from Flo's.

'Oh, dear,' Flo said.

'What is it?' Bryony asked.

'I'm not sure I really want to be here.' Flo took her sunglasses off and rubbed her eyes.

'I think it might be too late to back out now,' Bryony said.

'There's a car coming.'

They turned to look as a silver Volvo parked in the lane.

'That's his car,' Flo said and they watched as Mitch Lohman got out. He was carrying a canvas bag and he checked his watch. Bryony got her camera out.

'I'm ready for him,' she said and Flo put her sunglasses back on.

'Me too.'

Mitch came closer, crossing the lane so that he was on the same side of the hedge which edged the school playing field, and that's when they saw Sonny on the other side. The hedge was spindly and low towards the back of the playing field and it was this point that both Sonny and Mitch were heading for. The drop was about to take place.

'I can't believe Mitch is abusing his son like that. *My* great-nephew!' Flo whispered.

'It's so awful,' Bryony agreed. 'Poor Sonny.'

'Who's on playground duty? Why is nobody keeping an eye on what's going on here?'

Bryony looked around. No teachers were visible. There was a group of boys kicking a football nearby and two girls were cartwheeling across the grass, but nobody seemed to notice what Sonny was up to.

Flo clutched at Bryony's arm as she brought out her camera and began taking photos as Mitch approached the hedge. He bent down as Sonny approached from the other side, but they couldn't hear what was being said as Sonny slid his bag through the gap.

It was the work of a few seconds as Mitch unzipped the bag, took out the silver candlesticks and placed them in his own bag. He paused and Bryony and Flo watched as Sonny shook his head.

'Maybe he's asking where the piggy bank is,' Flo whispered. 'But he's not getting his grubby hands on my piggy bank, the swine.' Suddenly, Flo laughed. 'The *swine*, get it? Piggy bank –'

'Shush!' Bryony flapped a hand, but it was too late, Mitch had turned around.

'Who's that?' he asked, standing up to full height.

Bryony looked at Flo. Her hand was clapped firmly over her mouth.

'Leave this to me,' Bryony said. 'Meet me back at the shop as soon as he's gone, okay?'

'What are you going to do?'

'Wing it,' Bryony said and she stepped out from behind the tree.

'What are you doing?' Mitch called over to her.

Bryony smiled at him. 'I'm looking for the greater-crested...' she faltered, 'tree tit.' She swallowed hard.

Mitch's face creased up in disbelief. '*Tree tit?*'

Bryony nodded. 'There's been reports of it in the area and I'm trying to photograph it.' She held her camera up as if that was enough proof.

Mitch scratched his head and Bryony caught Sonny's eye from the other side of the hedge and winked at him, hoping he wouldn't give the game away.

'I've not seen no bird,' Mitch said, and Bryony flinched at his use of the double negative.

'Well, maybe I'll try the playing fields,' she said, nodding to him before moving away, and how hard that was when she knew exactly what Mitch had in that bag of his. But making a citizen's arrest wasn't part of the plan and so she walked swiftly away.

She waited a whole fifteen minutes before daring to walk back down the lane again. Luckily, Mitch's car was gone. Flo was no longer hiding behind the tree so Bryony made her way back to her shop and found Flo waiting outside.

'Did he suspect anything?' Flo asked.

'I don't think so.' Bryony said, unlocking the shop door. The first thing she did was to make them both a cup of tea. She then popped the memory card from her camera into the computer and went through the pictures.

'Look at this one!' Bryony said. 'His hand's wrapped around the candlestick like a python.'

'And look at the fat smile on his face,' Flo said. 'He's probably working out how much money he can sell them for.'

All of a sudden, a sob erupted from Flo, obviously taking her as much by surprise as it did Bryony because her hand flew to her mouth. But there was no stopping the emotion and tears soon coursed down her pale face.

'Oh, Flo!' Bryony said, folding her in her arms. 'What a time you're having. Nobody should have to go through this.'

'What am I going to do? What am I going to say to him?' Flo cried.

'I don't know,' Bryony said honestly, 'but you don't have to go through this alone. I'll be right there with you when you confront him. If you want me to be.'

Flo mopped her eyes and Bryony gave her a few moments to compose herself.

'What a dear you are,' Flo said at last. 'I don't know what I would've done without you these last few days. But I'm afraid I'll have to face Mitch alone.'

'Are you sure?'

Flo nodded.

'He won't – you know – hurt you?' Bryony asked hesitantly.

'I don't think so. He might be a thief, but I don't think he'd stoop to violence.'

It was then that Colin the baker walked into the shop.

'Oh!' he said at the sight of Flo.

'It's okay, Colin,' Bryony said. 'This is Flo.'

'Yes,' he said. 'Hello Flo. You've – erm – done something to your hair?'

Flo gave a tiny smile and removed her wig. 'Just having a bit of fun.'

'Erm, right,' Colin said, his brow furrowing.

'She's had a bit of a shock,' Bryony explained.

'Everything okay, I hope?' Colin said.

'It will be,' Bryony said. 'Did you want something?'

'No, no. Just wondered what you're doing tonight?'

'Oh, I'm busy now, Colin.'

'Right. Of course. Well, I'll see you later, Bryony,' he said, nodding before leaving the shop.

'What a sweetie he is,' Flo said.

'Yes,' Bryony agreed.

'You like him?'

Bryony paused. Flo seemed to have cheered up.

'As a friend.'

'Oh, dear – the *friend* word. I can see he has more than friendship in mind.'

Bryony sighed. 'Yes. He keeps baking me things. I'm going to get fat if it continues.'

'He is the best baker for miles around. I'm sure he's hard to resist.'

'I'm doing my *best* to resist,' Bryony told her.

'I see,' Flo said. 'Does Colin know that?'

'I get the feeling he does. Deep down.'

'But you haven't told him.'

'Not exactly.'

'Oh, Bryony – you must! You must tell him.'

'I know, I know. It just never seems like the right time and he's so sweet to me and I hate the idea of upsetting him.'

'But better to upset him now than later when he's invested all his time and love in you. To say nothing of his pastries.' Flo gave a little smile.

Bryony nodded. She didn't dare tell Flo the real reason she was keeping Colin dangling. It would make her look so bad and she wasn't a bad person. She was just planning a bad thing. Then, once that was over, Ben would know exactly how much he'd hurt her and she could tell Colin it was over. Then she could get on with her life.

'And then there's Ben,' Flo pointed out unnecessarily, interrupting her thoughts. '*Two* men vying for your attention. Both handsome and kind –'

'I think we should look at these photos again,' Bryony said.

'I see.'

Bryony looked at Flo.

'It'll sort itself out with Colin.'

'Not if you don't take action,' Flo said. 'Forgive me if I'm butting in, but you seem so unhappy, Bryony. You've been such a wonderful help to me and Sonny. We love having you at Cuckoo Cottage. You've made such good progress in the garden, but you can't hide away there forever.'

'I know and I promise, I'm going to make sure everything is taken care of. Soon.'

'Soon?'

'I have a plan.'

'What sort of plan?'

'I – I can't tell you.'

Flo frowned.

'Don't be mad at me, Flo,' Bryony said, reaching out to touch her arm.

'I'm not mad, my dear. I just want to help you as you've helped me.'

'But you are helping me. I love the time we spend together.'

Flo smiled. 'Me too.'

'Can I come round tonight? Groom the donkeys?'

'Of course. Belle and Beau would love to see you.'

They gave each other a hug.

'Now,' Flo said a moment later, 'what are we going to do with these photos?'

CHAPTER 15

May arrived in a glory of colour. The cottage gardens of Castle Clare were full of lilac, honeysuckle and irises. The cold winds of April seemed to have passed and the air was warm enough for windows to be opened and for washing to blow dry on the line.

May also meant it was time for the book club and Sam Nightingale had brought the chairs over from the village hall and had arranged the back room of the bookshop. Callie had filled the kettle and had made sure there were enough mugs and plates for everybody.

'I wonder who's been baking,' Callie said as Sam came through to check on things.

'Ah, yes – the book club is turning into a baking battle zone, isn't it?'

'In the best possible way,' Callie told him.

'At least nobody goes hungry,' Sam said. 'And Winston laps it all up. Cakes, rivalries – he's in his element here even if he hasn't read the book.'

'He's bound to have read this one or at least seen the TV adaptation,' Callie pointed out.

'I've been thinking about that issue. We'll have to choose some books which haven't ever been adapted as films or for the TV so that we get the full unadulterated reader experience,' Sam said.

'That's a good idea,' Callie agreed. 'Do you know who's coming tonight?'

'Honey for sure. Antonia too.' Sam grinned.

'So there's an evening's entertainment right there.'

'And Flo. Polly and Jago too.'

'Oh, I do love them together,' Callie said wistfully. 'They make such a wonderful couple.'

'Polly deserves a decent guy after all Sean put her through.'

'Has she heard from him since he disappeared?'

'No, thank goodness. I don't think she will either.'

'Good.'

Sam thought about the dark days his beloved sister had endured at the hands of her abusive husband, and how she'd tried to hold everything together for the sake of their son, Archie. Polly had helped Sam set the book club up and she'd told him that focussing on something so positive had helped her through a really rough time. That and Jago, of course. A book club was all well and good, but it couldn't begin to compare to a handsome young guitar-wielding biker.

'What are you smiling about?' Callie asked as she approached him.

'Just thinking of Polly and Jago and how happy they are.'

'As happy as us?'

'*Nobody* could be as happy as us,' Sam said, bending down to kiss her.

It was then that the shop bell tinkled.

'I swear that bell has a sensor for anytime I get close to you.'

Callie laughed. 'You'd better go and see who it is.'

He sighed and went through to the front room to see who had interrupted his romantic moment.

'Ben!' he said in surprise. 'Good to see you.'

'Hey! How's it going?'

'Good. We've got our book club meeting tonight. You're not here for that, are you?'

'Erm, yeah. As a matter of fact I am.'

'Oh, welcome to the group. You're the first to arrive.'

'Hi Ben,' Callie said, coming into the room.

'Hey, Callie.'

'Can I get you a cup of tea?'

'Love one. Thanks.'

They all trooped to the back of the shop and Callie got busy with the kettle.

'Hey – erm – Sam?'

'Yes?'

'Is Bryony part of the book club?'

'Funny you should say that,' Sam began, 'because I finally persuaded her to join. This will be her first meeting.'

'Really?'

'Is she the reason you're joining?' Sam asked. 'I mean, far be it for me to judge why a person attends book club.'

'I like books well enough.'

'I know you do. You sent a fair few to them to our Bryony when you were away, didn't you?'

'She told you?'

Sam nodded. 'There were beautiful editions. I was a little envious, I have to admit.'

Ben shuffled around the room for a moment, looking at the shelves of books. 'You've got a great place here.'

'Thanks. I like it.'

'You look good here, Sam. I mean – you look at home.'

Sam nodded. 'I feel at home.'

'That's good. That's good.'

Sam watched him for a moment. 'Are you okay, Ben? You seem a little nervous.'

'No, I'm good. It's just, well, you're lucky – to have this place and Callie. You've made a good life.'

'Thanks.'

'I mean, I heard about Emma and I'm sorry that you went through all that.'

'It wasn't an easy time.'

'No, breakups never are,' Ben said. 'But it's all come good for you now.'

'I hope so.'

They smiled, but Sam could still see that Ben was on edge.

'She won't be mad with me, will she?' Ben asked at last.

'Bryony?'

'With me just showing up like this.'

Sam removed his glasses and pinched the bridge of his nose. 'She might be. You know Bryony. She does *mad* well.'

'Oh, yeah,' Ben said. 'I know. But we've been talking a lot recently.'

'You have?'

'Well, when I say talking, I mean writing.'

'Really?'

Ben cleared his throat. 'Via a dating website.'

Sam frowned. 'How did that happen?'

Ben laughed. 'We were both on the same dating website and we kind of hooked up. I don't know – we started exchanging messages – short at first, but they've been getting longer. They're like real conversations – like the old days when we could talk about anything. But here's the weird thing – she won't talk to me in real life. I've suggested meeting up, but she always ignores my suggestion.'

'Maybe she's just not ready,' Sam suggested.

'But she's asked me out. We've got a date in the diary. That dance over at Torrington Barn.'

'Really?'

'Yep.'

'Okay,' Sam said. 'Well, that's good.'

'It is,' Ben agreed, but it's driving me crazy not being able to talk to her until then.'

'And that's why you're here tonight.'

Ben scratched the back of his neck. 'I really want to see her.'

'Are you sure this is the best way to go about it? I mean, what if she isn't happy? What if she –'

'Explodes?'

'I was going to say…' Sam paused. 'No, *explodes* is a pretty good word.'

Ben gave a droll laugh. 'I'm kind of hoping she doesn't.' He took a deep breath and then nodded. 'This is a bad idea, isn't it?'

Sam didn't know what to say. 'What do you want to do?'

'I want to see her, but I don't want to cause any trouble.' Ben cursed under his breath. 'I sometimes wonder if I should've come back at all.'

'Don't say that.'

'It's how I feel.'

'This will work itself out,' Sam said. 'You've just got to give it more time.'

'Time,' Ben said with a nod.

'She still loves you,' Sam said.

'What?'

'I don't think she ever stopped.'

'You serious?'

Sam nodded. 'Of course, she hates you too.'

'Right!' Ben said. They exchanged wry smiles. 'Look, I'd better get out of here before she arrives.'

'You sure?'

'As much as I'd love to stay.'

'Join us for another one, okay?'

'You bet.'

Ben nodded his thanks and Sam watched as he left.

'Hold the tea, Callie,' he called through to the kitchen where the kettle was boiling.

'What's happening?' she asked, coming out into the shop and looking around. 'Oh, has he gone?'

'He thought it best not to surprise Bryony by being here.'

'Poor Ben. He really wanted to see her, didn't he?'

'More than anything.'

'I have to admit, I was looking forward to seeing them together. After that Sunday lunch, I couldn't wait for the sequel.'

'You are a naughty lady!' Sam said.

'No I'm not,' Callie told him. 'I'm just a very curious person. Blame the writer in me. I just *have* to know how things turn out.'

Sam chuckled. 'You use that writer line a bit too often.'

'Do I?'

'You think it can get you out of all sorts of bad behaviour.'

Callie gasped. 'Sam Nightingale, I hope you're teasing me!'

He put his arms around her waist. 'I might be.'

She shook her head, pushing him away. 'There'll be no cuddles for you if you think I might be a bad influence on you.'

'Not even if I'm crying out for a bad influence? I'm just a lonely bookshop keeper leading a very sheltered life in a small market town. I think I need all the bad influences I can get.'

Callie play slapped his arm and then let him kiss her and, as if on cue, the doorbell tinkled and the sound of voices was heard. It was time for the book club to begin.

It was a wonderful turn out. Winston Kneller was there with his old black Labrador, Delilah. Flo had come laden down with fruit scones, all buttered and ready to eat, and Antonia Jessop had made cheese straws.

Polly and Jago were there too as was Bryony who received a rapturous welcome and Sam couldn't help but feel relieved that Ben had decided not to stay.

Hortense Digger, or Honey as she liked to be called, had entered the bookshop carrying a large tin.

Polly quickly came forward and took it from her, placing it on a small table which had been set in the centre of the room.

'It's just a little trifle,' Honey said. 'Well, not a trifle actually. A gateau.'

Honey stepped forward and opened the tin to reveal an astonishing strawberry gateau, its top glistening with ruby fruit.

'Wow, Honey – you've really excelled yourself this time,' Sam said.

'Bang goes my diet!' Callie said with a grin.

'It's in honour of Ma Larkin,' Honey explained. 'It had to be strawberries, didn't it? It's a shame that it's too early for the ones in my garden so I had to make do from the supermarket. I hope nobody minds supermarket strawberries.'

'I don't think you'll hear any complaints,' Sam assured her.

Sure enough, Winston's eyeballs were nearly out of their sockets at the rapturous sight before him.

'Well, tuck in everybody. There's plenty to go around,' Honey said as plates and forks were passed to everyone.

'Gateaux are deceptively simple to make,' Antonia announced as she helped herself to a good-sized portion.

'Not as simple as cheese straws,' Honey said, nodding to the plate on the table which she obviously recognised as one of Antonia's.

'A cheese straw is a perfect accompaniment to an evening cup of tea. Besides we're going to need something savoury after all this sweetness,' Antonia said, her nose doing a strange kind of pecking motion towards her slice of strawberry gateau.

There then followed the wondrous silence of happy eaters luxuriating in the food before them. The gateau, as large as it was, didn't stand much of a chance of survival and was soon completely devoured. Only then was everybody able to concentrate on the job in hand and Sam kicked things off.

'It's really great to have my sister Bryony here as a new member,' Sam said. 'I've been trying to get her to join the book club since we began. I think you've all met her and know her from the children's bookshop over the road.'

Everybody said that they did.

'"The more the merrier" as Ma Larkin would say,' Sam added and everybody laughed. 'So, what did you think the book?'

'Nice and short,' Winston offered.

'Yes. Officially, it's called a novella because it's under fifty thousand words,' Sam told the group.

'A *novella*,' Flo said, sounding the word with pleasure. 'What a beautiful word and a beautiful book too.'

'Did you know it's the first of five books about the Larkin family?'

Sam asked.

'I saw the TV series back in the nineties,' Winston said. 'With that Catherine Zeta-Jones girl.'

Antonia Jessop grimaced. 'Are *all* the books we read adapted for television and film?'

'Does that matter?' Polly asked.

'It just seems that some of us might take advantage and not actually read the book,' Antonia went on.

There were mumbles amongst the group.

'Are you accusing me of cheating at book club?' Winston barked. Winston rarely barked. He was a very affable sort of man and so this sudden bark took everybody by surprise, not least Antonia who shifted uneasily in her seat.

'Well, I wasn't pointing the finger at you precisely.'

'I read the novel. Novella. No point in joining book club if you don't read the books, is there? I have to admit that I joined initially for a bit of company of an evening and a nice bite to eat, but I quite like this reading lark.'

Sam grinned. 'You sound like Pop Larkin there, using the word "lark".'

'"Larkin by name, Larkin by nature,"' Winston said, quoting the book. 'See, I've done my homework.'

'Actually, Antonia raises a very interesting point about adaptations and it's something I've been thinking about too. We really should try and choose something that hasn't been made into a film or TV series. But we'll talk about that later, okay? Shall we return to our discussion?' Sam said. 'I thought we could look at the character of Charley.'

'Mr Cedric Charlton,' Honey said.

'Yes,' Sam said. 'What did we think of his metamorphosis into Charley?'

'Metamorphosis?' Winston said, giving a long low whistle. 'Sounds like I'm back in a classroom!'

'Sorry,' Sam said.

'I loved Charley,' Polly said. 'He was made so welcome by the Larkin family.'

'We never seem to find out about his own family, do we? He seems to be alone in the world,' Flo pointed out.

'It's a common theme in literature, isn't it? The outsider being welcomed by a family,' Jago pointed out.

'Good point,' Sam said. 'Yes, a lot of novels are about bringing together a disparate bunch of characters who then become a kind of family. What did you all think of that? What did you make of Charley being welcomed into the Larkin's home and family?'

'I loved it!' Flo said with enthusiasm. 'I adored reading about Charley at the kitchen table and the trouble he had with those geese.'

'Home Farm was a completely alien environment to him,' Bryony said. 'I think it's fun to see a character thrown into an unfamiliar setting.'

'Yes, and all he could worry about was his buff form!' Honey said with a laugh. 'And the gorgeousness that was Mariette Larkin.'

'The charm of the place, the fun, the relaxed atmosphere, soon works its spell on Mr Charlton, doesn't it?' Sam continued. 'It makes it impossible for him to leave. You know he's been won over, don't you?'

'I found it all a bit saccharine-sweet,' Antonia ventured. 'Too much jollity and happiness and not enough grit.'

'Yes, but it's meant to be a light-hearted read,' Callie pointed out, 'so I think Bates met his objective.'

'Too much reliance on puerile humour,' Antonia went on. 'Does anybody else object to the number of times Pop Larkin belches in the book?'

There were a few sniggers around the group.

'He does apologise each time,' Honey pointed out.

'I thought it was hilarious,' Flo said. 'He used a funny term at one point, didn't he? What did he call it?'

'Early morning breeze,' Callie said.

'That's right! I'm going to start calling mine that too. I mean, if I ever happen to belch at the breakfast table,' Flo said.

'Which you won't because you're a lady,' Winston said with a wink.

With all this talk of wind, it seemed inevitable that Winston's dog, Delilah, would have something to say about it, and a deadly doggy smell soon wafted its way across the room.

'Oh my lord!' Antonia cried.

'Oooops!' Winston said. 'Late evening breeze!'

Everybody laughed whilst covering their noses with hands, books and scarves until the worst of the odour passed.

'So is belching a theme?' Winston asked, his expression partly serious as if he was truly trying to learn something.

'Erm, I don't think so,' Sam said. 'More repetition for humour's sake.'

'I see,' Winston said. 'I'll look out for that in future books.'

'Well, you won't find it in anything sensible,' Antonia said.

'I take it you didn't enjoy the book?' Honey said to Antonia.

'That's right. Much too silly for my taste.'

'But Bates writes about some of the most important issues ever,' Callie said. 'Family, community, the desire to find one's place in the world. He ticks all the boxes for me.'

'Yes, well some people are easily pleased,' Antonia said, shifting her bony bottom on her chair and giving a sniff.

Sam cleared his throat. 'Any other characters stand out?'

'Pop Larkin,' Polly said. 'He and Ma are larger than life, aren't they?'

'I can't imagine what it's like to have a family like that,' Jago said. 'There's so many of them and they all seem to get on too!'

'Unbelievable,' Antonia said. 'Like *The Waltons*. I never liked that either.'

Flo gasped. 'You never liked *The Waltons*?'

For a moment, everybody started talking about John-Boy, Jim Bob, Elizabeth, Erin et al. It seemed that Antonia was very firmly in the minority when it came to the long-running US drama series.

Sam managed to steer the conversation back towards Pop Larkin and everybody – even Antonia – managed to agree that he was a wonderful father: supportive, generous, funny and kind and with a real head for business.

'But he should pay his taxes,' Antonia pointed out. 'One mustn't be allowed to get away with that.'

Callie bent forward to pass the plate of cheese straws around and the group continued their discussion about favourite characters and scenes from the book.

'What I love about H E Bates is that he wasn't confined to a particular genre or story length,' Sam said after a while. 'He wrote light-hearted novellas like the Larkin quintet, darker standalones like *The Triple Echo*, serious books about the War like *Fair Stood the Wind for France*, and non-fiction too: autobiographies and gardening memoirs.'

'You're so knowledgeable, Sam,' Honey said. 'How do you know all this stuff?'

Sam gave a little smile. 'A lifetime of reading helps.'

'So, what does the H and E stand for? I was trying to guess,' Flo said.

'Herbert Ernest,' Jago said.

Everybody looked suitably impressed at Jago's knowledge.

'I read it on Wikipedia,' he confessed.

'I loved the yard full of animals and how H E Bates doesn't just make them pretty pretty,' Flo said. 'He knows animals are hard work, doesn't he? Just like my garden-full. There's always something to worry about.'

'I liked the strawberry picking scene,' Honey said. 'There aren't enough strawberries in books.'

'Are we going to read the others in the series?' Winston asked.

'Not as part of the book club,' Sam said, 'but feel free in your own time. They're terrific books. So any suggestions for our next book? The meeting will be in July.'

'Something short again,' Flo requested. 'Maybe another H E Bates. A serious one?'

'I think we should vary things, Flo,' Sam advised. 'Different authors, different lengths and genres.'

There were a few murmurings amongst the group.

'We've had H E Bates from the fifties and Thomas Hardy from the nineteenth-century – how about something in between?'

'Like what?' Honey asked.

'Well, we've just finished something light-hearted so why not go for something a bit more intense?' Sam suggested.

'Oh, yes,' Antonia agreed. 'Please, let's have something we can get our teeth into.'

'What did you have in mind?' Bryony asked her brother.

'I was thinking of Virginia Woolf.'

'Blimey – isn't she difficult?' Jago asked.

'She can be,' Sam said.

'I think that sounds like an *excellent* idea,' Antonia said.

'One of her novels, *Mrs Dalloway*, is a very interesting work. It was quite revolutionary and really made her name as a serious novelist. It's short too although it's not as easy a read as the Bates we've just read.'

'What's it about, Sam?' Honey asked.

'It's a day in the life of Clarissa Dalloway,' Sam began, 'and she's preparing to host a party which is very important to her.'

'Oh, I like a party!' Flo said. 'Is it a happy book?'

'Well,' Sam paused, 'why don't you wait and see?'

'It has to be a happy book if it's about a party.'

Sam caught Callie's eye and she gave an anxious smile. She obviously knew her way around Woolf's seminal work.

'Sam – you know that one was made into a film?' Polly pointed out. 'Vanessa Redgrave played Mrs Dalloway.'

'Ah,' Sam said, 'I didn't know that. Well, no watching the film anyone, okay?'

Everybody solemnly promised to go nowhere near the film.

After a little more discussion about other books they'd been reading or been meaning to read, the group tidied away the mugs and plates and prepared to leave the shop. Sam had taken some orders for the paperback of *Mrs Dalloway* and had tipped Winston off to the secondhand copy he had in the shop for two pounds fifty. All in all, it had been a very successful evening.

Bryony was giving Flo a lift. She'd picked her up for the book club meeting after she'd dropped Sonny at a neighbour who lived opposite Cuckoo Cottage. As they walked down Church Street to where Bryony had parked, the church clock struck nine, its fourth note horribly out of tune.

'I wish they'd get that fixed,' Bryony said. 'It hurts the sensibilities.'

'Get what fixed?' Flo asked.

'That out of tune bell that sounds the fourth note.'

Flo frowned. 'Can't say as I've noticed.'

They continued to walk down the dark street and had just made it back to the car when Flo gave a sigh.

'What is it?' Bryony asked as they both got in.

'All that talk about Pop Larkin,' Flo said, shaking her head. 'I couldn't help thinking about Mitch. Perhaps I should lend him *The Darling Buds of May* to read.'

'You think Mitch will suddenly turn into Pop?' Bryony asked.

'No, I'm afraid I don't, but it might give him some ideas about being a good father.'

'I hate to admit it,' Bryony said as she started the engine, 'but Antonia might have had a point when she said the Larkin family were unbelievable.'

'No! Don't say that,' Flo said. '*Your* family is living proof that the Larkins really exist.'

Bryony smiled. 'I know I'm lucky, but so many people aren't. When we were talking about the book, I couldn't help thinking of Jago and how his father just left him and then Sean's behaviour towards Polly and how that means Archie doesn't have a father either. Although he has a wonderful father-figure in Jago now.' She paused. 'And then dear Sonny.'

'Yes,' Flo said. 'There seems to be a lack of good fathers around here, doesn't there?'

'Thank goodness for books,' Bryony said. 'They rescue us so many times, don't they?'

'And now we have the lovely *Mrs Dalloway* to look forward to,' Flo said. 'I'm so looking forward to reading about her gorgeous party.'

Bryony bit her lip and decided to keep quiet.

When she got home after dropping Flo off, she checked her messages on the Country Catches website. Sure enough, there was one from Ben.

I've been thinking about getting a little car, he wrote. *Georgia's been letting me use hers for when I teach in Ipswich, but I think she's getting a bit fed up of catching the bus to work now. Let me know if you hear of a decent one going cheap.*

Hey – remember when Sam took us both out for driving lessons in his first car and you nearly ended up in that ditch near Newton St Clare? I still remember the strange shade of purple Sam turned'

Bryony gasped as she read the message, her mind spiralling back to that embarrassing day.

Yes, well don't forget who passed their driving test first time and who had to take it twice! she replied, smiling as she hit the send button.

This thing with Ben – these messages flying between them – were getting a bit too familiar, she told herself, too *natural*. She had to remain distanced. She had to be focussed on her plan and, with that in mind, she reached for the phone and called home.

'Hi darling,' her mother said. 'What a lovely surprise. Is everything all right?'

'Of course,' Bryony said. 'I just wanted to hear your voice.'

'Oh, sweetheart!' her mother said.

'Actually, I wouldn't mind speaking to Dad if he's around?'

'Well, it's been dark for a while now so I'm pretty sure he's in the house and not the garden.'

Bryony laughed. 'Good.'

'I'll just get him for you.'

Bryony waited, listening to one of the dogs barking in the background and Grandpa Joe's voice asking who was on the phone. A few moments later, she heard her father's voice.

'Bry?' he said.

'Hey, Dad.'

'You okay, love?'

'I'm good,' she said, blinking the tears away. 'I wanted to ask you something.'

'Sure. Is it garden-related?'

'No, it isn't.' She took a deep breath. 'I wanted to ask you how you felt when Mum pulled that trick on you. You know – when she stood you up? I mean, I know you told me you felt you deserved it, but how did you really feel?'

There was a pause before her father answered. 'Well, I felt hurt if I'm honest. I mean I knew why she did it. But I was also worried because, for a while, I thought she'd broken up with me. I wasn't sure she wanted to see me again and that nearly broke my heart.'

'Oh, Dad!'

'But you know how that turned out,' he told her. 'We got our happy ending.'

'I know.'

'Why did you want to know about that, Bry?' he asked her.

'I just – I've just been thinking about it, that's all.'

'No real reason then?'

'No,' she lied. 'No reason.'

There was another pause.

'You still there, honey?'

'I'm still here, Dad, but I'd better go.'

'Well, you let me know if you need to talk about anything, okay?'

'I will. I promise.'

They said their goodnights and their goodbyes and Bryony hung up the phone, thinking of her father as a young man and of her mother who'd had the power to break his heart. She wouldn't have, of course, because her mother and her father had been madly in love and nothing could have kept them apart. Not like her and Ben. They weren't in love, were they? Not anymore. Or at least, she wasn't in love with him. And, if he'd ever truly been in love with her, surely he would never have left her. It was as simple as that. She couldn't believe in his love now and she couldn't ever forgive him.

She went upstairs, turning the light on beside her bed and catching her reflection in the mirror on her dressing table. At first, she didn't recognise herself. She looked haunted, there was no other word for it. Haunted by the past. And she knew there was only one thing she could do to escape it – she had to exorcise it, and if that meant breaking Ben's heart then so be it.

CHAPTER 16

Ben loved Cambridge and any excuse to visit was good enough for him. He loved the architecture – the pale golden stone of the colleges, and he adored the emerald green of the quads and parks, and the wonderful blue of the River Cam. It was a beautiful city and there was always something new to discover there, but sight-seeing wasn't on the agenda today. He was meeting Aria and they were on the hunt again.

They met outside the train station and Aria immediately embraced Ben, squeezing him tightly to her.

'I want to apologise,' she began, 'for the way I treated you in London.'

'You already have,' Ben assured her.

'Not in – what's the phrase? In body.'

'In person,' Ben corrected her.

'Yes. Only in text.'

'But you don't need to keep saying you're sorry. I know what you're going through.'

'But I was mean to you when you were trying to help me.'

'It's okay.'

'Have you forgiven me?' she asked, her face suddenly like that of a child.

'There's nothing to forgive,' he promised her.

'I don't know what I'd have done without you,' she told him. 'Being here – it's so strange. I think I would have given up by now.'

'No you wouldn't have,' Ben told her. 'You're strong, Aria. You can do anything you want and you've made it this far.'

'I know,' she said, 'but it's been easier because of you.'

'Hey, we all need a bit of moral support especially when we're far from home.'

She smiled. 'And I have a good feeling.'

'You do?'

'I think we're going to find him today.' She shrugged. 'This Cambridge place – it feels right.'

'Yeah?' Ben grinned at her enthusiasm. 'But we don't have much

154

to go on.

She smiled. 'The friend I told you about?'

'The one in Ruislip?'

'He called me. He's pretty sure Dario mentioned a place called St Augustine's. Do you know it?'

'St Augustine's? That doesn't give much away, does it?'

'Is it a college?'

'I don't think so. I mean, I don't recognise the name. It sounds more like a church.'

'What would he be doing in a church?' Aria asked.

'You'd know better than I would.' Ben reached into his pocket for a map of Cambridge he'd printed out from the internet that morning and then he got out his phone to look the place up.

'It's a church all right and it's bit of a trek,' he said. 'We could catch a bus into town and then walk from there.'

Aria nodded. 'Can we see some of Cambridge?' she asked.

'What, first?'

She nodded.

'Erm, sure,' Ben said, surprised that she didn't want to make straight for the address where her brother might be, especially if she had a good feeling that he'd be there.

'I want to see your English colleges.'

They caught a bus into town, jumping off and walking around for the best part of an hour. Tour groups gathered outside the entrances to the colleges, cameras and phones at the ready to take pictures and Aria joined in, her phone held up as she took photo after photo.

'It's so beautiful!' she enthused. 'I want to live here, study here.'

They spent a little while longer walking around the colleges and then Ben made a show of looking at his watch.

'Don't you think we should find this place?' he asked her.

She seemed surprised by his question, but then turned serious.

'Yes, of course.'

Ben nodded and led the way.

They passed the entrance to the Fitzwilliam Museum and Aria stopped to take a photograph of the impressive white facade.

Ben scratched his head. Was it his imagination or was she a little too relaxed about finding her brother? Perhaps he was being too harsh. Cambridge was a special place and it wasn't surprising that she was bowled over by its beauty.

She must have caught him looking at her quizzically because she apologised.

'I'm sorry. It's just so beautiful and I might not be here again.'

They continued walking and it wasn't long before they found the street they were after and there in front of them was St Augustine's. It was an austere-looking Victorian Gothic church and, as they crossed the road, they could hear the muffled sound of music coming from inside.

Ben opened the heavy oak door and they stepped inside, immediately enveloped by the scene.

'It's a playgroup,' Ben said, nodding towards the children who were sprawled out on a large rug beside some book cases on the far side of the church. The music was coming from a CD player and one of the adults in charge was teaching some of the older children some actions.

'Aria – is Dario likely to be here?' Ben asked.

'He always loved children,' she said. 'Maybe he's working here.'

'Can you see him?'

They both looked around, but could only see the woman who was patting her head and circling her tummy at the same time – a move Ben still hadn't mastered to this day.

'I don't...' Aria's voice petered out as a tall man with short dark hair walked out from a room at the back of the church. He was smiling down at a small boy whose hand he was holding. The boy had a tear-stained face and the man was whispering something to him and Ben heard Aria catch her breath.

'Is that him, Aria? Is that you brother, Dario?'

Aria didn't respond for a moment, but then turned to Ben. 'That's Dario,' she told him, tears in her eyes.

Aria wasn't the only one with tears in her eyes; Flo Lohman had them too as she looked at the photographs Bryony had printed out for her of Mitch stealing the silver candlesticks. She still couldn't believe that her own flesh and blood would do something like that to her and it was made even worse by the fact that he'd used Sonny to do the stealing.

She thought back to when she'd visited Mitch's home. It had been stuffed with antiques. Had they all been stolen, she wondered now? Had her nephew being taking whatever he wanted from little old ladies across the whole of Suffolk? She dreaded to think. But what should she do next? She still hadn't worked it out.

One thing she was certain of, though, was that Sonny was staying with her for the time being. Mitch might have planted him there for stealing purposes only, and might want to take him home at some point, but Flo couldn't bear the thought of her great-nephew being raised to be a thief. Besides she'd seen a real change in the boy since he'd been at Cuckoo Cottage. He was taking an interest in the animals and would often be out in the garden before her in the morning, collecting the eggs and feeding everyone. He was more talkative too. They had conversations now rather than him just responding in monosyllables. He was still painfully shy if any of Flo's friends dropped by, but she could see that he was growing in confidence now that he was away from the domineering personality of his father.

Flo walked around the rooms of her cottage, noting the things that were missing. After the recent drop, Sonny had sat down with Flo at the kitchen table and he'd told her everything he could remember taking. It had been quite a list and Flo had done her best not to cry in front of him. It wasn't so much about the things, although it was bad enough that some of her beloved family heirlooms had been taken, it was more about the personal violation – the fact that her nephew had been sizing up her belongings. Had he no feelings? Didn't he care that those things *meant* something to her other than the financial value of them?

She hadn't even realised that the gold locket, which had belonged to her grandmother, had been missing. It had her grandmother's initials carved into it and would be of little value to anyone else because of that, which would mean it would be sold for scrap – melted down with a heap of other pieces. But, to Flo, that piece was a direct link to her past. Although she only wore it on special occasions, it was very dear to her. She liked to softly brush her fingers across those initials, remembering happy times spent with her grandmother. You couldn't replace that sort of thing; it was just too precious, and she couldn't believe that her nephew had told Sonny to steal from her jewellery box.

As she looked at the little table in the living room with the gap where a silver photo frame had once stood, she wondered if she'd ever see any of her pieces again or if Mitch had already sold them. A part of her wanted to storm right across to his house now with a big cardboard box to take all of her things back, but there was the other part of her that was paralysed with fear.

What if she just ignored it? What if she pretended she hadn't noticed? Surely he'd stop at some point? He couldn't seriously take much more and not expect her to notice, could he? Surely then they'd be able to move forward with no unpleasantness.

Flo shook her head. There was no ignoring this issue. As much as she wanted to pretend it wasn't happening, she knew she had to face it head on.

'And that means facing Mitch,' she told herself. 'Heaven help me.'

A shaft of spring sunlight beamed in through one of the stained glass windows of St Augustine's.

'Dario!' Aria cried.

The man looked up and was momentarily blinded by the sun. He shielded his eyes to try and see who'd called his name and his warm smile instantly vanished. He whispered something to the boy whose hand he'd been holding and patted him towards the play mat where the other children were.

'Dario!' Aria cried again, running across the aisle towards him.

'Aria?' he said. He didn't sound pleased and Ben was instantly on his guard. He'd had a feeling this might happen. Dario had run away from an impossible situation. He'd buried himself in a foreign city and was obviously trying to make a new life. The last thing he'd want reminding of was a painful past. Ben knew the feeling all too well.

'Dario,' Aria spoke quietly now as heads were turning to see what was going on. 'Aren't you going to say something?'

His face looked dark with anger. 'What the hell are you doing here?' He also muttered something else in Italian which Ben was pretty sure wasn't appropriate in a church.

'I've come to find you, silly.'

'Don't touch me!' he said in Italian, surprising Ben as he moved away from her.

'We need to talk,' Aria said. She was speaking in Italian too now.

'I'm working.'

'Yes, I can see that.'

Ben took pity on her. 'She's come a long way, Dario.'

'And who exactly are you?' he asked Ben.

'I'm Ben Stratton. I'm her friend. We met in Italy. She's told me what's been going on and I've been helping her to find you.'

'What the hell did you bring her to me for? Are you insane?' Dario asked.

'What do you mean?'

'Ben,' Aria said, turning to face him. 'I think it's time you left. I need to talk to Dario alone.'

Ben nodded. He understood that, but he was loath to leave her there in case things turned nasty. He felt a duty of care towards Aria and so he hesitated at leaving her with an angry man in a city she didn't know.

'What if I wait over here?' he said to her, pointing to a pew on the other side of the aisle.

She said something really fast in Italian then, something he didn't quite catch, but he could see that she was angry and it was clear that she didn't want him there any longer.

'I'm not leaving, Aria,' he told her. 'Not until you've sorted things out with your brother.'

'What?' Dario exclaimed in English. 'Her brother? What the hell, Aria?' He turned to face her and then looked at Ben again. 'Her *brother*? Is that what she told you?' He cursed. 'She's more twisted than I thought.'

Ben was confused and looked to Aria for an explanation, but she only had eyes for Dario and so Ben turned to him.

'You're not her brother?' he asked. 'Then who on earth are you?'

Dario shook his head. 'I can't believe this is happening.'

'What? *What's* happening?' Ben asked. 'She told me she was looking for her brother, Dario. She said Dario had run away after things got violent with his step-father at home. You *are* Dario?'

'I'm Dario alright, but I'm sure not her brother.' He cursed again. 'Someone warned me about her once, but I stupidly didn't listen to them. I fell for her and then it was too late.'

'Dario – don't talk like that,' Aria said. 'It's not too late.'

'Get your hands off me!' Dario said, jolting away from her touch. 'Don't let her near you,' he told Ben. 'She's poison. She's been stalking me ever since I broke up with her four months ago. The only way I could escape her was to leave.' He gave a hollow laugh then. 'But even England wasn't far enough, was it?'

By this time, one of the women in charge of the children had stood up from her place on the rug and had approached.

'Dario? Is everything okay?' she asked in a gentle voice.

'No, it isn't. This woman needs to leave,' he said, speaking in English once again.

'I'm not leaving,' Aria said.

'You're leaving,' Dario said.

Aria reached out and grabbed him by the arm, but he shook her off.

'I told you I never wanted to see you again. Why is that so hard to understand? You're not right, Aria. You're controlling and you're cruel and I want nothing more to do with you.'

Ben had seen enough. It was time for him to leave. He walked towards the door, the voices of Aria and Dario getting louder by the moment. The distressed woman was doing her best to calm them both down and a couple of the children had started crying. Ben needed to get outside.

Once he was through the door, he marched right across Cambridge, passing the Fitzwilliam once again and the shops and the colleges they'd photographed. He took a couple of wrong turns in his anger, but finally made it back to the train station.

He was furious. He'd been used. Betrayed and used. When he'd first met Aria he'd trusted her with his story about his mother's partner – the story he hadn't even told Bryony – and she'd used his vulnerability to get what she wanted out of him. It had been a horrible, twisted thing to do, and he'd fallen for her lies and those big vulnerable eyes of hers. She'd reached out and it had been his instinct to want to try and help her.

But it had all been lies. Aria had manipulated him for her own end. Well, never again would he be fooled like that, Ben told himself. Never.

CHAPTER 17

'Are you looking forward to the dance?' Colin asked Bryony. They were in her bookshop on Friday and she'd just closed for the night.

'Yes, of course I am,' she told him.

'Yeah?'

She gave him a smile which she hoped was convincing.

'I can't believe it's tomorrow,' he went on.

'No, neither can I,' Bryony said honestly. It had come round far too quickly for her liking and she didn't feel ready. As she straightened a book display, which an over-zealous toddler had recently been rifling through, she couldn't help acknowledging how anxious she was. If only it was all over. If only it could be this time next week, with the dance long over and life back to normal again. But life would never be normal again, she thought, because she was going to do something that would set her on a course she could never come back from.

She'd been swapping more messages with Ben via the Country Catches website. It was mostly silly stuff, remembering times gone by like the day they'd sneaked out of school together. They'd been thirteen and it had seemed like the most rebellious thing to do in the world.

Who's idea was that? Bryony had written to Ben.

Yours! he'd written back.

No, no! I'd never have initiated something like that!

Think again! We had that Science test, remember? The one you hadn't revised for.

Oh, right! I'd forgotten about that.

So we caught a bus into town and went to that cafe. Is that still there? Ben asked.

No, it closed years ago.

That's a shame. I really liked that old place.

Bryony smiled as she recalled that day. The messages they'd been swapping had brought a lot of memories back to her and it was easy to slip into that happy past when she and Ben had been the centre of each other's worlds. But she mustn't let that influence her now, she told herself. They might well have been happy once, but that was a long time ago and Ben had been the one to destroy that.

'I was thinking,' Colin said, breaking into her thoughts, 'I'd love you to meet my parents.'

Bryony's head snapped up, but Colin's eyes were firmly fixed on the pages of the dragon book.

'Oh, Colin, I don't think that's a good –'

'I mean, we've been seeing each other for a while, haven't we? It's been a few months now.'

'Yes, but –'

'And maybe I could see your family,' he suggested. 'At one of these huge Sunday lunches you've told me about.'

Bryony cursed herself for having casually mentioned the great Nightingale tradition of Sunday lunch. Big mistake.

'Let's see, shall we?' she said, knowing full well that it wouldn't be on the agenda – not after Saturday night.

When Saturday night arrived, Bryony found herself looking at her reflection in the mirror, ready to leave for the dance. Colin said he liked her bright colours, but she wasn't totally convinced that he did. He was so conservative in his choice of colour, which was fine, but she always felt so out of place standing next to him. They didn't make a natural couple, she thought. She'd known that from the beginning, though.

Since the first time he'd asked her out, she'd known that it was all wrong and yet she'd gone along with it. Part of her had wondered if she could, perhaps, make it work with Colin. After all, he was a nice guy – sweet, kind and generous. He was certainly handsome too. But she knew that the all-important spark just wasn't there – no matter how hard she might look for it. She'd simply gone out with him because he was nice and because she was a bit lonely, and that was an awful thing to do to him and now she was planning something even worse.

Colin picked her up at quarter past seven, opening the car door for her and complimenting her on her hair which she'd spent some time arranging with clips and flowers. He really was sweet, she thought, once again battling with herself at what she was going to do that night.

Parking was in a field and Colin made a fuss of taking Bryony's arm and guiding her over the bumpy ground.

'I have walked across a field before,' she told him, straightening her shawl which was wrapped around her shoulders.

'Yes, but you've got pretty shoes on tonight,' he said.

It was lovely that he'd noticed. Bryony wasn't used to wearing something quite so dainty and she felt as if her feet were naked without her big biker boots. But even she had to admit that they wouldn't look right with her midnight-blue dress swirled with large red roses.

The medieval barn at Torrington was large with a lofty roof. Lanterns hung from the ancient beams and straw bales, with woollen blankets on, had been placed around the perimeter for people to sit on. A large table full of food and drink stood at one end of the barn and the band were setting up at the other end. It was busy but, as she scanned the place, she couldn't see Ben. He'd offered to pick her up in his sister's car, but she'd told him that she'd meet him there. For one dreadful moment, she wondered if he might not show up. What if he'd got wind of her plan? No, that wasn't possible.

'Here,' Colin said a moment later, 'I've got you a wine.'

'Thanks,' she said, 'that's just what I need.'

Ben straightened the collar of his checked shirt. Checks were alright for a barn dance, weren't they? He didn't want to turn up looking too overdressed, but neither did he want to look as if he hadn't made an effort for their big night.

He still couldn't believe he was going to see Bryony. The date had sneaked up upon him whilst he'd been juggling an overpacked timetable of teaching commitments, translation work and the whole Aria business.

Predictably, Ben hadn't heard from Aria. He'd wondered if she'd ring up and apologise, offering an explanation, but of course she didn't. People like her didn't feel the need to explain. They could just use you for their own purposes and then move on.

He remembered the look on her face when she'd spun him the lies about her appalling family life. What an idiot he'd been to believe her. He hadn't even questioned her. You didn't usually question people about such things, did you? You took it for granted that somebody was telling you the truth. Well, Ben had anyway.

He'd gone over and over everything in his mind like the time that guy in the restaurant had recognised Aria and she'd run away. Who had he been? Another of Aria's exes? Or maybe he'd just known the truth about her.

But now wasn't the time to dwell on Aria. He had to place her very much in his past because he had more important things to think about in the present and, with any luck, what happened tonight would also influence the future.

Georgia had said he could borrow her car seeing as it was such a special occasion, but she'd made him promise to wash it for her in return. He'd happily agreed and now, driving to Torrington, he couldn't help imagining Bryony sitting in the car beside him. What would they have talked about, he wondered? And would they get much of a chance to talk at the dance? He hoped the music wasn't too loud.

At that thought, he laughed out loud. He sounded old before his time, hoping the music wouldn't be so loud that they couldn't have polite conversation, but he so desperately wanted to talk to Bryony. Their messages to one another had been so open, so easy, it truly felt as if they were becoming close again and finding their way back to the people they'd once been; the young couple who had been madly in love and who'd wanted to spend their lives together.

Parking in the field, Ben made his way to the dance, marvelling at the ancient building and the simple but charming decorations that had been put up. The music was already playing and couples were swinging one another across the floor. Ben watched, captivated for a moment by it all, but there was only one person he was interested in finding that evening.

As the music stopped and everybody clapped, he saw her. There was his Bryony, beautiful in a blue dress smothered in red roses, her hair pinned up with pretty clips and flowers. He didn't think he'd ever seen her looking lovelier than at that moment. She was standing opposite a fair-haired man. Wasn't that the baker from Castle Clare? Well, Ben guessed he'd probably made a pretty good dance partner whilst Bryony was waiting for him, but it was time for him to step aside now.

Ben's mouth suddenly felt very dry and the palm of his hands very hot. This was ridiculous, he thought. He was actually nervous. He wanted to get this right. The baker guy had moved away and

Bryony was now standing by herself. It was perfect timing, he thought, as he crossed the floor towards her.

Bryony saw Ben immediately. She'd done nothing but think about this moment ever since the idea had popped into her head. The more she'd thought about it, the more the hurts from the past had surfaced. Just the night before, she'd dreamed of that last time she'd seen Ben before he'd left Castle Clare. He'd been wearing sunglasses when he'd come into the shop and he hadn't taken them off. She'd thought it was so he could avoid eye contact with her, which had been horribly cowardly. When she'd woken up, her face had been wet with tears and the mood of that day all those years before had clouded her present one.

Now, she tried to keep those memories fresh before her, remembering how much this man had hurt her. There was no point in feeling guilty about what she was going to do to him. He deserved this, didn't he?

'Hey,' Ben said to her, a big smile on his face as he reached her. He still had that awful travelling beard, she thought.

'Hello,' she said.

'You look beautiful,' he told her and she could feel her face flushing at his attention. 'But you always do.'

'Ben, I –'

'I can't believe I'm here – *we're* here. This was such a good idea of yours.' He took a step closer to her and reached a hand out to take hers. The touch of his skin on hers almost undid her. She'd forgotten how big and strong his hands were and how neatly her own small hands fit inside them.

'So,' he began. He looked nervous. 'When do we dance?'

She swallowed hard. She had to do this. Right now.

'Dance?' she said, feigning surprise.

'Yeah, we came here to dance, didn't we? That's why you invited me here, isn't it?'

'Well, yes, I'm planning on dancing, but I'm here with Colin,' she nodded towards the table at the far end of the barn.

Ben looked confused. 'What do you mean?' He turned to face the table. 'The baker? Colin the baker?'

'Yes. He's my date, Ben. We've been seeing each other for months now.'

'But you invited me here tonight. Didn't you? Or have I got something wrong?' He seemed to be struggling now, as if mentally sifting through their messages to each other.

'No, you haven't got anything wrong,' she told him.

'I haven't got anything wrong,' he repeated her words slowly and then nodded. '*Oh!*' His face darkened and he dropped her hand. 'I see. I see what this is now.'

Bryony watched, transfixed as he kept nodding. She couldn't move and she certainly couldn't stop what was happening. This was all her doing. This was exactly what she'd been planning. She'd wanted to hurt Ben. She'd wanted to see him crushed but, now that the moment had arrived, she realised that it wasn't what she wanted at all. The look on his face was one of agony and she felt something inside her cracking at the pain she recognised in his eyes.

It was at that moment that Colin came back, a glass of wine in each hand.

'Here,' he said, handing one to Bryony and then turning to Ben.

'Hello,' Colin said. 'Are you a friend of Bryony's?'

'You might say that,' Ben said.

'Colin, this is Ben,' Bryony said. 'We used to… date.'

'Oh, *used to*,' Ben said. 'That's funny, see, because I thought that's what this was tonight – a *date.*'

'I explained,' Bryony said, desperately trying to keep calm, 'I'm here with Colin.'

Ben stared at Colin then. 'He's the father of your son, I suppose?' he said.

Bryony frowned. 'What?'

'Your son.'

'Ben, I don't have a son.'

'But that boy in the shop –'

'That was Flo's great-nephew, Sonny. He's not mine. Ben…'

Ben took a moment to absorb this and then he gave a strange, half-strangled laugh. 'Wow. I see. You just let me *believe* he was your son. You didn't go out of your way to set me straight.'

'No – I never told you he was mine. Ben – you don't understand.'

But it was too late to explain. Maybe, for just a while, she hadn't gone out of her way to deny Sonny was hers but, the truth was, she'd forgotten all about Ben in the shop that day with Sonny.

166

'Forget it,' he said. 'Let's forget *everything*, shall we? We seem to do nothing but cause each other pain.'

Bryony watched, distraught, as Ben left the barn and then she turned to face Colin. He was just standing there watching her and she knew what he must have seen in her face – her love for Ben.

CHAPTER 18

There was one person in the bakery when Bryony went in on Monday morning and she waited her turn before approaching the counter. They hadn't talked after Ben had left the barn dance. Colin had simply offered to take Bryony home and she'd accepted. The short journey had been in stony silence and she'd managed to hold her tears back until she had closed her front door. But she knew she had to talk to Colin and now it was Monday – the start of a new week – and she was desperate to make her apology to him. It was, she realised, long overdue.

Colin looked up, the smile that had been in place for the previous customer vanishing.

Bryony twisted her fingers into knots, waiting until the customer left the shop before she began.

'I don't know what to say,' she told him, her voice sounding small.

Colin stayed put, seeming to prefer to have the counter between him and her.

'Colin? I won't blame you if you never want to speak to me again. I should never have treated you like that.'

'You used me, didn't you?'

She swallowed hard and then nodded.

'How long for?'

'What do you mean?'

'I mean, was it from the very beginning?'

She looked into his kind face and saw the pain there.

'Yes,' she said. 'But I liked you, I really did. I even tried to fall in love with you, but I was a mess. You knew that. You knew I was struggling with…'

'Ben,' he finished for her. 'You've never got over him, have you?'

'Yes I have,' she said defiantly.

Colin shook his head. 'You're incredible, Bryony. You're standing here in my shop, after everything you've done to me, and after what you've done to Ben, and you're *still* denying you're in love with him?'

She opened her mouth to protest but the truth was that she didn't know what to say.

'It's my own fault really,' Colin suddenly said. 'I kind of knew you could never be mine. There was always Ben in the background. Even though I knew he was thousands of miles away, I knew you still carried him in your heart.'

Bryony could feel tears threatening to spill and quickly blinked them away.

'I'm so sorry, Colin,' she said. 'I really am.'

'Yeah, me too.'

'You're special. You deserve to find somebody wonderful and I'm not her.'

'I kind of realise that now.'

She nodded. She deserved that. She actually deserved a custard pie in the face, but Colin was much too much of a gentleman to do something like that.

'You've every right to hate me,' she said and turned to leave the shop.

'Bryony!' he called after her and she stopped and turned around. His face was full of panic and she watched, bemused, as he fiddled with something on the counter and then walked towards her. 'I could never hate you.'

She took the little paper bag he handed to her and looked inside. It was a perfect little tart filled with seedless raspberry jam.

There was a light knocking on Ben's bedroom door. Well, it had started as being light, but it was now becoming heavier.

'Ben?' It was Georgia. Of course it was Georgia. 'Are you awake?'

Before he could say anything, the door was open and his sister was inside his room, drawing back the curtains.

'Oh, for pity's sake!' he cried, burying his face in the pillow.

'Come on, big bro – it's time you were up. Aren't you teaching today?

'I'm not going in.'

'No?'

'No. Now leave me alone.'

Unbidden, she sat herself down on his bed. 'You've got to stop this.'

'Stop what.'

'This moping. You've got to move on. She doesn't want you in her life. You can't blame her really.'

'Oh, brilliant! My own sister isn't even on my side.'

'I'm just trying to be objective here. I think you really did break her heart when you left.'

'But you know it was the only thing I could do.'

'Yes, *I* know that, but she didn't, did she? You never told her and she's been carrying the weight of that around all these years.'

'Yeah, well I know that now, okay? You don't need to keep reminding me.'

'I thought that might help you.'

'How do you work that out?' Ben asked.

'Because you're now equal; you've both broken each other's hearts. I guess there's some kind of resolution in that, isn't't?'

'You're weird.'

'I'm just trying to help.'

'If that's true then you'll get out of here and leave me in peace.'

Georgia sighed. It was obvious that she wasn't giving up so easily.

'Why don't you go and see Mum, Ben?' Georgia began again. 'She's desperate to see you.'

'Are you kidding? I've just had my heart pummelled by the love of my life, I've been deceived by a mad Italian stalker and now you want me to compound the situation with a visit to Mum?'

Ben saw Georgia bite back a smile. 'Just go and see her. Get it over and done with. It won't be as bad as you think, I promise you. You're building it up into something it isn't.'

'Yeah, right.'

'Or I could call her and tell her to come over?' Georgia said, getting up from the bed. 'I keep reminding you and you shouldn't keep putting it off.'

'Don't, Georgia!' Ben was suddenly sitting up.

'Then you'll go and see her?'

He pushed his dark hair out of his face. 'If it will get you off my back.'

'For a while,' she said, grinning at him.

He groaned. 'I can't believe I'm agreeing to this.'

'Surely it's better than moping around.'

Ben picked one of his pillows up and threw it at her. 'Get out of here. You've ruined my morning and now you've made sure you've ruined my whole day too.'

'Hey, that's what little sisters are for!'

Ben waited for Georgia to leave the room before getting up. He had a thumping headache; he'd had one since the dance on Saturday night and that horrendous encounter with Bryony. His heart ached too when he thought about that night. How could the picture he'd had in his head of what was going to happen that evening have differed so very greatly from the reality of it? Georgia had warned him about Bryony's suddenly friendly messages, but he'd assumed, like an idiot, that all was well between them. His ego had allowed him to believe that he had won her back quickly and painlessly. Now, however, he realised that the pain he was feeling at her revenge was an insight into that which she had felt when he had left her.

But perhaps his sister was right and he should stop moping, although two days to get over a broken heart wasn't excessive, he thought, swinging his legs out of bed. He showered and got dressed, staring at his reflection in the hallway mirror. He looked awful. There were dark shadows under his eyes and he had a hollow look about him, as if a part of him had died.

For a brief moment, he wondered if it might be best to leave Castle Clare again. His return had brought him nothing but grief. Perhaps it had been a mistake coming home. Maybe this wasn't his home anymore. But he knew the deep hurt that would cause Georgia if he upped and left so soon after arriving, and he had made a commitment with his teaching. He also hated to give up and leaving would be an admission that he had failed and he wasn't ready to do that. Not yet anyway.

Georgia had taken her car to work and so Ben made his way to the little garden shed behind the house and brought out his old bike. Georgia had said she kept in working order and occasionally used it to nip into town. It felt funny riding it again and he recalled the last time he'd been on it. It was just before he'd left home. He and Bryony used to go on bike rides together, cycling into the Suffolk countryside, laughing as they sped down hills and puffing as they peddled up them. They would take little packed lunches and at least two novels between them and find a quiet spot far from the madding crowd and sit and read and kiss.

He cursed the memory of that last bike ride with Bryony, but it clung to him as he pedalled the short distance to his mother's house. It was six long years since he'd last seen his mother and he hadn't spoken to her since that awful day when Paul Caston had struck him. He could still hear his mother's cry after him as he'd left the house.

Reaching his mother's house, he got off the bike and wheeled it into the front garden which was little more than a patch of weeds with a wheelie bin in the middle. It used to be pretty, he thought, filled with pots of geraniums in the summer and dahlias in the autumn. It was sad to see it so neglected now. Perhaps he should do something about it. His conscience told him it would be the right thing to do.

Summoning up his courage, he rang the doorbell and waited. It wasn't long before the door opened and there stood his mother. She looked older, of course, her once dark hair now threaded through with grey and worn in a shorter style. She was thinner too, her face looking gaunt. He'd braced himself for the physical change he'd see in his mother after six years but, no matter how hard you try to imagine a thing, it never really prepares you for the reality.

'Ben!' she cried. Her small eyes were suddenly bright with tears as she looked at him.

'Hey, Mum.'

Her hands flew to her face and she stood there just shaking her head for what seemed like an age. Ben cleared his throat.

'Can I come in?'

'Yes,' she said. 'Of course.'

He followed her into the narrow hallway of the terraced house. The wallpaper was peeling off the wall and the paintwork was scuffed, he noticed.

'Can I get you a cup of tea? You still like your tea?'

'Sure.'

They went into the kitchen and Ben noticed that some of the tiles behind the sink were missing. The old place really hadn't had any money spent on it, he thought. But then, his mum only worked part-time these days and her job in the office of a local solicitors wasn't exactly lucrative.

He watched in silence as his mum went about boiling the kettle and making the tea. When she turned around, she smiled at him.

'You've grown a beard,' she said unnecessarily.

'I've had it a while.'

'It suits you. You look like your father.'

'I hope not.'

His mother smiled. 'He had his faults, but he was still a handsome man.'

Ben found it painful to hear about the father who had abandoned him and his sister when they were so small. If there was ever a reason to shave his beard off, it was hearing that it made him look like his father.

They walked through to the living room and, once again, Ben noticed how shabby everything looked. The furniture was the same as when he had left only more knocked about and worn, and the carpet looked grubby and was threadbare in places.

'You been well?' he asked her as they sat down opposite one another.

'Can't complain. Been missing you.'

Ben looked down at his feet, feeling awkward.

'What was it like?' she asked him.

'What was what like?'

'Leaving Castle Clare?'

His mother was one of those special East Anglians who never felt the need to leave their own county. Actually, now he came to think of it, she had once had a day trip to Frinton on the Essex coast, but she hadn't enjoyed it.

'It was good,' he told her. 'I needed to – get away.'

'I know you did, love.'

He nodded, not knowing what else to say about his departure.

'He left a couple of weeks later,' she told him. 'But you know that. Georgia would have told you.'

Ben nodded.

'I should never have let him come between us as I did. I was blinded by him for a while. You of all people must understand that – how all-consuming it can be to love somebody.' Her pained expression touched him and wasn't all that dissimilar from what he'd seen in the mirror just a few minutes ago. 'Paul, you see – he was the first man to pay me any sort of attention after your father...

well, after he left. I mean, there were others, but I thought Paul was different.'

'It's alright, Mum,' Ben told her. He'd come round prepared for a fight – determined to have it out with her for the years of pain he'd been carrying but, looking at her now, all the fight left him. He could clearly see that she'd been just as hurt as he had. She'd paid as great a price and had lived with the regret.

'I'm so sorry,' she said and the tears began to spill. 'I should never have let him into our lives. I don't know what I was thinking. I guess I wasn't, was I? I'm so sorry!'

'Mum, it's okay. It's all over now and I'm back.'

'Yes, yes!'

He swallowed the hard lump that had formed in his throat. This was turning into a right old week for emotions, he thought.

'Let me help around the place, Mum,' he said, doing his best to keep his feelings in check.

'What?' She sounded confused.

'This old house – it needs – well, it needs everything doing, doesn't it?'

She made a funny sort of noise that was half-laugh, half-sob and then she smiled. How he'd missed his mother's smile, he suddenly realised. She looked half her age when she smiled.

'Ben – my Ben!' she cried, standing up and reaching out towards him. Ben stood up from the sofa and she wrapped her arms around him and sobbed into his shoulder. 'Never leave again, my darling boy.'

'I'm not planning to,' he told her and he was absolutely sincere about that. During the tumult of the last few days, he might have thought about leaving, but he knew now that he wouldn't. Castle Clare was his home and he was staying.

CHAPTER 19

Bryony pulled into the driveway of Campion House and breathed a huge sigh of relief. It was only Wednesday and yet it seemed as if the weekend was a lifetime ago. How she'd struggled through the last few days, she'd never know. The day after the dance, she'd called to excuse herself from her family's Sunday lunch, claiming a headache, which wasn't too far from the truth. She couldn't have faced anyone the way she'd been feeling. She'd made her excuses to Flo on Monday, knowing that one kind word from her dear friend would have sent her over the edge. Tuesday was a little easier. Bryony had gone through the motions of running her shop, but it had been purely perfunctory and, somehow, she'd got through the day although there had been that awkward moment when she'd been reading *Beauty and the Beast* to a group of children and had had to blink back the tears when the happy ending arrived.

Her mother had been distraught when she'd called her.

'Polly says you're not eating properly,' Eleanor had cried down the phone.

'I just missed lunch a couple of times,' Bryony said. 'It's no big deal. I wasn't hungry.'

'Come home,' her mother had said. 'Come home *now*!'

Trust Polly to have reported home, Bryony thought, although she was secretly touched by the fact that her sister had been caring enough to take charge. The truth was, Bryony needed the love and support of her family right now. It was what the Nightingales did best – they cared for one another. When the world turned against you and you were battling your way through it, you knew you weren't alone. You only had to reach out for help and it would be there.

She sighed now, taking her small overnight bag from the passenger seat and getting out of the car. The door was unlocked, but Bryony rang the bell before going in, just to let them know she'd arrived. Immediately Brontë and Hardy came charging down the hall to greet her.

'Hello there!' Bryony said, bending to kiss their soft heads. There was nothing quite like a doggy cuddle to lift the spirits.

'Darling!' her mother called, coming out of the kitchen at the back of the house and embracing her. 'How are you?'

'I'm good,' Bryony said.

'Yes?' Her mother took a step back. 'Polly says not.'

'Polly meddles too much.'

'Now that isn't true and you know it.'

Bryony nodded. 'I know.'

'Then she's right? I don't need to ask you that – I can see it.' Eleanor cupped her daughter's face in her hands. 'Are you sleeping?'

'A bit.'

'But not eating properly.' Her mother tutted. 'Well, we'll soon put that right. Why don't you go upstairs? Take your things.' Her mother suddenly frowned. 'Is that all you've brought with you?'

'I'm only staying the night.'

'One night? I thought you'd be here for the rest of the week, darling, and the weekend too. I've planned a whole week of meals to fatten you up.'

'I don't need fattening up,' Bryony protested.

'You do if Colin the baker's no longer feeding you treats every day.'

'I'm going upstairs,' she said.

'I'll put the kettle on, okay?'

'Thanks, Mum.'

Bryony breathed a sigh of relief as she climbed the stairs. There was no other place she'd rather be. Her mother had made up the bed in the room she'd once shared with Lara. As Lara was away at university, Bryony would have it to herself. Entering it now, a wave of nostalgia flooded her and she could almost hear the echoes of her younger self laughing in that very room – at some silly joke her sister had told. Lara was always the clown of the family. Gosh, she could do with a dose of that now, she thought, putting her overnight bag by the side of her bed and sitting down.

She stayed completely still for a moment, breathing in the familiar smell of home and looking at her sister's things on the other side of the room. As with all the Nightingales, books made up a fair proportion of Lara's worldly goods and Bryony recognised the titles which belonged firmly on a university curriculum for their wasn't a single Nightingale who hadn't taken time to study literature. But there were also some wonderful modern titles too, from the realm of the book club, because it was just as important to keep up to date with what people were reading and enjoying now. The classics of the future, her mother called them whenever her father questioned why she was reading yet another modern novel.

'You can't have your head in Hardy all the time,' she'd tell him.

Bryony got up and opened the bedroom window, breathing in the fresh May air and taking in the glorious view. She could just see the top corner of the greenhouse and the raised beds where, no doubt, her father would be. And what was she going to tell him? How on earth was she going to explain what she'd done? Especially when it had been inspired by a story he'd told her.

She closed her eyes, feeling the full weight of her regret once again. What had she expected to feel when she'd taken her revenge on Ben? Triumph? Satisfaction? She had felt neither of those things – just a deep sense of emptiness and self-hatred.

When she went downstairs, her mother was in the kitchen making jam tarts.

'We've still got heaps of bramble jam,' she said as Bryony walked into the room. 'I thought I'd better get it used before jam season is upon us again.'

'It smells wonderful,' Bryony said.

'The kettle's boiled. Help yourself to tea.'

'Do you mind if I –'

'He's in the garden,' her mother told her, instinctively knowing that Bryony wanted to talk to her father.

'Of course,' she said.

'Where else at this time of year?'

Bryony smiled. 'I'd be disappointed if he wasn't.'

A recent shower had soaked the grass and it turned Bryony's brown boots to black in a matter of seconds. It was good to be outside. She'd rung Flo to apologise for not coming round to help with the chores but, after Saturday, she hadn't been good company. She'd make up for it another time. She was missing her Cuckoo Cottage fix.

Making her way towards the greenhouse, Bryony spied her father before he saw her. He was bending over a raised bed, a serious expression on his face. Such concentration, she thought, such passion for the earth.

'Dad?' she called softly, not wanting to startle him.

'Hello Bry,' he said, opening his arms to embrace her as she approached and, oh, how good it felt to be wrapped up in such a hug. It was just what she needed and, seeming to sense this, her father held her for a little longer than usual.

'What a treat to have you home. Can I expect your help in the garden?' her father asked her.

'Yes please.'

'Good.'

Finally, they broke apart.

'Dad?'

'Yes?'

'I've done something horrible,' she said. 'So horrible.'

He frowned. 'I can't believe that,' he told her.

'Well, it's true.'

He guided her towards an old bench under a beech tree and they sat down. She noted her father's flask there. Even though he was only a short walk from the kitchen, he liked to have his flask out in the garden with him so he could sit and observe the work he'd done and that which still needed doing whilst he sipped his tea.

Slowly, calmly, Bryony recounted the whole sorry story of her and Ben – from the dating website emails to the barn dance confrontation. Her father listened in silence, nodding, but not saying anything until she'd finished.

'And you were inspired by the story I told you about your mum?' he said.

'I'm so sorry, Dad. I feel like I've betrayed you too. You trusted me with that story and I abused that trust.' She could feel tears threatening again. She had cried more during that last week than she had when Ben had left Castle Clare.

'I still can't believe I did that,' she whispered. 'I feel horrible. I had it in me to do those things so I must be a horrible person.'

'Do you think your mother is a horrible person?' her father asked her.

'No, of course not.'

'But she did something similar, didn't she?'

'It wasn't nearly as bad as what I did,' Bryony said, 'and she loved you and you two got together.'

'But she didn't know we would at the time.'

'I bet she did,' Bryony said. 'Just as I know Ben and I never will.'

Her father took a deep breath and reached for his flask, unscrewing the lid and pouring a measure of tea into the cup. He handed it to Bryony and she took a grateful sip.

'Now, I'm not saying what you did was right, Bry,' he told her, 'but you've been carrying around an awful lot of hurt this last few years. Ben knows that.'

'But I led him on, Dad. We were writing to each other and it felt...' she paused, trying to recall how she'd felt as she'd been writing those messages to him. She hadn't been scheming then, not really. Her words had truly come from the heart and she'd needed to talk to him.

'It was like the old version of us, swapping news and asking each other's opinions,' she said.

'So, you were honest in your messages to him?'

'*Yes.*'

'Tell him that.'

'But I knew what I was planning.'

'And you knew that it was wrong,' he pointed out.

'I still did it, though. I knew what I was doing,' she said. 'There's no excuse for it.'

'You still love him, don't you? And he loves you.'

'Not now. Not after this.'

'Are you sure about that?'

'How could he?'

'Because it's very easy to love you, Bryony.'

'Oh, Dad!'

He put his arm around her shoulders and hugged her close.

'I have a feeling that the two of you are meant to be together,' he said. 'Despite him taking off around the world and despite you needing to take your revenge for that. I don't think any of that matters – I think you two can get over all that.'

'You do?'

'Don't you?'

Bryony shook her head. 'I have this big empty feeling inside me. It's like my life is over.'

'Oh, honey, it's not over. This chapter might be. But you read novels – you know that sad chapters are followed by happy ones.'

'Not always,' she said. 'Sometimes you just get more sad chapters like in *Jude the Obscure*.'

'But you are most definitely *not* a Hardy heroine,' he told her. 'You're more like a –'

'What?'

'An Austen heroine – bright, witty and wonderful. You'll get your happy ending, Bryony.'

Bryony smiled at that. 'You think so?'

'Absolutely. You've just got to believe it.'

Flo was missing Bryony's company at Cuckoo Cottage. Belle and Beau the donkeys were totally in love with her and the hens, ducks, geese and pigs all ran towards her whenever she arrived. Bryony was very much a part of the fabric of Flo's place now. But young people had their own lives to lead and Bryony had sounded teary when they'd spoken on the phone on Sunday. Flo suspected that it was serious man trouble

Was there any pain like young love, Flo wondered? She remembered the pangs of romantic love. Flo might have chosen never to marry despite two – or was it three – proposals? She couldn't quite remember if Michael O'Connor had actually popped the question or not, but she still knew that the heart was a fragile thing.

Family could cause you as much grief as any romantic relationship. Flo knew that only too well especially in the last few weeks. As she picked up Peggy and Beatrice the hens who had somehow managed to get into the fenced-off vegetable garden, Flo ruminated on the situation she now found herself in. She still hadn't confronted Mitch, but the time was fast approaching when she should. For one thing, she wanted to retrieve her possessions before he sold them; for another, Sonny was getting anxious.

'What do I say when he asks for the stuff?' Sonny had asked her on Monday morning before they left for school. His father was expecting another drop.

'You simply say that there isn't any more stuff,' Flo told him.

Sonny looked anxious. 'He'll shout at me.'

'Then you tell him you're going to call for a teacher.' Flo had kissed him. 'Don't worry, I'm going to sort this out once and for all and then he'll never bother you with this again, I promise.'

But Flo had been putting it off. Sonny had said that Mitch's face had turned an alarming shade of red when he'd been told there was no more stuff to steal. He'd used some choice words which Sonny had repeated. Flo had gasped and had told her great-nephew that the hens would stop laying if those kind of words were ever heard again at Cuckoo Cottage.

As she pulled out a couple of dandelions from between the cabbages, she made a decision. She would see Mitch that evening. She would go round to his house and, if he was out, she would simply sit in her car until he came home. Sonny could spend the evening with the neighbour across the road. She was always happy to have him.

Wiping her hands on her dress, Flo returned inside.

'Sonny?' she called. He was in the living room with Threddy the cat on his lap. 'I'm going round your dad's, okay?'

'Do I have to go?'

'No, sweetheart. You can go across to Lindy's.'

Sonny smiled. 'Can I take Threddy?'

'No, Lindy's terrier would only chase him. Do you want to take anything across with you? Your homework or –'

'I've done it.'

'Good boy.'

'I'll just take a book. Bryony gave me a really good one.'

Flo smiled. It was lovely that he was enjoying reading so much.

'Okay then,' Flo said. 'Let's do this.'

CHAPTER 20

Flo had never been more nervous in her life than when she was sitting outside Mitch's house. He was in. She could see the living room light was on and, through the net curtain, she could see the wavy blue light from the television set. She should go in. Right away. What was she waiting for? She was only prolonging the agony because she wasn't going to leave without facing him.

'Get on with it, old woman,' she told herself, leaving the sanctuary of her car and making her way to Mitch's front door. She knocked, then knocked again, wondering if he could hear her above the blare of the TV.

A moment later, he opened the door.

'What are you doing here?' he asked.

Flo was furious that he'd ask such a question. Surely, as a father, his first concern should be that Sonny was okay. But Mitch obviously wasn't thinking of his boy.

'We need to talk,' Flo told him, pushing past him and entering the house.

'You can't just barge in here!' Mitch shouted after her, slamming the front door shut.

Flo made her way into the living room and, finding the remote control, switched the TV off.

'Hey! I was watching that.'

Flo ignored him. Instead she dived straight into her mission.

'Tell me what this is, Mitch.'

'What do you mean?'

'All this stuff in here.' Flo motioned to the mountains of bric-a-brac, her eyes peeled for anything that belonged at Cuckoo Cottage.

'This is my business,' he told her, stuffing his hands in the pockets of his jeans. 'I'm a dealer.'

'And where do all these things come from?'

'Where do you think they come from? Other dealers, people who want to sell their stuff.'

'So you buy it, do you? You buy things from people who want to sell things?'

'That's right.'

'Well, then we have a problem because I didn't want to sell to you. I still wanted *my* things.'

Mitch frowned. 'What are you talking about?'

'I know what you've been doing,' she told him. 'I know how you've used your own son to steal from me. He's confessed and I've seen it with my own eyes so there's no point denying it. You're a thief, Mitch, and you've stolen from your own family.'

He muttered something under his breath which Flo didn't quite catch. She probably didn't want to catch it either, she thought.

'Goodness only knows where all these things have come from,' she went on. 'I bet I could find a dozen old women you've stolen from, just like me, if I dug around a bit.'

'Who do you think you are – Miss Marple?'

'Oh, you can joke about this all you like, Mitch Lohman, but I'm deadly serious. This ends right now.'

She could feel tears in her eyes as she confronted him, feeling both weak and strong in the same moment.

'I don't know what your problem is,' he said. 'You're going to leave everything to me in your will anyway, so what's the difference?'

Flo couldn't quite believe what she was hearing. 'What's the difference? Are you serious?'

'I don't want to wait around forever.'

Flo gasped. Who was this man standing before her? Surely he couldn't be related to her in any way? If it hadn't been for young Sonny, Flo would have wiped her hands of her nephew a long time ago. It pained her to admit it, but he'd always been bad news. And that's why she'd made a decision.

'Listen to me, Mitch,' she began, her voice a lot calmer than she felt. 'You can keep the things you stole from me.

Mitch frowned. 'Yeah?'

'Apart from my grandmother's gold locket, you can keep it all. On one condition.'

'What?' Mitch grunted.

'I'm keeping Sonny.'

Mitch seemed to be considering this as he gazed down at his feet. She'd expected some kind of token fight from him or maybe even an incredulous laugh, but he simply nodded.

'He's better off with you anyway,' he said at last, looking up at her.

'Yes he is,' Flo said. 'I'm glad we're agreed on that. You can see him whenever you like. You know where he is. I'm not taking him away from you; I'm simply taking care of him.'

Mitch nodded and then cleared his throat and looked shifty.

'What?' Flo asked.

'That locket.'

'Yes?'

'I can't give it to you.'

'What do you mean?'

'I sold it.'

The words hung in the air between them. For one dreadful moment, Flo thought she was going to faint.

'Then you'd better get it back,' she told him.

'I can't do that.'

'You'd better do that, Mitch Lohman. You get that locket back or I'll report you to the police. I've got photographic evidence too,' she said, reaching inside the bag she'd been clutching. She produced one of the photos Bryony had taken. 'That's a copy,' she told him, 'and there are plenty of others.'

Mitch looked at her, a sort of fear mingled with respect in his eyes.

'You'll get that locket back or I'll write you out of my will. Don't think I won't!'

Mitch looked genuinely floored by this. 'I don't know if I can –'

'I'll expect it back by the end of the week,' she told him. 'I take it we understand each other.' She picked up the remote control and switched the TV back on and then, without a backward glance, she left his house.

When Flo got back to Cuckoo Cottage, she put the kettle on and sat down at the kitchen table. She was shaking. Her confrontation with Mitch had taken every ounce of courage in her, but she was so glad that she'd faced him. She'd let her nerves calm a bit and then she'd go and pick her Sonny up.

Her Sonny.

She genuinely thought of him as hers now and she was excited at the thought of their future together. Mitch might have shredded her nerves good and proper, but Flo realised that she had a lot to be grateful for.

Bryony spent just two nights at Campion House. She knew she could easily have stayed longer, being mollycoddled by her family and sinking into the cosy routine of home once again, but she really shouldn't do that. She had to face up to what she'd done and the sooner she did that, the better.

Whilst she was there, she'd come across the old copy of Arthur Ransome's *Coot Club* on one of the bookshelves in the bedroom. It was the one she and Ben had read together at Wroxham on the school trip.

Flipping through the pages, she'd gasped as she came across a pressed flower. It was a daisy – one of the daisies he'd picked for her to make a chain to wear around her neck. He'd made one for her head too. A daisy crown, he'd called it, for his fairy princess. She'd laughed and called him a silly romantic and he'd shrugged. He'd never been afraid to show his feelings.

'Oh, Ben,' she'd whispered, closing the book. 'What have I done to us?'

With those words still echoing in her mind, she popped her 'Back in 10 minutes' sign in the door of her shop on Friday lunchtime and crossed the road towards Josh's.

'Hello, sis,' he said as she walked in. 'Look at the state of this book.' He handed her a paperback which was currently riding high in the bestseller lists.

'It's all creased,' she observed.

'Mucky too. And they had the nerve to send it out for me to sell as brand new!' Josh tutted. 'Who have they got packing their books these days?'

Bryony couldn't help smiling at her brother's indignation. He was usually indignant about something.

'You see the clothes shop has closed?' he continued, nodding out of the window at the shop next to Well Bread.

'Yes, it's a shame. I wonder who'll take it next.'

'As long as it isn't a rival bookshop,' Josh said, rubbing at an invisible mark on the cover of another of his books.

'Josh,' she began.

'Yes?' He was examining some other books now and shaking his head at small imperfections.

'That day you brought Ben to Sunday lunch –'

'I'm not apologising for that again,' he declared.

'I'm not asking you to.'

'Good.'

'Where did you pick him up from?'

Josh frowned. 'Why?'

'Why do you think? I need to talk to him and he's ignoring all my messages.'

'I'm not surprised,' Josh said.

'Why? What's he told you?'

'Nothing. I've not spoken to him since that Sunday lunch.'

'Really? Then why did you say you're not surprised he isn't speaking to me?'

'Because I've heard.'

'What have you heard?'

'That you took your revenge out on him good and proper.'

Bryony placed her hands on her hips. 'Did Mum tell you that?' Bryony knew that her dad would have told her mum.

Josh shook his head. 'Polly told me.'

'What?' Bryony cried. So, she thought, Dad must have told Mum and she must have told Polly who then told Josh. 'God, I hate living in this family sometimes. Does anyone *not* know?'

'I wouldn't have thought so.'

She sighed in despair. 'Are you going to tell me where he lives or not?'

Josh turned to face her. He didn't look happy. 'You're putting me in a really awkward situation here, Bry,' he told her. 'Ben's my mate.'

'And I'm your sister,' she stated. 'What do you think I'm going to do? I just need to talk to him.'

'Yes, but I might be implicated if you fly into a rage and murder him.'

'I'm not going to murder him. If anything, he might murder me.'

'Can I have your first edition Dodie Smith if he does?'

'You've got to give me his address first.'

'All right, all right.' Josh walked to his shop counter and picked up a pen and scribbled a note on a piece of paper which he handed to her. 'I'm not visiting you in prison.'

'Fine. Just make sure you send me plenty of books.'

As Flo had sat dithering in the car outside Mitch's house so too did Bryony outside Ben's. Well, Georgia's, she thought. Bryony had always got on with Georgia. She was one of life's fun people, with an

186

ever-present smile on her face. Only they hadn't talked in years and she probably wouldn't be smiling when she saw Bryony.

Ringing the bell a moment later, Bryony tried to gather her thoughts. She was there to apologise. That was good, wasn't it? That was putting things right. Nobody could hate her for that. Still, she couldn't help feeling nervous.

'Bryony?' Georgia said as she opened the door.

'Hello Georgia.'

'What are you doing here?'

'I've come to see –'

'Not me, I bet.'

'Is he here?'

'No, he's not.' Georgia was abrupt, but she didn't sound angry and Bryony felt sure she could detect a little tenderness in her eyes. 'Would you like to come in?'

Bryony really felt like weeping with relief. She hadn't been rejected or punched on the nose.

'Yes, thank you.'

She followed Georgia down a hallway towards the kitchen.

'Tea?'

'Thank you.'

Georgia went through the motions of making the tea and Bryony looked around the tiny room.

'How is he?' she asked at last.

Popping tea bags into a pair of mugs and pouring boiling water over them, Georgia sighed, 'I won't lie – he's pretty cut up about all this. It was a pretty mean thing to do to him.'

Bryony bit her lip. 'I know it was. Oh, God – what have I done?'

'Well, you've wasted a hell of a lot of time for a start.'

'Do you think he'll see me?'

'I'm not sure,' Georgia said.

'I need to talk to him, Georgia. I *have* to. I made a mistake – a *huge* mistake – and I need him to know that. You've got to let me see him. I must talk to him.'

Georgia was watching her as she spoke, her eyes wary but seeming to understand the desperation Bryony was feeling.

'I want to show you something. I think you'll like it,' Georgia said, disappearing out of the room.

Bryony couldn't begin to imagine what Georgia was going to get and was surprised when she returned a moment later with a large photo album.

'Come with me,' she said and they took their mugs of tea together with the photo album into the living room, sitting next to each other on the sofa, the album on the small table in front of them.

'I made this because I thought Ben's travels deserved posterity,' Georgia said. 'He didn't know I was doing it but I kept all the photos he sent me. He used to email and text me photos all the time. I don't think he realised I was keeping them to print out.'

She motioned to Bryony to open it. And there he was – her intrepid hero. Standing high in the mountains with an enormous rucksack on his back, resting by a mammoth waterfall, looking hot and humid in the middle of a jungle. Her Ben in all those strange lands. And in each and every photo was that irrepressible smile of his which she'd missed so much.

And there he was with a camel, an elephant, a snake of ginormous proportions. There he was in a city, a desert, by an ocean. He'd left Castle Clare and he'd seen everything. And did she wish she'd gone with him? Would it have been the best adventure of her life?

As she looked at the pictures, she remembered some of the postcards he'd written to her.

You'd love it here. Well, not the humidity and the insects and the spiders, but you'd love the people and the places.

Oh, no. Bryony would not have liked the creepy crawlies.

She turned the page and saw a photograph of Ben in a temple in Istanbul.

The colours – I wish I could bring all the colours home for you. You've never seen such incredible textiles and patterns.

Oh, yes – there was a part of Bryony which would have loved to have been part of Ben's adventure and to have seen all the things he had seen. He'd once written and told her that the cities and the scenery were all very well, but it was the people who made his trip so special. He couldn't get over how welcome he'd been made. He'd once stumbled across a village in the mountains of southern Spain and been invited into a humble little home and shared the family's food and been given shelter for the night

They had next to nothing. All they had was their company and their kindness and the food they'd grown and foraged from the wild.

Bryony's eyes misted with tears as she remembered the words he'd written to her.

'He really wanted you to go with him,' Georgia said.

'I know he did, but I just couldn't.'

'All his postcards to me said how much he was missing you. I kept telling him to move on. I told him that when he came back too, but he still kept going on about you. I don't think he'll ever stop loving you.'

'I think he might have stopped now,' Bryony said. 'After what I did to him.'

'Look,' Georgia said after a moment, 'he'd kill me if he knew I'd told you so you mustn't say anything, but he's teaching today. I'll give you the address.'

'Really?'

'He might be denying it at the moment, and I still haven't personally forgiven you for that mean trick of yours, but I truly think you guys are meant to be together. I mean, if *you* two can't make it to a happily ever after then there's no hope at all for the rest of us.'

'I won't mess it up this time,' Bryony told her. 'I promise.'

'You'd better not!'

They held each other's gaze for a moment and then Bryony leaned towards Georgia and hugged her.

'Thank you.'

Bryony looked through a few more pages of the photo album.

'You know,' Georgia said, 'there was always one thing that puzzled me.'

'What's that?' Bryony asked.

'Didn't you notice?'

'Notice what?'

'That he was wearing sunglasses the day he left?' Georgia said.

'Yes, I did.'

'But you didn't ask why?'

'I thought he wanted to avoid eye contact with me,' Bryony said, remembering the horrible goodbye scene in her shop.

'That wasn't why he was wearing them.'

'Then why?' Bryony asked.

Georgia shook her head. 'You'd better ask Ben. He might finally be ready to tell you.'

CHAPTER 21

Bryony didn't waste any time. After thanking Georgia again and giving her a big hug, Bryony left with the address of the college written down. That fifteen-minute drive was the longest in her life and she cursed every slow-moving tractor and traffic light that held her up. Georgia said Ben would be home that evening, but Bryony simply couldn't wait that long. Nothing else seemed to matter to her but seeing Ben as soon as possible.

Reaching the college, she parked her car and walked into the building. She was looking for the English department, but didn't want to ask anyone for fear of being thrown out. How difficult could it be? Ben had navigated his way around the world; surely Bryony could find a classroom.

It didn't take her long and, as luck would have it, she timed it for the end of a lesson when the bell went and a dozen students filed into the corridor, leaving the door of the classroom open. And there he was: her Ben, standing with his back to the door as he sorted through a pile of books which had been messily heaped on his desk. He was wearing a jacket she didn't recognise. He looked smart. The role of teacher became him well and she bet her life that several of the students had big crushes on him, beard or no beard.

She watched him for a moment, not daring to speak, and then he looked up. A brief elation lit his eyes, as if he'd forgotten all about their last encounter, but then a frown darkened his face.

'What do you want?' he asked.

Bryony walked into the room. 'To talk to you.'

'I thought you'd said all you wanted to say to me at the dance.'

'No, Ben. I said all the wrong things to you then and I've come to apologise because I didn't mean them.'

'No? Look, Bryony, if you want to talk to someone, why not try that nice baker of yours?'

'Colin? I've told him how I feel.'

'Good, I wish you both well.'

The anger of his words hurt her, but it was the least she deserved.

She took a deep breath, refusing to give up now.

'I've told him,' she began. 'I've told Colin how I feel about you. He didn't need telling as it turned out. He knew from the start. I think everybody knew. Except me.'

She watched the expression change on Ben's face. There was a slight softening around the eyes which encouraged her to continue.

'I found that copy of *Coot Club* we took to Wroxham. One of the daisies you picked for me was still in its pages. It's as bright as ever.'

'What is this? You suddenly want a trip down memory lane?'

'Yes,' she said. 'I want us to talk, Ben.'

'I thought we had been talking – I thought all those messages you sent me were the real thing.'

'They *were*,' Bryony assured him. 'That was the real me talking to you.'

'Yeah? And here I was thinking you were just reeling me in so you could dump me and have your revenge.'

Bryony swallowed hard. She almost couldn't bear to look at the pain she saw in his eyes, knowing that she had caused it.

'Ben, I'm sorry. I'm so sorry. I should never have done that to you. I knew it was wrong – right from the beginning I knew it was wrong, but you'd hurt me so much! You'll never know the pain you caused me when you left. I thought my life had ended.'

'*I'll* never know the pain I caused you?' he said and gave a hollow laugh. 'I'm feeling it right now.'

'I'm sorry,' she said again. 'I wish I could undo it.'

'And I asked you to come with me, remember? I didn't just leave you.'

'But you put me in an impossible situation, Ben. You left without any warning. Mum had just given me control of the shop and Polly had just had Archie and needed extra help. I couldn't leave all that. I didn't *want* to leave all that.'

'Fine. You made your choice. Just like you did at the dance.'

Bryony bit her lip. This wasn't going well and she didn't know how to rescue it. But then she remembered something.

'Why were you wearing those sunglasses?' she asked him.

'What sunglasses?'

'The day you came to say goodbye.'

Ben started fiddling with some papers on his desk. It was clear he knew what she was talking about.

'At the time, I thought you were trying to avoid eye contact with me, but Georgia said it was something else.'

'You've spoken to Georgia?'

Bryony nodded and Ben cursed.

'Why were you wearing them, Ben?' She walked towards him until only the desk stood between them. He was still fiddling with his papers and Bryony reached a hand across the desk and placed it on his, stilling his action. She saw him flinch ever so slightly, but he didn't remove his hand. 'Tell me,' she said. 'I need to know.'

It seemed like an age before he began to speak.

'You remember my mum started seeing a new guy?'

Bryony nodded. 'Paul, wasn't it?'

'Paul Caston,' Ben said, a barely disguised look of hatred on his face. 'Georgia and I knew he was no good the minute he walked into our mum's life, but she was blinded by his artificial charm. He was always buying her things. Stupid little gifts like glass unicorns and ceramic roses. She thought it was true love, but I knew she was just pleased to have a man in her life after dad. It must have been tough for her and I wanted her to be happy, but there was nothing in Caston that was good. You could always smell booze on him for a start. He seemed to have a can of something or other permanently glued to his hand. He'd start really early too, swigging his disgusting cans at the breakfast table. The house stank. I told Mum he was a dangerous drunk but she always defended him. She said he'd been laid off from work recently and was going through a rough patch. But he was just using Mum.'

Ben paused before continuing.

'He moved in shortly after they started going out. He ate all our food and did all his washing at ours. I don't think he had his own place. I think he just moved from one gullible woman to the next.'

'And your mum didn't see this?'

'You don't see what you don't want to see, do you?' Ben replied. 'Georgia and I tried to keep out of his way, but you could see he resented us being there. He wanted Mum all to himself and we got in the way. He was like a kid – jealous and petulant if he didn't get his own way. Anyway, after a couple of months of this nonsense, I told him to leave.' Ben paused.

'And what happened?' Bryony asked. She was still holding his hand.

'He told *me* to leave.' He gave a shrug. 'After that, we both seemed to lose our temper at the same time, only I never raised a hand. But you could see Paul had been itching to take a swing at me for weeks. I could smell the booze on him as he punched me in the gut. I called him a drunken pig. Well, I actually called him something else.' He gave a grim grin at the memory. 'Then he punched me in the face. Gave me a black eye.'

'Oh, Ben! And that's why you were wearing the sunglasses? To hide the black eye from me?'

'And that's why I had to leave,' Ben said. 'I couldn't stay. Not after that. One of us would have killed the other. I'm sure of that. And I couldn't bear to be near him. I told Georgia to get away from there and not to come back. I hated leaving her almost as much as I hated leaving you, and I desperately wanted to protect Mum, but she just wouldn't listen to me even after I showed her my black eye.'

'But why didn't you tell me all this, Ben? You should have told me what was going on.'

'It was family stuff. You didn't need to be involved.'

'How can you say that? We were together, weren't we? That's exactly the sort of thing couples should face *together*. You can't cherry pick what you share. If you're truly with somebody, you should get the whole package – not bits and pieces. Not highlights.'

Ben took a deep breath. 'I guess I wanted to protect you from it all. From Paul Caston. I didn't want him sullying your life and, when I was with you, I certainly didn't want to talk about him. What we had was so good, so pure.'

She held his gaze for a moment and she could see the old Ben looking out at her.

'Oh, Ben!' she whispered. 'We could still have something good. It might not be as pure anymore, but it could be good. I think there's still something between us.' She paused. 'Don't you? I tried to deny it. All those years you were away, I tried so hard to move on. I dated – *disastrously* – and I did my best to forget about you, but the truth is simple. There isn't anybody for me but you, and I regret not going with you so much. I should have been there with you, by your side, in all those places, but I was afraid. I was too afraid to just up and leave home like that.'

'I know,' he said in a soft voice. 'You were always happiest at home.'

'I couldn't even begin to imagine leaving Castle Clare and I know that might make me dull and boring –'

'You're not dull and boring,' he interrupted. 'I knew it was a big ask.'

'I should have gone with you.'

'No. No. It wouldn't have been right for you. It wouldn't have worked. I realise that now.'

There was a pause.

'I wish you hadn't stopped writing to me,' she confessed.

He frowned. 'But you never wrote back.'

'I might have done.'

'What, after two years of *not* writing to me?'

'I reckon year three might have produced a short note.' She gave a tiny smile and Ben shook his head.

Bryony squeezed his hand. 'Can you forgive me?'

They held one another's gaze. His expression had softened now.

'We've wasted a lot of time, haven't we?' he said.

'We can make up for it.'

'You know I was seeing other people when I was away?' he told her. 'After I stopped writing to you, I mean. I thought you'd moved on and I tried to as well.'

Bryony nodded. She hadn't expected him to remain a monk.

'Anyone special?' she dared to ask.

'Nope,' he said. 'How could they be when they weren't you?' He moved out from behind the desk and, with one swift moment, he'd captured her face in his hands and kissed her fully on the mouth. Bryony almost buckled at his touch. She'd forgotten what it was like to be kissed by Ben. His was the only kiss she'd ever craved and his touch was the only one which lit her up so completely.

'Ben!' she cried. 'I've missed you so much.'

He ran a hand through her hair. 'I'm here now.'

'And you forgive me? I need to hear you say it if you do.'

'I forgive you,' he told her, kissing her again. 'Do you forgive me?'

'Yes. Yes! Of *course* I do. I love you!'

'Good!' he said. 'Because I love you too.'

Suddenly, they were both laughing like the children they used to be – the Ben and Bryony who had grown up together, who had defied school teachers to sit next to one another, who had swapped books and read aloud to each other on river banks. Years of tension, recriminations and regrets dissolved in that one moment. They were together again and, this time, it would be forever.

CHAPTER 22

'Who's he?' Grandma Nell asked from the end of the dining table.

'It's Ben,' Grandpa Joe explained as he placed a spoonful of peas on her plate. 'Bryony's Ben. They're back together again.'

'Oh, she likes him now, does she?'

'That's right.'

'And that's him there, is it?'

'Yes,' Grandpa Joe said patiently.

'He's shaved that beard off,' Bryony said as she helped herself to roast potatoes.

'I wish you'd given it to me,' Archie said.

'Maybe you'll have your own one day,' Polly told her son.

Archie stroked his face as if trying to imagine it and Bryony smiled as Ben's hand sneaked towards hers under the table and held it.

Bryony still couldn't believe that she and Ben were together again. Since their happy reunion in Ben's classroom they had hardly been apart, spending as much time together as possible. After all, there was six years of catching up to do and they were determined not to waste a single moment. Ben told her all about his travels. He also filled her in on the whole Aria business. Bryony had been outraged for him and then felt awful at having been the second woman within a week to hurt him so badly and had apologised all over again. He'd milked it for a moment. Just a moment.

Bryony had told Ben all about Polly's ex-husband Sean and how the wonderful Jago had come into her life at just the right moment. She'd also told him about every single awkward customer who'd come into her shop over the last six years. In return, Ben told her about every single travel delay he'd had. They'd commiserated with one another, confessing that, at the time of each awkward customer and every travel delay, they'd longed to reach out to each other and share the moment.

They'd longed to share every single wondrous moment too. Ben had stored up so many amazing stories and Bryony wanted to share all her family funnies too. They talked themselves hoarse and laughed until their bellies ached.

Ben and Bryony. Together again.

The Nightingale family were thrilled but not at all surprised to welcome Ben back into the fold.

'So, when's the wedding?' Grandpa Joe asked.

'Grandpa!' Bryony cried.

'What? It's a valid question. We're not getting any younger at this end of the table,' he told them with a chuckle, leaning towards Nell to give her a kiss on the cheek.

'What was that for?' Grandma Nell barked, taken aback.

'Because you're you,' Grandpa Joe told her.

'I hope you don't turn into them,' Josh said, 'all lovey-dovey at the dining table.'

'It's cute,' Bryony told her uptight brother. 'And you wouldn't be here if it wasn't for all things *lovely-dovey*.'

Josh held his hands up. 'I'm stopping this conversation right now.'

Everybody laughed at that.

'I'm so glad to see you back together again,' Eleanor told them. 'It's –' she paused, '*right*.'

Lara, who was home from university for the weekend, beamed at them. 'Like Gabriel Oak and Bathsheba Everdene – you found your way to each other in the end. Pass the carrots, Sam.'

'Oh, God! I hope not like that,' Josh said.

'Yes, there weren't *quite* so many tragedies on the way,' Sam pointed out as he passed the carrots to his youngest sister. 'I see you more like Pop and Ma Larkin – you're a natural fit. You're meant to be.'

'I hope that's not your way of saying I'm plump, Sam,' Bryony said.

Sam grinned. 'It's my way of saying you two are *perfick* together.'

'We'll need a bigger table soon,' Frank announced.

'Oh, no!' Eleanor cried. 'I like it like this. It's so cosy.'

'I like it too,' Polly said, smiling at Jago who was sitting next to her.

'Tell us some more of your travelling tales, Ben,' Callie said.

'Yes, yes!' Archie shouted.

Ben cleared his throat and told them about the volcano he'd walked up, and about the South American trail he'd explored. As rhubarb crumble was served, he told them about some of the exotic dishes he'd eaten and the copious amounts of wine he'd drunk – just to be sociable, of course.

'But one thing struck me wherever I went,' he told them.

'What?' everyone said at once.

'People's hospitality. No matter where I was in the world, people made me feel welcome. Take one family in Italy, for example. I was staying with them when I was teaching in Rome. The parents were lovely and they had five children.'

'Like us!' Lara said.

'Yes. I thought of them as the Italian equivalent of you guys,' Ben said. 'But there was one big difference.'

'What was that?' Jago asked.

'They weren't you.'

Silence greeted Ben's statement.

'No matter where I went or who I met, it wasn't here and they weren't you.'

Bryony felt as if her heart had stopped at his words and she could feel tears threatening as he squeezed her hand.

'Oh, Ben!' Eleanor said.

'You old fool,' Josh teased, trying to make light of the moment.

'Maybe,' Ben said, 'but nowhere was quite like this. This feels like home to me.'

Bryony could see that he was visibly moved by this confession and she leaned towards him to kiss his cheek.

'No more kissing at the table, please!' Josh begged.

'It'll be you next,' Eleanor warned.

'That'll be the day,' Josh scoffed.

'He's married to his bookshop,' Lara told them.

'That's right.'

'I pity the poor woman who tries to come between you and your books,' Frank said.

'So do I,' Josh agreed.

'It'll happen,' Eleanor said. 'Mark my words.'

Once lunch was cleared away and tea had been served in the living room, Bryony got up to check on the dogs. She loved being around them and was beginning to wonder if the time might be right to have her own. For a moment, she pictured her future with Ben. They could get a little place together and have a dog, just like Polly and Jago. She was just dreaming about the future as she let Brontë and

Hardy have a quick run in the garden when she heard a voice calling her.

'Sweetheart?'

Bryony turned around. 'Dad!'

He crossed the lawn and enveloped her in a warm hug.

'What was that for?' she asked.

'Do I need a reason to hug my own daughter?'

'No, of course not!'

'I'm just so happy for you,' he told her. 'I knew you two would find your way back to each other.'

'You had more faith than I did,' Bryony confessed.

'You look happy,' he told her.

'I am,' she said. 'Happier than I've ever been in my entire life.'

They walked towards the end of the garden together, stopping to look back at the house. 'I thought I'd lost him. Twice. But never again, Dad.'

'He's home to stay, isn't he?'

'He says so and I believe him.'

'You can take the boy out of Castle Clare –'

'But you can't take Castle Clare out of the boy,' Bryony finished. 'It has a way of either keeping you here or drawing you back again, doesn't it?'

They walked around the vegetable beds, her father telling her what he'd planted where and that's when Bryony remembered Flo. It seemed an age since she'd seen her friend and so much had changed since she had.

'I've got to go,' Bryony suddenly announced.

'Already? You mother won't be happy.'

'She'll understand.'

They went back inside, gave the dogs' paws a quick rub with a towel and walked back through to the living room.

'I'm afraid we should get going,' Bryony announced, nodding towards Ben.

'Oh, darling, already?' Eleanor said.

'You're not coming on the dog walk?' Sam asked.

'Afraid not.'

'Where are you going?' Lara asked.

'To see Flo and Sonny,' Bryony told her. 'I feel awful. I've not seen them for ages and they've had so much going on.'

'Ah, yes,' her dad said, 'that thieving nephew of hers.'

When Bryony had stayed at Campion House earlier that week, she'd told her parents about Flo's recent trials.

'What's happening with that?' Sam asked. He'd obviously been filled in by the family.

'I'm not sure,' Bryony said.

'Well, let us know,' Polly said.

'I will,' Bryony promised.

Ben stood up. 'Thanks for a delicious lunch,' he said.

'Our pleasure, Ben,' Eleanor told him. 'We'll see you next week?'

'Of course you will,' Bryony said. 'And all the weeks after that too!'

Cuckoo Cottage had never looked prettier than on that May afternoon when Bryony and Ben arrived together.

'Come in, come in!' Flo said, ushering them inside with enthusiasm. 'What a lovely surprise.'

'Hello, Miss Lohman,' Ben said.

'Oh, Ben! How lovely to see you. And call me Flo, for heaven's sake! My, what a handsome man you are.'

'He's shaved his beard off,' Bryony told her.

'Ah! And you look good without it. Good with it too, mind,' Flo said.

'It wasn't going down well with the women in my life,' Ben confessed as they walked through to the kitchen, 'and I decided that it had to go.'

Bryony smiled. 'It tells me he's home,' Bryony said.

'How's that?' Flo asked.

'It was his travelling beard,' Bryony explained, 'and shaving it off means that he's now home to stay.'

'And you're back together, I take it?'

'We are,' Bryony said.

'Well, that is good news,' Flo said, a huge smile on her face. 'Oh, my!'

'What is it?' Bryony asked as Flo's hands flew to her face.

'What about that nice baker?'

Bryony could feel herself blushing. 'I think he knew we'd never work out.'

'Oh, dear, oh, dear.'

'She's a real heartbreaker, isn't she?' Ben teased, earning him a thump in the arm from Bryony.

'I apologised profusely to him. I felt so awful.'

'She apologised to me too,' Ben said. 'She's very good at apologising.'

'I've behaved very badly,' Bryony acknowledged.

Flo moved towards her and hugged her. 'You have a big heart, my girl. Never forget that.'

'Oh, Flo!'

'Ben – did she tell you what's been going on around here and how she's helped me?'

'She did indeed. It sounds like you two could set up your own private investigation company,' Ben said.

Flo laughed. 'Well, I don't know about that.'

'Did you see Mitch?' Bryony asked as Flo turned to put the kettle on.

'I did. It wasn't easy, but we've come to an understanding and Sonny is to stay with me from now on.'

'Oh, that *is* good news,' Bryony said. 'And did you get your things back?'

Flo shook her head. 'I let him keep them.'

'Why?' Bryony asked.

'Because he let me keep Sonny.'

It was Bryony's turn to hug Flo. 'It's *you* who has the big heart.'

Flo finished making the tea and they sat around the kitchen table.

'There was one thing I told Mitch I wanted back,' Flo said.

'What was that?' Ben asked.

'My grandmother's gold locket. But I don't suppose I'll see that again. He said he'd sold it.'

'You really should call the police,' Bryony said.

'No, no,' Flo insisted. 'It's all done now. Time to move on.'

It was then that Sonny came in from the garden.

'Hello,' he said as he saw them all sitting there.

'Hello, Sonny,' Bryony said, noticing the difference in the boy at once. He looked happy, confident even, and he was holding a couple of eggs in his right hand.

'Sonny, come and meet Ben,' Flo said.

'Hello, Sonny,' Ben said.

'Hello,' Sonny said. 'Would you like an egg?'

'That's very kind of you,' Ben said with a laugh.

'I'll get you a box to take some home,' Flo told him.

'What's happening with that neighbour thief of yours?' Bryony asked, thinking of the pale bony hand which popped through the hedge to steal Flo's eggs.

'Didn't I tell you?' Flo said. 'He's stopped stealing. I told him I'd set man traps all around the garden and he was liable to get his hand stuck in one of them if he kept poking them through the hedge.'

'You didn't!' Bryony said with a nervous laugh, not knowing whether to believe her or not.

'I jolly well did! And do you know what? Shortly after that, the donkeys stopped braying. It's the strangest thing. They don't seem bothered by the trumpet anymore. I actually have a suspicion that they're in love.'

'Belle and Beau in love?' Bryony said. 'That's so romantic!'

'Perhaps donkeys in love don't bray,' Flo said. 'Anyway, problem solved.'

It was then that they heard a knock at the door.

'Just a minute,' Flo said, getting up and walking through to the hallway. A moment later, she came back into the kitchen. 'Someone's just posted this.' She was holding a padded envelope.

'What is it?' Sonny asked.

Flo opened it and reached inside, gasping as she took out a small blue box and opened it.

'It's the locket,' she said, her eyes misting with tears. 'My grandmother's locket.'

'The one Mitch stole from you?' Bryony asked.

Flo nodded and took the locket out of the box, opening it carefully.

'Grandma,' she said, her fingers hovering over the image of her beloved relative.

Bryony and Ben stood up, looking over Flo's shoulder at the old sepia photograph in the locket.

'She's beautiful,' Bryony said.

'She's home,' Flo said. 'Just like you, Ben.'

Ben smiled and Sonny walked up to Flo, hugging his arms around her waist.

'It's wrong to steal,' he said. 'I told Dad that.'

'Yes, darling,' Flo said, bending to kiss the top of his head. 'It's wrong to steal.'

Ben cleared his throat. 'There *is* one exception.'

'What's that?' Flo asked.

Ben took Bryony's hands in his and looked into her eyes, making her feel giddy and gorgeous and so very loved.

'You can have your heart stolen,' he said, 'and that can't be wrong because it feels like the most wonderful thing in the world.'

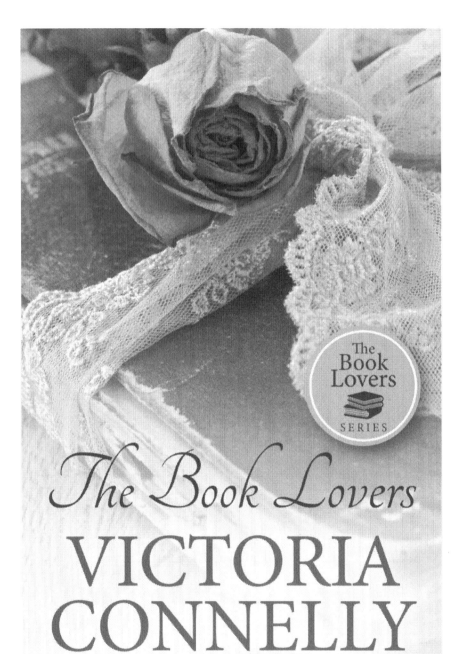

The Book Lovers

VICTORIA
CONNELLY

VICTORIA CONNELLY

LOVE
in an
ENGLISH
GARDEN

ABOUT THE AUTHOR

Victoria Connelly is the bestselling author of *The Rose Girls* and *The Book Lovers* series.

With over half a million sales, her books have been translated into many languages. The first, *Flights of Angels*, was made into a film in Germany. Victoria flew to Berlin to see it being made and even played a cameo role in it.

A Weekend with Mr Darcy, the first in her popular Austen Addicts series about fans of Jane Austen has sold over 100,000 copies. She is also the author of several romantic comedies including *The Runaway Actress* which was nominated for the Romantic Novelists' Association's Best Romantic Comedy of the Year.

Victoria was brought up in Norfolk, England before moving to Yorkshire where she got married in a medieval castle. After 11 years in London, she moved to rural Suffolk where she lives in a Georgian cottage with her artist husband, a springer spaniel and her ex-battery hens.

If you'd like a free ebook and to hear about future releases, sign up for her newsletter at www.victoriaconnelly.com. She's also on Facebook, Twitter and Instagram.

BOOKS BY VICTORIA CONNELLY

The Book Lovers series
The Book Lovers
Rules for a Successful Book Club
Natural Born Readers
Christmas with the Book Lovers

Austen Addicts Series
A Weekend with Mr Darcy
The Perfect Hero
published in the US as Dreaming of Mr Darcy
Mr Darcy Forever
Christmas with Mr Darcy
Happy Birthday, Mr Darcy
At Home with Mr Darcy

Other Fiction
The Heart of the Garden
Love in an English Garden
The Rose Girls
The Secret of You
A Summer to Remember
Wish You Were Here
The Runaway Actress
Molly's Millions
Flights of Angels
Irresistible You
Three Graces
It's Magic (A compilation volume: Flights of Angels,
Irresistible You and Three Graces)
Christmas at the Cove
Christmas at the Castle
Christmas at the Cottage
A Dog Called Hope

Short Story Collections
One Perfect Week and other stories
The Retreat and other stories
Postcard from Venice and other stories

Non-fiction
Escape to Mulberry Cottage
A Year at Mulberry Cottage
Summer at Mulberry Cottage

Children's Adventure
Secret Pyramid
The Audacious Auditions of Jimmy Catesby